RUNNING WITH A SWEET TALKER

Brides on the Run, Book 2

JAMI ALBRIGHT

She's a take-no-prisoners fireball. He's a sweet-talking charmer. It could be love...if they don't kill each other first.

Hotshot lawyer Luanne Price may not believe in happily ever after, but she'd do just about anything to earn her absentee father's love. So when he waltzes back into her life with a plan for her to marry his business associate, she foolishly agrees. But on the wedding day things go south. Fast. Luanne's desperate to get away, even if that means hitching a cross-country ride with the infuriating Jack Avery.

Jack needs to get Luanne out of his system. He'll watch her tie the knot and forget about her. Once she's married to another man, then she'll be off-limits forever. Solid plan. Until he spots her army-crawling through the bushes to escape the Wedding of the Season.

He knows he should let someone else deal with the runaway bride. But if there's one thing Jack has never been able to do, it's resist Luanne. Will their romance rev up on the open road, or will Jack and Luanne crash and burn?

Publisher: Jami Albright
www.jamialbright.com

Cover designer: Najla Qamber Designs
www.najlaqamberdesigns.com

Editor: Serena Clarke
www.serenaclarke.com

❀ Created with Vellum

For Chris
You are everything a hero should be.
I love you.

Chapter One

J ack Avery stared at the scene before him while sucking on a cherry lollipop his godson Aiden had given him. His third-floor window gave him the perfect vantage point to observe the bride sprinting a serpentine pattern across the lawn of the wedding venue. Luanne Price was beautiful, brilliant, and surprisingly agile in a banana-cream-pie dress as she leaped over a fallen log in her path.

"What are you up to, tough girl?"

Not his business.

She'd already caused him enough distraction. Why he found a woman who gave him so much shit attractive, he'd never know. But something about her smart mouth lit him up like a Roman candle. This woman intrigued him. He couldn't remember the last time that had happened. Lately, the beautiful and docile women he dated had begun to bore him to death. They paled in comparison to the feisty pixie who had just scurried behind the flower-covered altar. "What the hell?"

Why did her every move fascinate him?

Stupid, Jack.

He was ten kinds of crazy to even contemplate getting involved with her for any reason. Thankfully, in a little more than an hour she'd be someone else's problem.

That was the reason he was here today. To see Luanne tie the knot. It would be tough to watch, but then it would be real, and she'd be off limits. He didn't fool around with married women. Ever. His mama would come back from the grave and slap him into next week if he ever did.

He leaned closer to the window of the suite and watched as she hiked up her dress and ran out of sight to avoid a couple of waiters. The glimpse of tan leg she gifted him with ignited images of all the things he'd never get to do with her. Another man would have that privilege.

Jealousy tore at his insides. The irrational urge to beat his chest and bellow *mine* concerned him. Luanne wasn't his. She barely gave him the time of day. And when they did converse, she bloodied him with her words. In spite of that, he fantasized about arguments with her that ended with the two of them sweaty and naked. It was damned inconvenient...and dangerous, considering he'd probably end up dead after such an encounter.

But what a way to go.

Gavin Bain sauntered into the room. "Hey, man. Where's my kid?"

Jack's friend was his number one client and the hottest thing in music right now. He looked every bit the badass rock star, even in a thousand-dollar suit and tie.

Jack pulled the sucker from his mouth with a pop. "He's out siphoning gas from cars in the parking lot."

"Good. The boy needs to learn life skills."

Gavin wasn't fooling him for a second. He may seem casual about his toddler son, but nothing could be farther from the truth. That three-year-old, and Scarlett, Gavin's wife, were his whole world. "He went down for a nap about thirty minutes ago."

Another flash of white caught Jack's eye as Luanne threw herself against the trunk of a huge oak tree. She quickly poked her head out and then jerked it back like a CIA operative on a recon mission.

Seriously, what was she doing?

The answer came in a brain-scorching lightning strike.

"Hot damn, she's running," he mumbled.

"Jack?"

"Huh? What?" He couldn't tear his gaze from the runaway bride. Especially when she dropped to the ground and belly-crawled through the flower bushes.

"I said I can stay with Aiden until the sitter gets here if you have something else to do." Gavin's brow wrinkled. "What's so interesting out there?"

"Yeah. Great. Gotta go." He grabbed his suit jacket from the back of the sofa and barreled for the door.

Gavin chuckled. "Okay. Don't let me stop you."

He wouldn't.

He was on a mission

He had a bride to catch.

* * *

The prick of twigs poking into Luanne Price's arms as she shimmied on her belly through the azalea bushes was only a slight annoyance. What were a few scrapes compared to the gaping wound in her heart? She needed to put that away and concentrate on escape. A few more precious inches and she'd be at the parking lot and home free. Army-crawling through the shrubbery wasn't how she'd pictured leaving her wedding, but desperate times and all.

The thought of *dear old Dad* and his devil's deal with her fiancé spurred her forward. If she could get to her car, she could run and not look back. Thank goodness she had put a hide-a-key under the back bumper, just in case. Ironic that fleeing her own wedding would be her just in case.

Her manicured fingers clawed the soil as she pulled herself along the ground. A tiny twinge of guilt dogged her. This dress looked like a cake topper and wasn't her style at all, but it had cost five thousand dollars, and she was ruining it in her escape. But guilt evaporated when she saw a break in the bushes. One last surge and she'd be free.

Once clear of the greenery, she inspected the damage to the dress. Surprisingly, it wasn't too much the worse for wear. She quickly forgot about her dress when the sound of the wedding quartet warming up reached her ears. Damn! It was time to move.

She crouched low and used the other cars as cover as she duck-walked to her little red Corvette. But her elation at seeing her baby was short-lived when she noticed it was blocked in on all four sides. How would she get out of here? Walking wasn't an option if for no other reason than Jimmy Choo did not make walking shoes. The rhine-stone-encrusted beauties she wore were made to be admired, not for functionality.

She peeked over the hood of her car to make sure she hadn't been discovered. With every beat of her heart, her blood pressure ticked up another notch. At this rate, she'd be leaving here in an ambulance.

Calm the hell down, Luanne.

Whistling and the masculine tap, tap, tap of shoes on asphalt caught her attention, and she dropped out of sight. Her butt hit the hard, warm pavement with a thud. The July Texas sun beat down on her bare shoulder as she huddled as close to the front tire of her car as possible. She prayed whoever it was would walk by without noticing her.

The whistling and tapping stopped. "Luanne Price, fancy meeting you here."

She cursed the escape gods. Of all the people to see her in this humiliating state, Jack Avery was the absolute worse. Well, he wouldn't rattle her. No matter how fine he looked in that black suit and gold tie that set off his whiskey eyes. Damn him and his McDreamy good looks.

She smoothed her short hair from her sweaty face. "Hello, Jack."

"Car trouble?" He pushed back the sides of his jacket and slid his hands into the front pockets of his pants.

"I noticed one of my tires was low when I got out of the car earlier. It's been buggin' me all morning, so I came to check on it." She made a show of inspecting the tire. What the hell was she supposed to be looking for? The only thing she knew about cars was how to turn them on and how to drive fast.

He leaned a hip against the driver's door. "Yeah, I can see how that would consume your thoughts. Why let a pesky thing like a wedding get in the way of good car maintenance?"

"Exactly." His accessing stare unnerved her. She went back to inspecting the tire and tried to ignore him. "Well, it was good to see you, Jack."

Take the hint, Jack-ass, and go away.

He didn't.

Paper crinkled and a red lollipop appeared in front of her face. "Want one?"

She pushed his hand aside. "No, thank you."

"Aiden gave me these damn things, and I can't stop eating them."

Against her will and better judgment, she followed the motion of his tongue as he licked the sucker.

"They're nothing but pure sugar."

Lick.

"Probably all kinds of bad for you."

Lick.

"But I'm addicted."

Lick.

"I seem to be having trouble with impulse control lately." He winked. "Know what I mean?"

"Um...no." Sweat beaded on her upper lip. She wiped it away with the back of her hand. "Tire looks fine. I guess I better get back inside, the wedding starts in a bit." She gave him her best pageant smile.

"Yeah." He turned his face to the sun. "Beautiful day for a wedding."

He wouldn't take the hint and leave. Or maybe he was calling her bluff. Well, two could play that game. "Yes, it is."

He straightened and buttoned his jacket. "May I escort you back inside?"

"No. I'm going to sit a bit longer and enjoy the sunshine." She waved him off with a flick of her hand. "You go on ahead and have a good time." She smashed down the skirt of her dress that poofed around her face. The thing had enough volume to float a boat.

"The sun is nice. I think I'll stay and enjoy it with you." He turned, rested his butt on the car and crossed his arms over his chest.

Why wouldn't he leave? She ventured a look in his direction and couldn't help but appreciate the sight. The sexy dimple in his chin had probably been the undoing of many women—that and the devil's glint in his mischievous expression. As much as it chapped her behind, she was no exception. She tried and failed to settle the butterflies whipping around in her stomach, but it was no use.

Since the day she'd met his arrogant ass, she'd done everything she knew to get beyond her unhealthy attraction to him. He was the exact kind of man who could break her, and she didn't touch those men with a ten-foot pole.

As if her thoughts drew his gaze, their eyes locked. Her body ignored the siren going off in her head. Every part of her that should be ignoring him saluted and reported for duty.

"You have a little something there." He pointed toward her head.

Her hand flew to her hair, and she patted her head. "Where?"

"Here." His fingers gently pulled a sprig of grass from behind her ear. A tremor ran down her neck when he lightly brushed her earlobe with his fingers.

"Thanks," she breathed.

A sly smirk appeared on his face. "No problem."

Jerk. He knew he got to her, and it rankled. "I want to look my best for Doug." She gave him a tight-lipped smirk.

"Uh-huh. Then you might want to wipe that smudge of tire grease from your upper lip." He waggled his finger in her face.

She slapped it away and wiped her mouth. "Go away, Jack."

"I think I'll stay for the fireworks." He popped the lollipop back into his mouth.

"Fireworks? There aren't going to be any fireworks." Not that her father hadn't tried.

He grinned around the sucker. "Oh, I think there will be when everyone figures out the bride's bolted."

"I'm not running." She so totally was.

"Please. I know a runner when I see one." He surveyed the area around them. "It doesn't look like you're going to get very far, Thumbelina."

She hated it when he called her that. He only did it to annoy her.

That was Jack in a nutshell—annoying. He could make the Pope cuss. "Don't you worry about me, Jack Avery. I can take care of myself."

"I was going to offer you a ride, but I guess you don't need my help." He rapped his knuckles on the top of the car. "No need to hang around if there isn't going to be a wedding. I've got places to go and people to see."

"And women to objectify." Petty, she knew, but still satisfying.

His laughter filled the air. "See ya later, trouble." He sauntered away, jingling his keys.

Panic at seeing his retreating back knotted her muscles. She needed help, but not from him. If she'd learned anything from her father, it was that nothing was free. The last thing she wanted was to be indebted to Jack.

Shouts from the house slammed into her like a missile. Her heart rate, which had ironically stabilized in Jack's presence, hit the stratosphere. Doug and her father were yelling her name.

Strike that. The last thing she wanted was to marry Doug Divan. Decision made. "Wait."

Jack pivoted to face her, still playing with his keys. The shit-eating grin he wore made surrender a bitter pill to swallow. But she gulped it down, along with her pride. There'd be plenty of time to get both back at his expense...later...when she was a hundred miles away. "I could use a ride."

He sauntered back to her. "Well now, Luanne. I don't know if I'm inclined to help you anymore. You were pretty mean to me." He had the nerve to pout.

She hated him.

But she also needed him.

With will she didn't know she possessed, she unclenched her teeth and beamed at him. "I'm sorry I was mean, Jack. Could you please get me the hell out of here?"

He offered her his hand. "On one condition."

"What's that?"

"Tell me why you're running."

Chapter Two

J ack fought the urge to hum a tune. He didn't want to examine why helping her made him happier than anything in a long time. And why was he helping her? He had to be in his hometown in five hours. Beauchamp, Louisiana was a three-hour trip from Zachsville, so he didn't have all day to get Luanne home and then on the road. It's not like he could call and say he wouldn't be there to present the scholarship he'd created in his mother's name.

From the corner of his eye, he saw his passenger fidgeting. "You doing okay over there, Luanne?"

"As fine as I can be stuffed into this huge dress and tiny sports car. What exactly are you compensating for with this vehicle, Jack?"

"Not a thing, Thumbelina. Not. A. Thing." He flashed her *the smile,* the one that worked with every woman but her.

She rolled her eyes. "That's what they all say, pretty boy. Just get me home in one piece, please."

"Alright, but you're no fun."

His Porsche 911 ate up the twenty miles between the wedding venue and Luanne's house. He tried not to speed, but, please, in this car it was a crime to go the speed limit.

"So what's your plan?" He watched in fascination as she peeled false eyelashes from her lids.

She shrugged. "I don't have one past gettin' away from Zachsville."

"What about your law practice?"

"I've cleared my case load for the next month. We'd planned a three-week honeymoon in Europe. So I have some time to figure out what I'm going to do." She played with the eyelashes she'd removed. They looked like two caterpillars resting in the palm of her hand.

"You gonna tell me why you're running?"

The look she gave him nearly put him in the grave. "No offense, but I'm not spilling my secrets to you, Jack."

He chuckled. "Why do people always start a sentence with *no offense* when they're about to say something offensive? Besides, that was our deal." He smoothed his hand over the top of the steering wheel. "Tell me. I'm kind of a neutral party. It might help."

"I doubt it. But if you must know, I caught Doug with another woman right before you found me."

"You must be heartbroken."

"I'm devastated," she said on a tiny sob, then turned to look out the window.

Bullshit. Oh, she was upset alright, but somehow he knew it had nothing to do with that idiot she was supposed to marry. If she didn't want to talk about it, that was her business. He might be unhealthily fascinated with her, but whatever was going on with her was messy, and he didn't do messy.

Then she swiped a tiny tear from her cheek, and he was a goner.

Damn. Apparently he did do messy with this woman.

* * *

Luanne grabbed the top of the monstrosity she was wearing, and readjusted it. "I've got to get out of this dress. You can't believe how uncomfortable this thing is."

"It's not the type of dress you said you—"

"No! We will never speak of that." She held her hand up between them. "Do you hear me, Jack Avery? Never."

"I've wanted to talk to you—"

"I mean it, Jack. No more."

"I'm sorry I—"

"I'm warning you, Jack."

"You don't have to be embarrassed."

"Oh, my Lord, you're not going to stop until I talk about the single most mortifying night of my life. Are you, asshole?" She threw her arms open. "Go ahead, Jack, complete my humiliation." She knew it would probably be best to clear the air between them and purge the entire event from her life. But the thought of reliving that night was more than she could take today.

"That's not what I'm trying to do. I'm just saying, I understand. You had too much to drink and said some things that were...a little out of character."

She buried her face in her hands and groaned. "Please stop talking."

"Fine. But it wasn't that big of a deal."

That was total crap, and they both knew it. It was a huge deal. One that made him lay skid marks from her front door to the end of her street. "Can we talk about something else, please?"

"Sure, let's talk about that loser Doug Divan. You really dodged a bullet with that one."

She picked up a St. Christopher medal from the console and examined it. "I'm afraid to ask, but why do you say that?"

"Do I have to spell it out?" He plucked the medal from her hand and slipped it into his coat pocket.

Whatever. She didn't want to see his stupid charm anyway. "I guess so, because I have no idea what you're talking about."

"Your name would've been Luanne Divan and darlin' you would've lost any and all street cred with a name like that." He snuck a peek at his watch.

"Good point." It had never occurred to her what the two names might sound like together, since she'd never intended to take Doug's name.

"Actually, it's that weasel who dodged the bullet." He laughed. "You would've chewed him up and used his bones to build yourself a new shoe closet."

He was right. It was the most appealing thing about her ex-fiancé. She would've run the show, exactly the way she liked it. "Never underestimate the appeal of a finely constructed shoe closest, Jack. Women have married and killed for less."

"Can I ask you a question?"

"Can I stop you?" She gave him her man-eater stare but knew it wouldn't stop him.

"Why would you ever consider marrying him?"

"You wouldn't understand."

"Try me."

She picked at one of the many ruffles on her dress. "It was my father's idea."

His look of confusion almost made her laugh. She understood. Why would an intelligent, professional woman let her father choose the man she would marry in this day and age?

"He...ah..." How to explain this without sounding completely pathetic? She may as well tell him the same lie she'd been telling herself for the last six months. "He was concerned about me and wanted to make sure there would be someone to take care of me after he was gone."

"Ha!" Jack's bark of laughter boomed through the car. "Why in the world would he think you needed someone to take care of you? You're the most capable woman I've ever met." He turned off the highway onto the main drag of her little town.

Happy sparks sizzled and popped in her chest at his high praise. "Thank—"

"For that matter, why would *you* think you needed someone to take care of you? Or was it about that thing I'm not allowed to talk about?"

"Oh for the love of... No, Jack, it's not about that." Thank God, they were almost to her house.

One more mile and he'd need that St. Christopher medallion as protection against *her*.

Chapter Three

Jack attributed the sickness in his gut to the number of cherry suckers he'd eaten and not the fact that he'd be dropping Luanne off at her house in a few blocks. He had no idea why he wanted to keep her around, but something about her sad expression when she spoke of her father got to him. There was definitely more to that story than she was telling, and for some unknown reason he wanted to know it all.

Stupid.

He had his own father issues to deal with. A difficult discussion about his dad's drinking was one of the reasons for this trip home. He understood the man was grieving, but judging by the last few phone calls, it was getting worse. And his mother would never forgive him if he didn't try to intervene.

His father could hold a grudge. So if he didn't handle the situation perfectly, they might end up not speaking until his dad got over it. Not for the first time, he wished he could talk to his mother. Grief stole his breath and yanked at his limbs like a drowning man in a riptide. It was like that—one minute he'd be fine, and the next, the quicksand of sorrow would suck him under.

Luanne cleared her throat. "Jack, I...ah..."

He yanked himself out of his misery and focused on her. "Yeah?"

"I want to thank you for helping me."

"That tasted pretty bad, huh?"

She laughed. "Horrible. I hope I never have to do it again."

He glanced at his watch once more. He was still okay on time.

"Are you taking medication?"

"What?" Jack gave her a confused look.

She pointed at his hand resting on the steering wheel. "That's the second time you've checked your watch in the last twenty minutes."

"Oh. No, I need to get home to Louisiana by seven."

Her dress made a ruffling sound when she turned in her seat to face him. "You're from Louisiana?"

"Yeah."

"Really?" He voice was high and incredulous.

"Yes, Luanne. I think I know where I grew up."

"Weird. You don't have an accent."

"No. I don't. You don't get taken very seriously in my business if you sound like a broke-ass, swamp-dwelling, backwoods Cajun when you walk into a meeting."

She made a disgusted sound in the back of her throat. "Guess you're not very proud of where you come from."

"That's not it at all."

"Okay."

"It's not."

"I believe you."

He could tell she didn't believe him. He had put more bitterness into that statement than he'd intended. "Anyway, the Beauchamp, Louisiana School Board is honoring my mother at their yearly banquet."

"That's nice. Is she a teacher?"

"She should've been, but no. She managed the elementary school cafeteria for twenty-five years. After she retired, she volunteered by tutoring kids with reading issues. She passed away six months ago."

Her hand went to her chest. "I'm sorry, Jack. I didn't know."

He shrugged. "It's fine. I don't talk about it. But you see why it's important I be there."

"Absolutely. How far of a drive is it?"

"Three hours. I was wondering...and I hope you don't mind, but would you g—"

"Oh, no, Jack."

"I didn't ask anything yet."

"I know, but you can't possibly think it's a good idea for me to ride to Louisiana with you. We'd kill each other."

"That's not what I was going to ask you." Oh, this was priceless. He followed the path of crimson as it crept into her cheeks.

"You weren't?"

"No. Why would I ask you to go home with me?"

She adjusted the air vent to blow on her pretty pink face. "I don't know."

"I was going to ask you to give me a call when you get settled."

"Well, why didn't you just say so? Why all the *I was wondering* and *I hope you don't mind* buildup?"

"Because I knew you'd give me crap about asking you to call. I don't know if you're aware, but you can be difficult sometimes."

"Difficult? I'm not difficult and I'll prove it." She plastered on a pleasant expression. It appeared to take a gigantic effort, but she did it. "Of course I'll call. Thank you for your concern."

"I'd appreciate it." He turned onto her street. "So, what are your plans?"

"I need to get home, grab some clothes, my phone, and my wallet."

He looked her up and down. "Do you have your keys stashed away in that dress somewhere?"

"Funny." She yanked the bodice of the dress back into place. "I keep one hidden on the porch."

"What are you going to do about a car?"

She went back to playing with the eyelashes in her hand. "I'll have Charlie Riggs bring me a rental car from his shop."

"Doesn't he own the feed store?"

"Yes, but he also has rental cars."

"Makes perfect sense. Why is your phone and wallet at your house?"

"I didn't want to have to keep up with all of my stuff today, so we left our bags at my house. We were going to grab them on the way to the airport." An evil smirk eased across her face. "I guess I'll have to leave Doug's things on the lawn, outside his suitcase, ripped to shreds, and on fire."

He chuckled and shook his head. "You scare me sometimes, Thumbelina."

"Be afraid, Jack. Be very afraid."

* * *

"Who's that?" Jack asked, slowing the car.

"What? Oh, that's Tank, my dad's assistant." Luanne gathered her voluminous skirts and prepared to exit the car. "He does everything for my dad but wipe his ass. Come to think of it, he may do that too." Jealousy over this meathead's relationship with her father pinched and poked her heart. She was pathetic. What was next? Insane inferiority over the checkout lady at the Piggly Wiggly because her dad told the woman to have a nice day?

"Why is he here?"

"I don't know. Maybe my dad forgot something at the house, and Tank came by to get it."

"Does he have a key?"

"No."

"Then why would he be here? You're supposed to be twenty miles away getting married."

"I don't know. I'm sure he has a good reason." She pointed toward the curb. "You can let me out in front of the house."

"I don't like it."

"You don't like what?"

"That your dad's goon is here waiting on you."

"Goon? You're paranoid. I've known Tank for years. Except for his murderously awful personality, he's harmless."

"Luanne, the guy's as big as a brick shit-house. Why isn't he playing in the NFL?"

"He could have," she said in her best good 'ol boy accent. "He's the best damn linebacker to ever play for Zachsville's football team. Raider

Pride!" She nearly choked on her spot-on impersonation. "Too bad he's lazy and entitled, with zero ambition," she added. "He got into some trouble at UT and expected it to be brushed under the rug. It wasn't, and he had to come home. The Raider's Booster Club was thrilled when he moved back. They believe Tank Thompson's non-existent progeny are the future of Zachsville's athletic program."

"When did he go to work for your dad?"

"About a minute after he got back to Zachsville, where he's gotten an education in assholery. He gets high marks in that, but then again, he learned from the best."

"And I shouldn't be worried?"

She waved off his concern. "No. He's an asshole to everyone else. He mostly ignores me. I'm too small and scrawny to garner his attention. I'm not good breeding stock for the big man. Thank God."

Jack stopped the car in front of her house. "Maybe I should stay until Charlie Riggs brings the rental."

"Don't be ridiculous. You need to get on the road. I'll be fine."

She opened the door and glanced back over her shoulder. "Seriously, Jack, thank you. Be safe, and I hope they honor the hell out of your mom. She sounds like she deserves it."

He never took his gaze from Tank, who was speaking into his phone. "Okay. You be safe, too."

She watched the car crawl away from the curb. If Jack had pushed the vehicle it would've moved faster. "Sheesh. Men." She hiked up her dress and headed toward her visitor. "Tank—"

"Luanne, you need to get into the car."

"Why?"

"That was your father on the phone. He's on his way to take you back to the wedding. He told me to hold you until he gets here."

"Hold me? Is he crazy?"

One blond eyebrow crawled up Tank's bullet forehead. "He is not."

Would her father actually force her to marry Doug? Yes, she'd let him orchestrate this sham of a wedding, but seriously, wasn't it obvious she didn't want to get married anymore? "Well, I'm sorry to disappoint him, but I'm not going back." She went to the flower pot where she kept her extra key. It wasn't there.

"Looking for this?" Tank dangled the keyring from his finger.

Fury had her stomping toward him. "Give that to me, Tank Thompson."

"What? This?" He swung the key out of her reach.

She fought the urge to jump and grab for it like a child. Instead, she held her hand out like the adult she was. "Yes. Give it back."

"I don't think so." He walked to the curb and dropped the key down the storm drain.

Her brain couldn't make sense of what was going on. Her father was coming to drag her back to the wedding. She had no way to get into her house. And Tank might truly be dangerous. Panic began to inch its way around her chest. "You're insane. I'm calling the police." She took off toward her neighbor's house to borrow their phone.

Two steps were as far as she got before a beefy pair of arms wrapped around her waist and lifted her off the ground.

"I guess you didn't hear me."

What the hell? "Put me down, you meathead." She wriggled and kicked, but in Tank's iron grip it had zero affect. This was a nightmare. She couldn't see her father, she'd never been able to tell him no. If she went back she would end up Luanne Divan.

Tank swung her around like she weighed nothing and deposited her into the back seat of his Range Rover. He buckled her in, slammed the door, and locked it with the fob. The interior of the vehicle was like a sauna and made getting a deep breath difficult. Her cold, numb fingers fumbled with the seat belt. One click, and she was free, or so it seemed. But the child safety lock was engaged on both back doors. They wouldn't open. A frustrated scream ripped from her throat, and she banged impotently on the window. Her anxiety ratcheted up with every step Tank took toward the driver's door.

Just as he got to the front of the car a black streak knocked him to the ground.

Jack.

She fought to crawl into the front seat, but couldn't get her dress out of the way. The smell of new car and stress sweat curdled her stomach. A cocktail of fear and adrenaline made her head swim, but determination not to be this meathead's victim propelled her past those things.

Miles of lace and crinoline hampered her crawl over the console, not to mention the fight ensuing between the two men on the lawn. Her muscles strained for every inch of progress. Finally, she tumbled into the front seat and jumped out of the car.

Neither man seemed to notice. Jack sat on Tank's chest, pummeling him with blows, but Tank deflected as many as Jack landed. The lawyer had him in height but the ex-linebacker was strong as an ox. Tank bucked, reared up, and threw Jack over his head.

The minute Tank gained his feet, he pulled a stun gun on Jack. A mother-lovin' stun gun.

Ohmygodohmygodohmygod.

What was she going to do? She didn't have her phone to call the police, and she wouldn't leave Jack to run to the neighbors. *Where* were her damn nosey neighbors?

The two men were circling each other. Tank was saying something to Jack, but she couldn't hear anything over the blood hammering in her ears.

She had to do something. Standing there like a helpless damsel and letting Jack get hurt wasn't an option. There was no other choice. Time to put up or shut up. She yanked up her dress and made a running leap for Tank's back, screaming like a wild woman. Her arms and legs went around him and she hung on for dear life.

For a second Jack stood still with his head cocked like he couldn't actually believe what he was seeing. Tank spun around, trying to throw her like a bucking bull.

"Don't just stand there. Do something!" Desperation was laced through her shriek. There was no way she would last for a full eight-second ride.

Her would-be rescuer kicked out and knocked the stun gun from Tank's hand while the bigger man thrashed around trying to dislodge her. He got tangled in the fabric of her enormous dress, and they both went crashing to the ground.

Her moment of heroism had passed. A blur of grass and dirt came at her face, and fear froze her heart. Time to get away from her father's goon. With the forward momentum of the fall, she rolled out of the combat zone.

Jack coldcocked Tank with a right cross. Luanne was stunned as the ex-football player's eyes rolled back in his head and he went limp.

"Is he dead?"

"No. I only knocked him out. Holy shit." Jack flicked his hand up and down and flexed his fingers. "Let's get out of here." He reached down and grabbed Tank's car keys.

He tried to take her hand, but she shook him off. All she could do was stare at Tank's motionless form.

This loser tried to kidnap her.

He'd put his hands on her.

He'd threatened her, and now he would pay.

She marched to where the stun gun lay on the ground. In one move she picked it up and flicked it on.

"Luanne?"

She ignored Jack. This was between her and Tank.

"Luanne. You don't—"

"Shut up, Jack." She marched over to Tank, placed the weapon to his crotch and pulled the trigger. Tank groaned and curled into the fetal position. "Don't ever put your hands on me again, you scumbag." She dropped the stun gun, stepped over him, and calmly walked past Jack toward his car. "Jack, I'm gonna need a ride out of town."

"Ooookay."

Once she'd crammed her body and dress in the car, she glanced at Jack. He stared at her from the driver's seat with some emotion she didn't have the energy to decipher. She pushed her hair from her sweaty forehead. "What?"

He chuckled and shook his head, jammed the key in the ignition and slammed his foot on the accelerator. "Like I said, sometimes you scare me, Thumbelina."

Chapter Four

Luanne dabbed at the cut near Jack's hairline with a wet paper towel, while he griped and moaned. Her patient sat on the closed toilet lid of the gas station restroom they'd pulled into as soon as they were out of town. The smell was almost as bad as his complaining. Almost.

"Ouch. That big son-of-a-bitch has a nasty left hook."

"I don't think you need stitches. A Band-Aid should work." She rifled through the plastic grocery bag from the convenience store and pulled out some antibacterial ointment and Band-Aids. "Hold still."

"Damn it, that stings. Are you sure you got the right thing?"

She held the tube in front of his face. "It's the right thing. Don't be such a baby. Now, put that bag of frozen peas on your jaw and let me handle this."

"What the hell happened back there?"

"I don't know. Tank said he was supposed to keep me there until my dad arrived." The bitter reality soured her gut. It clogged her throat and reduced her words to a whisper. "I knew my father wanted this wedding, but I never dreamed he'd try to force me to marry Doug."

"That's seriously screwed up."

"I guess since he arranged the whole thing he's bound and determined to see it happen."

"What?"

"Nothing." She wasn't talking to Jack about her screwed-up relationship with her father.

Her hands shook as she opened the bandage box. He wrapped his warm fingers around hers. "Hey, it's okay. We're out of town and pretty soon you'll be a whole state away."

She nodded. She couldn't trust her voice. It was all so surreal, and the fact that Jack was the one who'd saved her was almost too much to deal with. She now owed him for two huge things. It made her itchy and irritable. Nothing good ever came from owing anyone anything. The bandage went on and she began cleaning up the supplies. "You pretty much got your ass kicked, Jackie Boy."

"You saw me take him down, right?"

"Yeah, after I helped you."

"You looked like a rabid marshmallow."

They both laughed.

She grabbed the sweetheart neckline of her dress and yanked it back into place. I've got to get out of this dress."

"I could help with that." He tried to waggle his brow and winced.

"Shut up, Jack."

"You're no fun, Thumbelina."

His comment rolled off of her—a sure sign of how stressed she was. What was she going to do? She didn't have her ID or wallet. She had no car, no clothes and no way to get any of those things. "Can I borrow your phone?"

"Sure." He dug it from his pocket and handed it to her.

She scrolled through his contacts. "You don't have Scarlett's number?"

"No. If I need Gavin I call him, not his wife. Besides, Gavin would kick my ass if I called to chat with his wife."

"Okay. I guess I'll call Gavin."

She pulled up his contact info and dialed. It rang, then she heard his voice say, "Hey—"

"Gavin, thank—"

"You've reached my cell. Leave a message at the tone. If this is my wife, I'm thinking dirty thoughts about you." *Beeeeeep.*

"Oh, brother."

Jack peered into the mirror, inspecting Luanne's handiwork. "You get his voice mail?"

"Yes. They're ridiculous."

"I know. That boy is whipped." He gingerly poked at a bruise on his temple. "Good luck getting him to call you back. He never checks his messages. You should text him."

"Good idea." While she typed out a text, she couldn't help but notice that even after a fight Jack still looked like he could model for *GQ.* "They're both whipped. The best thing about *Gavlett,*" the name the two of them had given Gavin and Scarlett, "is Aiden. That kid's a hoot."

Jack smiled at her in the mirror. "He is. He called me a tooty head the other day."

She grinned. "Smart boy."

"Geez, let's get out of here. It's like a smelly sauna." He grabbed his jacket from the hook on the door and opened it for her.

After the fetid stench of the bathroom, the motor oil and gas saturated air of the convenience store parking lot smelled like heaven.

She dialed Gavin's number a second time and left a message for Scarlett to call her on Jack's phone. There was no telling how long it would take her friend to call her back. She knew what she had to do, and it just about killed her to do it. "Jack?"

He turned to her. "Yeah?"

She chewed her lip. Her stomach rolled and flopped. "Can I borrow some money?"

He shrugged. "Sure."

"I'll pay you back. I mean, I'm good for it. It's only that I couldn't get my purse or anything and I don't have any money on me." She held her hands out to prove she wasn't hiding a purse or money bag.

He unwrapped a piece of gum and popped it into his mouth. "I know. How much do you need?"

She was shocked. He wasn't going to make her work for it? Had

Tank hit him harder than she thought? "I don't know. Not much. I only need some clothes. Nothing fancy, though."

"Hold on." He jogged into the store.

She could see him talking to the clerk and the clerk pointing this way and that. A minute later he jogged back up to the car. "Get in."

"What were you doing?"

"Asking the guy if there was a shopping center in this Podunk town."

"I don't need a shopping center, just a small shop where I can get something to cover my body other than this dress."

"Good. Because there isn't a shopping center, but there is a Charity Mart." He opened the car door. "Ever been there?"

"No, have you?" No way Jack in his tailored suits and gazillion dollar sports cars had ever been to Charity Mart.

"You haven't lived until you've bought an entire secondhand outfit, a television, and a push lawnmower from a thrift store."

* * *

Jack perused the aisle of the Lido, Texas, Charity Mart. After he'd begun making money at sixteen, he vowed he'd never step foot into a thrift store again. Everything about this place screamed desperation to him. Maybe he was projecting, because that's how he'd felt all those years ago when this was the only place his mother shopped.

It had all been fine until the day Paul Sanders, an older boy in middle school, noticed Jack wearing one of his old shirts. It was one of Jack's favorites, a Dallas Cowboys football jersey with Troy Aikman's name and signature on it. Unfortunately, he hadn't noticed that Troy had autographed it to Paul.

The whole experience had been horrible. For one thing, he never knew they were truly poor until that moment. It'd crushed something inside him. For another, he'd been talking to Laurie Teagan when Paul made his announcement. Twenty years later and he could still feel the hot pricks of mortification on his face.

The only good thing to come from that nightmare was the discovery of his superpower. Even though he was dying of embarrassment inside, he'd grinned at Paul and said, "I'm sure it looked good on you, but it looks better on me." There was a moment of stunned silence, then Paul laughed, ruffled Jack's hair, and said, "You're alright, kid." After that he became the older kid's official mascot, because he was funny, charming, and hid every negative emotion he'd ever had.

He'd learned a valuable lesson that day. It doesn't matter if you're dying on the inside, it's what people see on the outside that matters. Charm may be deceitful, but it's the best weapon to have in your arsenal.

Exhaustion grabbed at him and he rubbed an ache at the base of his skull. The remaining adrenaline from the fight pulsed through his veins and made his head hurt. He hadn't acted that out of control since...well, never. Not even in high school when Chuck Waverly hit on his girlfriend right in front of his face. He'd wanted to beat the shit out of the rich mama's boy, but he'd only plastered on a cocky grin, shrugged, and said, "Take her if you want her." It almost killed him, but if everyone knew how he really felt about Staci Adair, then he'd appear weak, and weak and poor were a socially deadly combination.

Plus, going after Chuck probably wouldn't have done any good anyway. It was only a matter of time before Staci, the love of his young life, was lured away by Chuck's convertible and fancy dinners. He'd only accelerated the inevitable. No way could he have competed with that back then. He brushed his finger over the fringe of a woman's poncho and wished Chuck and Staci could see him now.

He caught a glimpse of himself in a five-dollar gold-framed mirror that his mother would've snatched up in a heartbeat. Older, wiser, and more successful, he'd made something of himself, damn it. He'd constructed a life anyone would envy. Not a normal life, because who wanted normal, but an exceptional life. One that didn't resemble his poverty-stricken childhood and was blessedly drama free. Sure, his clients had boatloads of drama, but that was their shit. He was in total control of his life.

Well he had been until a few hours ago, when he'd let his...curiosity? lust? heart? get the best of him and gone after a sexy pixie. Now, he'd lost all control and had a starring role in a runaway bride drama.

He examined the dressing room door that hid the source of his troubles. "You doin' alright in there, Luanne?"

"I'm fine. I can't believe all the stuff you can get here. Some of these clothes have barely been worn." She waved a blouse over the top of the door. "This is a Michael Kors blouse, it's missing a button, but with some needle and thread it would be perfect, and it's only five dollars."

He shook his head and grinned. She sounded just like his mother.

Look at these shoes, Jack. They've barely been worn.

This jacket is nice. Yes, it has a little rip in it, but I can sew that right up.

There's not a thing wrong with this bike, nothin' a little air in the tires and spray paint won't fix.

"Yeah, it can be a real treasure trove of gently used things." *And a bottomless pit of self-loathing.*

"I know. I found this Ralph Lauren dress. I don't even need a dress, but for $9.99, I can't say no."

Why did hearing the glee in her voice make his heart speed up? "You enjoy spending my money. I feel like a sugar daddy."

She snorted. "A low-rent sugar daddy."

"You wound me, Luanne."

The lock clicked and the door cracked open, revealing her beautiful face. "Ha. Yeah, right. I think your gigantic ego can handle it."

He caught a glimpse of the creamy skin across her shoulder and his mouth watered. "Having trouble with that zipper?"

"Yes. Stupid thing got stuck." She turned her back to him. "Can you help me?"

It was time he shook off the sad-sack memories of the past and focused on the perfect distraction the universe had given him. "Sure."

"Thanks...what are you doing?"

"I'm coming in." He shoved into the dressing room and slid the lock into place. "Unless you want the whole store to see your naked backside."

"Jack." There was a warning in her voice that he probably should listen to, but something about this woman made him reckless as hell.

"Turn around, Luanne." He almost lost it when her bare back came into view. It was a playground he wanted to explore. "No bra?" The words barely made it past dry vocal chords.

"I only had a strapless for the dress and it cuts into me, so I took it off." Did she sound a little breathy too?

The zipper sank to a tantalizing depth. Twin indentations on either side of her spine appeared right above a tiny scrap of white lace. Lace that enveloped a perfect ass and hid delights he'd only ever been able to dream about. The recklessness raging through him traveled south. Great, now his other brain was fully onboard this ill-advised course. His thoughts scrambled until he stopped thinking altogether. "Good decision."

He took a hold of the rough metal zipper and grazed her soft, creamy flesh. Warmth pulsed through his body and he quickly abandoned the idea of covering her up. Lost in a blast of desire, he trailed a finger up her spine, the velvety path, the sexiest thing he'd explored in a long time.

Gooseflesh broke out on her skin. "Jack?"

This was madness. He should stop. But no amount of money in the world could've made him walk out of that dressing room. Luanne stood stock still. Their eyes met in the mirror. Hers were dilated and bright with desire, and he knew his were too.

She licked her lips. "I—"

"Shh." He tunneled his fingers through her hair and bent to kiss between her shoulders. She smelled like the worst and best decision he'd ever made wrapped in a candy coating. Electricity shot to his groin. He had to taste her.

He flicked his tongue out and groaned. Everything about this crazy, independent, fierce woman drove him insane and the decadence of her skin was no exception. Unable to stop, he sank his teeth into the side of her neck. Not enough to hurt, but enough to telegraph exactly what he'd like to do to her.

She tilted her head to give him better access. "You like that?" he breathed across her skin.

"Mmmm."

"I can make you feel—"

"Sir." *Knock, knock, knock.* "Sir, you can't be in there. We've had some complaints."

Luanne jerked up and whacked his chin with her head. Hard. The room tilted and spun, he saw stars, then he slid down the wall.

His last thought was *Damn it, I hate Charity Mart.*

Chapter Five

"I don't know why you didn't let me drive." Luanne adjusted her position in the seat so she could look at Jack.

"I've told you twenty times that I'm fine. Besides, no one drives this car but me." He pinned her with a look. "Ever."

With a quick salute she said, "Aye, aye, Captain." She infused the statement with enough sarcasm to choke a horse. Like she'd even want to drive his stupidly fantastic car. "So if you're fine, why are you being such a sourpuss? I said I was sorry, and besides, the salesclerk startled me." Thank God she had. Her back still tingled where he'd touched her. His fingers...and his tongue...and his love bite. And he'd been so kind to her. Maybe there was more to the arrogant playboy Jack Avery than she'd originally thought.

"No offense, Thumbelina. It takes a lot more than the likes of you to take me down."

Nope, still an arrogant jerk.

He clicked on his blinker and made a right turn onto a beautiful tree-lined street. "And another thing...I don't know why you wouldn't let me pay for your clothes. It wasn't a big deal."

Ahhhh, there it was. The real source of his attitude. He wanted her to be even more in debt to him than she already was. "If it wasn't a big deal, then why are you so pissed off? Besides, if you're going to be mad at anyone you should be mad at the store manager. She's the one who said I could use my wedding dress as payment."

She'd wanted to kiss the saleswoman for making the suggestion. She didn't want to be beholden to Jack, or to anyone else for that matter. Nothing like learning early that survival was for the ones who could take care of themselves. Bitter lesson to learn for a kid barely out of diapers.

Baby, Mama can't get out of bed today. I'm too sad.

But I'm hungry, Mama.

There's some dry cereal on the table, you can eat that.

Without milk?

Yes. You're not a baby anymore, so you don't need milk.

She'd been three.

But she'd shown her mother how big she was and gotten the milk all by herself, and cleaned up the spill she'd made too.

She was scrambling eggs by the time she was five. A growing girl couldn't live on cereal alone.

So, yes, she could take care of herself.

They turned onto another tree-lined street with antebellum mansions on each lot. "You grew up here?" Figured. Jack certainly gave the impression of being born with a silver spoon in his mouth and both fists.

He snorted. "Not hardly."

"What does that mean? Are these too small for the Avery family?"

He flashed a cocky grin.

"Pretentious ass."

His shoulders rose and fell. "What can I say?"

"You're hopeless."

"Listen, I'm sorry you have to come with me to this thing for my mom, but I don't have time to get you settled in a hotel before it starts."

"I told you that you don't have to *settle* me anywhere."

"Yeah. How are you going to pay for a hotel? Exchange another article of clothing?"

Wow, an arrogant ass and nasty to boot. She didn't know what she'd thought she saw in this guy, but it must've been a hallucination.

He glanced into the rearview mirror before he changed lanes and turned into the parking lot of the Alexandria Civic Center, then whipped into a space in front of the building. He sat with both hands still on the wheel and stared at the front door. "I'm sorry. That was rude."

"Yes, it was." She wouldn't let him off the hook so easily.

He didn't move. She wasn't sure if he was even breathing. Finally, he turned and a brief streak of raw pain flashed across his face, but was gone almost as quickly as it had appeared. "I'm not myself, but I shouldn't take it out on you."

She knew what those words cost him. This man was in pain. He may be an arrogant ass, but there were deep secrets behind that playboy face. She reached and straightened his hair, then quickly pulled her hand away. "I'm sorry about your mother."

He shook off her concern. "Thanks, but really, I'm okay."

Instead of aggravating her, his instant denial broke her heart a little. Probably because of that flash of misery a few moments earlier. *Damn it.*

This was too much. She didn't want to think of him this way, as a wounded boy missing his mama. So she changed the subject. "You look pretty good for a guy who's been in a fight, been coldcocked, and rescued a kick-ass damsel in distress."

He blew out a breath like he was glad she'd changed the subject, and gave her a wink. "You think I look good, tough girl?"

She shook her head. "You're incorrigible." She checked her makeup in the visor mirror.

"Guilty as charged, counselor." He unhooked his seatbelt. "Ready?"

She flipped the visor back into place. "I'm glad I decided to buy this dress today. It would've been awkward to walk in with those shorts I bought with *Moneymaker* on the ass."

He gawked at her. "You got those?"

"Oh, yeah, and I found the cutest tube top to go with them."

"What?" he croaked out. "You did?"

It felt good to laugh. A full-on belly laugh at that. Even when he was busy aggravating the crap out of her, he could always make her laugh. She shoved his shoulder. "No, you idiot."

He laughed too. "Okay." His fingers plowed through his hair, and he sucked in a chestful of air then puffed it out. "We should go in now."

The banquet room was full. People milled about, and round tables held centerpieces of books with candles stacked on them. At the front of the room was a long table for the VIPs, and behind it was a huge picture of a pretty woman with her gray hair pulled away from her face. Her whiskey eyes sparkled like her son's and it made Luanne's heart hurt. She couldn't have been more than fifty-five.

"Jack Avery, you good-lookin' devil." A woman old enough to be his grandmother sidled up to them and planted her cane directly in front of him. Luanne almost died when the geriatric gave him a lascivious once-over.

Instead of being embarrassed, Jack widened his stance and put his hands out to the side for her inspection.

"Heavens, boy, if I were forty years younger..."

"You'd still be too beautiful for me." He winked. "How are you Mrs. Parker? Woo-wee, woman. You're lookin' hot as fire. You know poly-ester and loafers get me every time."

The older woman leaned on her cane and laughed so loud people all over the room stared. She wiped a tear from her wrinkled cheek. "Boy, you're as bad as ever. Now give me a kiss and help me to my seat before I fall down."

He bent and placed a lingering kiss on Mrs. Parker's cheek, then offered her his arm. "Mrs. Parker, this is my friend Luanne Price. Luanne, this completely inappropriate woman is my fifth-grade teacher, Amelia Parker."

She poked Jack in the ribs. "You know it, buddy boy. Nice to meet you, Luanne."

"It's nice to meet you too, Mrs. Parker."

Jack placed Mrs. Parker's free hand in the crook of his arm. "Come on beautiful, make me look good."

Luanne walked behind them, shaking her head. He was slick as a snake, just like her father. The open wounds on her heart burned and bled. She'd lost track of the times her father had charmed her into believing every word he said was true, only to find out it was all a lie.

She watched Jack's teacher snuggle into him and his black head bend to her curly gray locks and whisper something. Mrs. Parker giggled like a teenager. To be fair, he wasn't exactly like her father. No way would Marcus Price have put himself out for her like Jack had today. Nor would he have broken his neck to get to an award ceremony for his dead mother. Hell, the man couldn't be bothered to make it to holidays for his mother who was alive and well.

Once they had Mrs. Parker situated, and Luanne had been introduced to the woman's friends, they made their way to the front of the room.

They stopped in front of the head table. "Your mother was lovely," Luanne said.

"Yes, she was." He gazed at the photo like if he wished hard enough she would speak to him. After a moment, he peered down at Luanne with a sheepish grin on his face as if he'd been caught unawares, but was willing to give her that tiny sliver of himself. "Lovely inside and out." It tugged at a feeling she didn't want to acknowledge.

"Jack!" A very pregnant woman with a clipboard waddled up to them. "Thank God you're here. We thought y'all weren't coming."

He flashed his signature you're-not-really-mad-at-me expression. "Sorry, Rosemary."

"Well, that's alright, cher," she said, obviously flustered by his complete attention. She looked around. "Where's your father?"

"He's not here?"

"No. I thought he'd be with you."

"I just pulled into town and haven't been by the house. I called earlier and left a message that I'd meet him here." Jack pulled out his phone and scrolled through the messages. "He didn't text me back. Let me call him." He stepped away, leaving Luanne and Rosemary standing there.

"Hello, I'm Luanne." She extended her hand.

Rosemary juggled the clipboard and took her hand. "Rosemary. You're with Jack?"

"Yes, but not—"

"Well, that officially makes you the most envied woman in Beauchamp, Louisiana. I don't think I've ever seen Jack with a woman, other than prom and homecoming dates."

"You've known him a long time?" She should set the woman straight and tell her they weren't dating, but the chance to learn more about Jack was too tempting.

Rosemary laughed. "Does since birth count? Our mothers were best friends." She glanced at Jack's mom's picture, and her eyes glistened with tears. "Robin was the absolute best person to ever live. We all miss her. How's Jack doin'? I know he and his dad have had a real bad time dealing with her death."

Thankfully she was saved from answering when Jack returned. "We can go ahead and get started."

The ice-cold anger rolling off of him was so uncharacteristic that Luanne did a double take.

Rosemary hugged her clipboard to her chest. "Oh, no, what's wrong?"

"Nothin'."

Had she ever heard Jack drop a letter from a word? No, she hadn't, and it freaked her out.

"Jack, you know you can tell me." Rosemary placed her hand on his arm.

He looked around and lowered his voice. "He's drunk, Rose." His hands went to his hips and he hung his head. "Of all the nights."

His childhood friend wrapped him in a hug. "It'll be alright. I'm sure it's all too much for him. He'll be better tomorrow."

He drew a huge breath in and let it out slowly. "You're probably right."

She smiled up at him. "Better?"

Jack nodded and a weird expression played on his lips. "Your baby kicked me. Not gonna lie, Rose, that's kind of freaky."

She patted her stomach. "Well done, baby. Uncle Jack can always use a good kick in the pants."

Luanne's mind raced for a way to escape this intimate conversation that she had no business being a part of. "I'll stand at the back and watch from there."

"Nonsense," Rosemary said. "There's plenty of room for you at the head table. I'll move some folks around so you can sit next to Jack."

The uncomfortable look on Jack's face probably mirrored her own. But neither of them said anything.

"You have your speech?" Rosemary asked.

"Yes."

"Okay. I'll go tell them we can start." She kissed his cheek. "Remember why we're here."

Luanne and Jack found their seats and made small talk with the people around them. Then dinner was served. It looked amazing, but Jack hardly ate. She, on the other hand, scarfed down her food like a lumberjack.

As dessert was being passed out, Rosemary went to the podium. "Thank you all for coming. I think we can agree the Civic Center staff has outdone themselves." She stepped back from the mic and led the room in applause. "This banquet is to honor all the folks who volunteer at all of our schools here in Beauchamp. As the principal of Joanna Colquitt Elementary, I'd like to thank you all from the bottom of my heart. You all make the wheels turn—without you, the whole system would grind to a halt." The teachers and other educators applauded.

"Tonight is also about honoring one of our own, Robin Avery. Robin worked for the Beauchamp school system for twenty-five years and volunteered as a literacy pal for many years. Everyone loved Robin. Her sunny smile and positive attitude kept morale up around Joanna Colquitt for many years. As you know, we lost Robin this year to cancer." Her voice caught and she took a minute before continuing. "I'll never understand why God takes the good ones so early, and Robin was the best. Her son Jack is here tonight to honor his mother in a very special way."

The crowd stood and clapped as Jack made his way to the podium. The thunderous appreciation for his mother reverberated off the walls.

"Thank you, Rosemary, for the lovely words about Mom." He took a breath and surveyed the crowd. "You know she would have hated all of this." Everyone laughed. "But she would've also been touched, as I am. Mom was gifted, talented, and extremely smart. She also had a ninth-grade education. Did you know that?"

He leaned toward the microphone. Luanne knew without looking at the audience that they were hanging on Jack's every word. Hell, *she* was hanging on his every word.

"Her family was very poor, so after her freshman year in high school she had to drop out of high school to work. When she was twenty-eight she got her GED. I remember she and I would do homework together, me learning my letters and addition, while she studied for the exam."

He paused and his Adam's apple moved up and down several times.

"Education was incredibly important to her. Trust me, you did not want to bring home a B when you were capable of making an A, and pack your bags if you brought home a C. I can still hear her saying, 'Jack Henry Avery, do you know how lucky you are to be able to go to school and learn? Education is a blessing. Now get to your room and do your homework so you don't grow up to be an idiot.'"

Laughter floated through the room, and Luanne caught a stray tear before it fell from her lashes.

"She gave me a love of learning and so much more. Things I will forever be grateful for, things I don't know if I ever thanked her for..." He stopped, lowered his head, and squeezed his eyes shut. For several long seconds, the emotions of the room balanced on the tip of a needle.

When Jack looked back at his audience, the familiar devil-may-care grin was back in place. "She was one of kind. The best mom, wife, and friend anyone could ask for. So, in honor of my mother and to further the education of the bright minds of the Beauchamp school system, I've set up the Robin Marie Avery Scholarship Fund. I'd like to introduce the first two recipients, Josey Weber and Nick Nguyen."

Before the last words were out of his mouth, the crowd erupted into applause and everyone got to their feet as the two kids made their way to the stage. Shrill whistles and shouts of celebration filled the room. The kids both shook Jack's hand and he gave them each a check. The girl's family snapped pictures, while recording the whole thing on their phone. Nick's family was crying with joy. Once the hand-shaking was done, Jack excused himself and made his way back to his seat.

When he sat down she reached over and lightly brushed his hand under the table. It was all she could afford to give him. He was too dangerous, too complicated. Over the past few hours she'd realized something awful. Jack may have the schmooze factor like her father, but there was one hugely fundamental difference. And no matter how hard he tried to hide it, or she tried to ignore it, the truth stared her in the face.

Jack Avery had a good heart.

Damn it.

Chapter Six

Jack couldn't wrap his mind around the fact that his dad had got drunk and missed the scholarship ceremony. They'd been talking about it for weeks. Granted, every time he spoke with his dad he'd seemed more and more distant, but he'd chalked that up to grief.

Luanne yawned from the passenger seat. He hated that he'd have to deal with his dad with her as an audience, but setting her up in a hotel and sorting her issues would take time. Time he didn't want to take. He had to make sure his dad was alright. "I'm sorry you have to witness this thing between me and my dad."

She waved away his concern. "Please. You've met my father, right? Besides, I'm exhausted. If you point me toward the nearest bedroom, I'll take my problems there, so you can have some privacy with your dad."

He chuckled. He'd had the privilege of meeting Marcus Price at a BBQ at Scarlett and Gavin's house. The man was a boa constrictor waiting to tighten his coils while smiling to your face. "Yeah. Okay, thanks. I honestly don't know what's happened to him. He doesn't drink, other than a couple of beers during a ballgame or something. What I mean is, he's not a drunk."

"I get it. This was probably really hard for him and he, I don't know, needed some help to get through it and drank too much."

"Maybe. It's just..."

"What?"

"It's just that when I spoke with him earlier he seemed so angry. My dad's probably the nicest guy in the world. I've rarely heard him raise his voice. But he was ranting about my mother and me when we were on the phone."

"What did he say?"

"I don't know. It was all so slurred and convoluted."

"I'm sure he'll be okay when we get there. The ceremony probably brought up some sad memories for him."

"I hope you're right." Jack turned into the driveway. He cringed at the thought of her seeing the tiny yellow house he grew up in. He'd tried multiple times to get his parents into a nicer place, but they'd both refused. Seeing the house today was jarring. Since his mom's death his father had let the place go. It really did look like the Averys were from the other side of the tracks.

He turned the car off. "Well, here we are, home, sweet home." Bitterness curled around every word.

"This is where you grew up?"

"Yep. Surprised?"

"A little."

"I wasn't lying about my mom and her drive to see me educated. I knew from an early age that you had a better chance of escaping this..." he waved his hand in the direction of the house, "with a framed diploma on the wall. I worked hard, graduated, went to college and never looked back. But it didn't always look so run-down. My dad hasn't kept it up."

"I'm sort of sorry I called you a pretentious ass."

He shrugged. "It's fine. I am a pretentious ass, but it's a learned behavior, not something I grew up with."

They exited the car and made their way up the rickety steps to the house. Through the door he could see all the lights were on, except the one in the living room.

He slid his key into the lock and opened the door. He pointed to a door down the hall. "You can use my bedroom. I'll sleep on the day bed on the back porch. The bathroom is next to it. It should be clean, I have someone come and clean the house twice a month. Rummage around for anything else you might need. The kitchen is straight ahead."

"I can't take your room. I'll sleep on the back porch, or the sofa."

"It's fine. You'll have more privacy in my room."

She nodded. "Thank you, Jack. I really don't know how to repay you."

"I'll think of something."

"Pig," she said, without heat. "Since I'm already racking up a bill, do you think I could borrow your phone? I need to try and get in touch with Scarlett."

"Sure." He reached into his pocket and withdrew his phone. "Five missed calls from Gavin's phone. You're in trouble Ms. Price."

"I never heard it ring."

He checked the toggle on the side of the phone. "I turned it off for the wedding. I guess I never turned it back on."

"I better call her. She's probably got the Highway Patrol looking for me." A tap of her finger and the phone came alive. "Thanks for letting me use it."

"No problem. Ignore the porn. It's research for work. I promise."

She chuckled and gave him a wave over her shoulder as she made her way down the hall. "Good night, Jack."

"Good night." He followed her movements and almost forgot about the trouble he had brewing with his father. Almost. "Dad?"

"Who dat?"

He followed his father's Cajun greeting into the small living room and flipped on a small table lamp, casting the room in a golden hue. His dad sat sprawled on the sofa with a bottle of Jack Daniels in one hand and a piece of paper in the other.

"What's up, Dad?" What the hell was going on? He'd never seen his dad like this.

"Nuttin'."

"Something is obviously going on or you wouldn't be sitting here in the dark, drunk as a skunk, and smelling like you haven't showered in a couple of days."

"Mind your own damn business." Spittle followed the statement from his father's lips.

Jack stepped back like he'd been punched in the gut. His father never spoke to him in this manner. He strode over to take the bottle from his dad's hand. "Give me that. It's not doing you any favors."

The drunken man wrestled for the bottle but lost. "Just get da hell out of here. You're not my son."

"What? Dad, are you sick? You're talking crazy."

The house phone rang on the small table next to the sofa scaring the shit out of Jack. He lifted the receiver. "Hello."

"Jack, it's Rosemary. How's your dad?"

"He's drunk and talking out of his head, but I think he'll be fine in the morning."

"Okay, if you need anything let me know."

"I will." He returned the phone to its stand.

"Stop talkin' about me like I'm not here, boy. Show me some respect, goddammit, is that any way to talk about your father?" He stared at the paper in his hand, then crumpled it in his fist. "Not your father..." he mumbled, and then began to cry.

Panic flooded Jack's veins. Something bad was going on with his dad. He knelt beside the sofa so he was eye level with his father. "Dad, tell me what's wrong. It's alright, you can tell me."

The elder Avery shook the fist with the paper in Jack's face. "This is what's wrong. This is the end of my life. Your mother lied to us, Jack." He got nose to nose with his son. "She lied," he growled. The words sounded like they were being dragged over broken glass.

Jack restrained his dad and took the sheet of paper from his curled fingers. "What is this?" It was a letter addressed to his mother.

"Go on, read it. Every last thing was a bald-faced lie."

Robin,

My name is Kyle Harris. I'm Mitch Rawlings' partner. I know it's been years since you and Mitch have spoken and there has been a great deal of water under the bridge, so this letter probably comes as a shock to you.

I'm writing to inform you that Mitch is very ill, life-threateningly ill. He's very brave, but the illness is taking its toll on him.

Robin, I know I am overstepping my bounds, but I love Mitch and I can't stand to see him in pain. I think it is time that Jack finally finds out who his real father is. Mitch is a good man and I would hate to think he would die without ever getting to know his son, or his son knowing him.

I realize I am only a bystander in this drama, and I can't even image how difficult it was for you to find out your fiancé was gay, but times are different now. I know I'm asking a lot, and I understand if you want no part in this...

It went on, but Jack never saw the rest. The room swayed and his legs went out from under him. He landed with a thud next to his father. The air trapped in his lungs finally escaped. "What the hell, Dad?"

All his dad could do was cry. Jack knew how he felt. He raised the bottle to his lips and took a long swig. Tears pressed against his own eyes, fire clogged his throat, and his world took a sharp left turn into what-the-fuckville. "It can't be true. She wouldn't have lied to us like that. She just wouldn't have."

His father nudged a box with his foot. "It's true, Jack. The proof is in this box. She kept the letters that went back and forth between them. You aren't my son. Your real father is a gay syrup farmer in Vermont." He staggered to his feet.

"Dad."

His father stared down at him like he'd never seen him before. An imaginary fist gripped Jack's throat. "I don't care what this letter says." He kicked the box of correspondence off the table. "Or what those letters say. You're my dad. We'll figure this out together."

"No. We won't. I'm sorry, Jack, but every time I look at you all I see is her betrayal. I think it would be best if you weren't here in the morning. I need to deal with this by myself."

Then the man Jack had worshipped his whole life walked out of the room.

Chapter Seven

Stepping into Jack's room was like stepping into a high-school yearbook. It took Luanne a moment to process the space. His trophies sat on shelves, pictures of him and his buddies were pinned to a corkboard above his desk, and black and gold pom-poms stuck out of a vase on a shelf. The centerpiece of it all was Jack's letterman jacket, framed and hung above his bed.

Next to the bed was a photo of Jack in a white tuxedo, with a pretty blonde with jewels in her hair and a flowy pink dress. Rosemary. Her back was to his front and his arms were wrapped around her, while her hands rested on his arms. It was the classic prom pose. There was another picture of him and Rosemary facing each other, standing in front of a horse stall, laughing their heads off.

But the picture that caused a knot to form in Luanne's throat was of Jack in his graduation regalia, hugging his mom. They both had their eyes closed like they were trying to memorize the moment. Could a man who obviously loved his mom this much be all bad? That was a question for another day. She had way bigger fish to fry today.

She pulled up the contacts on Jack's phone and dialed Gavin's number.

Gavin picked up on the first ring. "Hey, dickhead."

"Hey, good-lookin'."

"Luanne?"

"Yes."

"Why do you have Jack's phone?"

In the background she heard Scarlett say, "Is that Lou? Give me the phone."

"Yeah, it's her—"

"Lou, where are you?" Scarlett's tone was frantic.

"In Beauchamp, Louisiana, with Jack."

"What? How did you end up with Jack? That's the last person I expected you to be with."

"He offered me a ride and I took it."

"*He offered me a ride* is not an answer. You better start talkin', sister."

"I saw Doug with another woman right before I ran."

"That piece of—"

"It's not about Doug. I'm not in love with him."

"Yes, I know. I believe I told you not to marry him."

"Well, turns out you were right, but not because he isn't the love of my life. I don't do love and you know why. But my father..." Could she tell Scarlett, actually say the words out loud? She had to tell someone— it was eating her alive. "I was hiding in one of the rooms in the back of the event center trying to clear my head—"

"Because you were making the biggest mistake of your life."

"Noted. Do you want to hear this, or not?"

"Sorry, yes."

"Anyway, Doug and his girlfriend were in the hall makin' out when my dad caught them."

Scarlett sucked in a breath. "Oh, crap. I bet Marcus nearly killed Doug."

Misery crisscrossed her heart. "Yeah, that's what I thought would happen too."

A moment of hesitation. "It didn't?"

"Oh, my father tore Doug a new one, but it wasn't because he was cheating on me, it was because his cheating might stop the wedding and ruin their deal."

"I don't understand."

She wished she didn't understand either, but unfortunately this pain was all too familiar. "The long and short of it is my dad needs the Divan's business. Doug needs a respectable wife to appease his family and take over his father's company. I was the solution to both their problems. Once Doug was running the company, he and my dad would do the deal of the century and make tons of money." Humiliation oozed over her. That part of the tale was bad, but it was the rest of the story that tore her heart from her chest. "He told Doug he could have all the affairs he wanted after we were married, Scarlett. It's just so..."

"Disrespectful. Hurtful. Callus."

"Yes." Her legs refused to hold her anymore, and she sat down hard on the bed.

"Hot shit-fire! I hate that man."

As miserable as Luanne was, she bit back a laugh. Scarlett was learning the fine art of cussing from her rock star husband, and she hadn't quite gotten the hang of it. "Yeah...well...we've never been close, but I did think he had my best interests at heart when he proposed the idea of marrying Doug, and I do love my father. Did...I *did* love my father."

"Oh, Lou, I'm so sorry."

Luanne swiped another irritating tear. "It's okay."

"No, it's not. You deserve better than this."

The tenderness in her friend's voice was her undoing. The floodgates opened and the tears fell unchecked down her face. "He sent Tank to my house to bring me back to the wedding. The idiot threw my house key into the storm drain then got physical when I said I was calling the cops. That's when Jack jumped him and they fought, and Tank pulled a stun gun on Jack. I jumped on Tank's back to distract him, then Jack knocked him out and we ran. Jack had to be in his hometown for a ceremony for his mom, so we took off for Louisiana."

"I heard about Tank. The whole *town* has heard about Tank. I can't believe your father did that."

She wiped her face. "Believe it. Jack was taking me to my house so I could get some money and clothes, then I was going to rent a car and get out of town. But because of what happened with Tank, plus the fact that my dad was on his way to get me, we got the hell out of there without any of my things. I have nothing with me. I traded my wedding dress for some clothes at Charity Mart, so at least I'm out of that ridiculous thing."

"You're wearing second-hand clothing?"

"Desperate times, my friend, desperate times. Anyway, do you think you could wire me money tomorrow?"

"Sure. Where do I send it?"

She laughed. "I have no idea. I'll ask Jack and call you in the morning."

"What's your plan?"

"I don't really have one. I can't rent a car or catch a plane because I don't have a driver's license, so I'm sort of stuck with Jack for now. I think he plans to stay here for a few days, then..."

"Why don't you get him to take you to our cabin on the lake—it's on his way back to Austin. Let me know when you'll be there and I'll get the caretaker to meet you and give you the key."

Relief poured over her. She had a solution and she wouldn't have to rely on Jack for anything but a ride. "Can you meet me there?"

"Oh, honey, I'd love to, but we leave for our trip tomorrow, remember?"

"I forgot."

"Yeah, we're taking Aiden to that place with the mouse."

"Is he in the room?"

"Yes." Scarlett lowered her voice to a whisper. "We can't say the name in front of him or he loses his mind. There's no telling what he's going to do when we get there. I'll call when I get back and if you're still there I'll come then. Wait, how will I get in touch with you?"

"I'll buy a cheap phone after you send the money and text you the number."

"Okay. How are things with Jack? I'm surprised you haven't killed him yet."

"They're fine, but I'm really pissed at him."

"Shocker."

She laughed. "Yeah, well, he's saved me twice, and that really screws with my plans to hate him forever."

"Shame."

"I know."

"What are you going to do about your father? He was furious, but in that smarmy Marcus Price kind of way. He and Gavin almost got into it, because he thought I knew where you were and tried to bully the info out of me."

She picked at loose string on the bedspread. "I can imagine Gavin's response to that."

"Yeah, well, let's just say that your dad got up close and personal with The Delinquent, and he backed off quick."

"I bet he did." The thought of Gavin 'The Delinquent' Bain ripping her father a new one brought her a sick sense of satisfaction.

"Um...Lou, there's something else you should know."

There was more? "Tell me."

"It appears there's a chance that Tank could lose a testicle due to the...um...shot you gave him."

"What?" She couldn't stand Tank, but she hadn't meant to do permanent damage.

"Yes, and...well, the Zachsville Raiders Booster Club is out for blood. They're sure if Tank loses a testicle, then he won't be able to have kids, and you know what they always say about his unborn spawn."

"Those kids are the future of Zachsville's athletic program," they said together.

"They're pressuring Will Sinclair to press charges."

"What does Will say to that?"

Scarlett snorted. "Will told them he wanted the whole story before he made any kind of decision. Will's the best DA Blister County's ever had. He's not going to kowtow to a bunch of overzealous sports fans. I wouldn't worry about any kind of legal repercussion, but the public backlash is another thing. I'd lay low for a while if I were you."

She nibbled her fingernail. "How was Gigi?"

"Your grandmother was flitting around your father trying to calm him down."

"I should call her." Mutant butterflies began to duke it out in Luanne's belly at the thought of that conversation.

"Yes, you should."

"Can you text me her number?"

"You don't know your grandmother's phone number?"

"She got rid of her landline, and I don't have her cell number memorized. Do you know Floyd or Honey's cell numbers?"

"Um..."

"Exactly. No one memorizes numbers anymore. They're all programmed into our phones."

"Have you and Jack talked about what happened after our wedding?"

Mortification shot up her neck, prickling and stinging. "He tried to, but I shut him down."

"Don't you think you should clear the air between you?"

She jumped up from the bed. "And say what, Scarlett? Hey, Jack, remember that time I got drunk at my best friend's wedding, sucked your face, then lost my freakin' mind while we were on our way to my house to get it on? Yeah...well...sorry about that. 'Kay?" She paced around the room. "I mean how do you come back from that? And how do I explain it, without telling way too much about myself? No thank you. He already has enough ammunition to bury me."

"Did he try to rub your nose in what happened? I'll kick his mother-lovin' ass."

She picked up a cologne bottle from the top of the dresser and sniffed. It smelled musky and old, like it hadn't been used in a very long time. "No. He was actually pretty nice about it, but who knows when he'll try to use it against me. It's best to let sleeping dogs lie."

"Okay, but for the record, I think you're wrong."

She replaced the cologne bottle and picked up a leather bracelet with flowers burned into the band. When she turned it over, she saw the name Valerie written in black sharpie. Interesting. "So, noted."

"I'll text you your grandmother's number."

"Thanks, I love you."

"I love you too."

Once they disconnected she stared at the phone. She needed to call her grandmother, but it was the absolute last thing she wanted to do.

The phone vibrated in her hand and her grandmother's number popped onto the screen along with a message from Scarlett.

BTW, be careful around Jack, he can charm the pants off a saint.

A snort escaped her. Yeah, she'd almost found that out in the dressing room of the Charity Mart.

She tapped the screen to make the call. Her grandmother answered on the first ring.

"Hello."

The bedsprings squeaked when she plopped down on it this time. "Gigi, it's Luanne."

"Luanne, your father is fit to be tied."

"I bet he is." Of course her grandmother would be more concerned about her baby boy's welfare as opposed to her well-being. No matter that Marcus Price was a fifty-year-old man.

"What does that—"

"Luanne, this is your father."

Damn.

"Yeah, so?"

"So? I'm worried sick about you and all you can say is so?"

Don't fall for it, don't fall for it, don't fall for it.

But it was so hard. Something about her father acting all concerned about her turned her to mush.

That's how you got into this situation.

She hardened her heart against his endearing tone. "I'm sorry you're worried, Marcus, but I assure you there's no need."

"Marcus? What is heaven's name is going on, Luanne?" Her father actually sounded hurt. Give the man an Academy Award.

"Stop! Just stop."

"I—"

"I heard you, Dad. I heard you with Doug and his girlfriend in the hallway. You remember, when you were selling me to the higher bidder?" She hated the tears in her voice.

There was a long pause, and then she heard her grandmother's screen door open and close. He must've gone outside.

"Sweetheart, I don't know what you think you heard, but that never happened." His assertive, soothing tone lapped through the phone line.

"I heard you. You told him that he could cheat with whoever he wanted after we were married, but that he better not screw up this deal for you." She wished she sounded as confident as he had. That was what she'd heard. Right?

"Luanne, honey, what kind of father would say that? Certainly not one who took you in after your mother died, who paid for your excellent college education, and who set you up with your own law practice right out of law school. You simply misinterpreted what I meant."

"But..." She rubbed at her forehead. Her head dictated what she knew to be true, but her stupid heart wanted to believe she had misunderstood. He always confused her. And despite everything, she loved him.

"Truth be told, I'm glad you ran out on Doug. That boy needs to be taught a lesson, and I think he's learned it. So you can come on home to the people who love you, so we can work this out."

The caress of his words chased her anger away, and all she wanted to do was please him.

"You're right—"

"Besides, your grandmother depends on you so much. You're our one true connection."

"Dad, I'll get Jack to take me to the bus station tomorrow. I should be home in the afternoon, but we need to talk."

"No. No daughter of mine is going to ride the bus. I have someone on the way to Mr. Avery's parents' home as we speak. They'll see you safely home, doodlebug."

That melty feeling in her chest was her heart going all gooey over the nickname. "Okay, but I'm not marrying Doug. Maybe I don't understand what I heard, but I know what I saw. I'm not anyone's sloppy seconds."

"That's my girl. He's already gotten rid of that bimbo, and I've had a come-to-Jesus meeting with the boy. We'll take it one day at a time. I only want you home where I can take care of you. See you tomorrow."

"See you tomorrow."

She disconnected the call with joy in her heart. A warm glow snuggled around her. Her father *did* care about her.

Jack's room was like a cozy cocoon around her moment of contentment. She flopped back on the bed. Her father's conversation rewound in her brain, and she sifted through the words to find every morsel of affection. Each one soothed the desperate places in her heart that longed for his approval.

She relished his concern for her, but with every replay, the sour notes behind his sweet tone broke through her happy haze. She wanted to ignore them. She was being too sensitive, too needy. That's what he'd always told her.

Stop your crying, Luanne. Why do you have to be so sensitive? You're too needy, just like your mother.

Never mind that she'd just lost her mother, or that he hadn't shown up for Christmas, even though he'd promised. Never mind the million other promises he'd made and broken. Never mind, never mind.

Unease prickled the underside of her skin. She flipped to her side to try to get more comfortable. But no matter how she lay, the unease in her belly wouldn't go away.

Clarity fought its way to the surface.

And truth kicked down the friggin' door to her mind.

"Son of a bitch." One of the pillows from Jack's bed sailed across the room.

He'd done it again. Totally sweet-talked her into believing something that wasn't true. When would she ever be able to see through his bullshit? It didn't matter that she was a grown woman, the little girl heart inside her was destined to believe every corrupt word out of his mouth.

Nausea roiled in her belly. He'd used all the things he'd ever done for her against her. Again. She grabbed the remaining pillow to muffle the frustrated scream that clawed its way out of her throat.

Played.

She'd been played.

The images on the far wall blurred as she tried to wrap her mind around what had just happened. People would be shocked to see badass Luanne Price reduced to a blubbering fool, a mass of ignorant devotion, with only a few words from the last man in the world she should ever trust.

He'd said he sent someone to get her. He would find her. She had no doubt. What to do? What to do? Her overwrought brain chased for solutions that all led to one place.

Jack.

* * *

The old cypress floorboards creaked as she approached the lump on the floral sofa. Jack was sprawled with an empty Jack Daniels bottle dangling from the fingers of one hand and a half-full bottle of the same poison in the other.

"Hey, Jack." She kept her voice down, not wanting to disturb the older Avery.

Jack didn't say anything, only rolled his head to meet her gaze. His eyes were red and glassy.

"You alright, Jack?" She could tell he wasn't but she needed to give him an out if he didn't want to confide anything to her.

"I'm dandy. How are you, Thumbaweena?" He cracked up laughing. "Thumbaweena. Get it? Cause you're a wee, little thing."

Indecision froze her. She'd never seen Jack so undone. Most of the time he seemed to skate through life as if he hadn't a care in the world. "Yeah, I get it. Good one."

"I know, right? You never laugh at my jokes. Why is that, Lulu? Are you missin' your funny bone? Want me to help you find it?" He waggled his eyebrows and then snorted.

She sat on the coffee table in front of him. "Hey, buddy, why don't you give me that? I think you've had enough." She reached for the bottle, but he clutched it to his chest.

"I'm not done yet." His words were slurring more by the minute. "It still hurts."

Alarmed by the pain in his voice, she placed her hand on his knee. "What hurts, Jack?"

Had he and his father physically fought? She did a quick search for injuries. He looked fine, except for his flushed face and red eyes.

"My heart hurts." He took a big swig and then made a face like it was the worst thing he'd ever tasted.

"Why does your heart hurt?" Seeing him in this much pain made did something unfamiliar to her chest.

He dropped the empty bottle, then picked up a piece of paper and shoved it at her. "Here."

It was a letter addressed to his mother. She skimmed the page and her breath caught. Her gaze jerked up to him. "Jack," she whispered.

"She lied. She lied to me my whole life." Another swig. Another scowl.

"I'm sorry."

He looked at her like he'd forgotten she was there, then let his head fall back on the sofa. "Fuuuuuck."

"Is this why your father was drinking? Did he know?"

"Yes. No." He shook his head. "I mean yes, this is why he was drinking, great idea by the way. And no, he didn't know." He took another long pull from the bottle and then wiped his mouth with the back of his hand. "He wants me gone, told me not to be here in the morning. He can't stand to even look at me." The pauses in his speech lengthened. His lids kept dropping and staying closed, then he'd try and blink them open, only to close them again.

Taking her life into her own hands, she again tried to pry the bottle from his grip. This time she was able to take it with no problem. He slumped to the side so that his head was resting on the arm of the sofa. She pulled an afghan from a nearby chair and covered him. "Rest, Jack. We'll sort this out in the morning."

When she stood to leave he grabbed her hand. "I'm glad you're here, Luanne."

She pushed his hair from his forehead. "I'm glad I'm here too, Jack." She could admit that to him now, because judging by the amount of alcohol missing from those bottles he wouldn't remember this conversation in the morning.

Long minutes passed as she stood there making sure he fell asleep and didn't try to go for the whiskey again. So much for Counselor Avery coming up with a plan. He was in no condition to do anything and his problems were as big as hers. Apparently, the combo of alcohol and heartbreak caused snoring. Jack was done. She'd have to figure something out in the morning.

But she knew the morning would be too late. Her father's man was probably only hours away already. Jack's car keys on a small table just inside the room caught her eye.

Her gaze went to Jack.

To the keys.

Back to Jack.

How mad would he be? Did she care? His father said he didn't want Jack here in the morning, and what kind of friend would she be if she didn't try to help him? Right?

She snatched up the keys and looked back at the sleeping man on the sofa. "We're going on a road trip, Jack. I hear Vermont's nice this time of year."

Chapter Eight

L uanne rubbed her dry, scratchy eyes as she paced around the concrete picnic table. Exhaustion seeped through her pores. She'd driven all night and only stopped now to call Scarlett to give her an update.

The pink and golden rays of sunrise danced through the branches of the trees surrounding the roadside rest stop, and birds sang their morning song. Jack's phone pressed to her ear repeatedly vibrated with incoming texts. She ignored them and waited for Scarlett to answer.

"Hello."

Crap, it was too early for any decent person to be calling. "Hey. I'm so sorry to wake you, but I have cell service now and don't know if I'll have it later today. We've had a change of plans."

"We've?"

"Jack and I."

"You and Jack?" Instantly, Scarlett sounded way more awake.

Luanne ran her fingers through her hair. "Yes. It's a long story and not entirely mine to tell. But what I can tell you is that my father pulled his sweet-talkin' routine on me last night, and I nearly fell for it."

"You called your dad?" Scarlett's shock pierced her eardrum.

"He was at Gigi's. When I called her he highjacked the phone. He said...it doesn't matter. The point is I can't see him yet, and he said he was sending someone to pick me up. Which would've meant a Justice of the Peace wedding for me and Doug when I got back to Zachsville."

"He said that?"

"Not in so many words, but I know that's what he wants."

"He's really not letting this go, is he?"

Luanne used the seat of the picnic table as a step and climbed up on the concrete slab to sit cross-legged. "No. He must be up to his neck with this business deal."

"So now what's your plan?"

"That's part of what I can't talk about, but we'll stop tonight and I'll call and let you know what I can."

"Okay, tell me where to send the money when you can. I don't like the thought of you going cross-country without any resources."

She glanced over at the car containing her lifeline. "I'm not alone. Jack's with me."

Scarlett snorted. "Yeah, that makes me feel better."

She didn't want to talk about Jack. Her feelings toward him were very confused. On the one hand he was Jack, the annoying yet gorgeous thorn in her side. On the other hand, he was Jack who'd just found out his mother had lied to him his whole life, and she couldn't help but feel bad for him. "I'll call you later then. Oh, wait. When are you leaving for your trip?"

"Our flight's at noon."

"Okay, if you're not available when I call later I'll leave a message. Thanks."

"You don't have to thank me. Take care of yourself."

"Love you, bye."

She placed the phone on the table, leaned back on her hands, and enjoyed the morning rays on her face. What was she going to tell Jack? He wasn't going to be happy. She'd made the decision to leave his father's house, she'd driven his precious car, and she'd put him in danger without his consent. Yep. He was going to be pissed.

The staccato beat of her pulse was a direct result of guilt.

Guilt and anxiety.

But didn't he deserve to meet his father? And his father's family. She'd found the second page of the letter underneath Jack when she'd manhandled him up and maneuvered him to the car. Had he even seen it?

Not only did he have a father he didn't know about, but he also had a grandmother and aunt who were anxious to meet him. So much family. Wanting him. The broken, lonely little girl inside her ached for a long-lost family to want her too.

Stupid, Luanne. This is about Jack, not you.

Still, if he did this to her, she'd be furious. She chewed on her thumbnail. Yep, this could get ugly. Indecision pulsed through every mental argument and a bead of hot sweat rolled down her temple. Enough. Time to brazen it out.

When in doubt, grow a pair of balls.

* * *

The incessant pounding of the bass drum shattering Jack's head would not stop. He might have been able to ignore it if it weren't accompanied by a piercing pain in his neck and shoulder. Slowly, he peeked one eye open, but all he could see was black leather. His attempts to get into a better position were met with resistance in the form of something long and round shoved against his ass.

What the hell?

He moved his hand behind him to investigate the object in question, but stopped short when pain shot through his shoulder. Gingerly, he turned his body and saw the stick shift from his Porsche. How had he gotten into his car? Oh, God. He hadn't tried to drive somewhere, had he? Panic gripped his gut. He never drove drunk.

Relief washed over him when he realized he was in the passenger seat. But how had he gotten in the car? Maybe he'd decided sleeping in the car was preferable to sleeping in a house with a father who wanted him gone.

The events of the night before scrolled through his head like a movie on an old projector, yellowed and harsh. The alcohol, the letter, his father telling him to be gone in the morning, and the alcohol...so much alcohol. He tried to swallow down the fiery bile chugging up his throat, but his mouth was so dry.

An eighteen-wheeler's horn blasted nearby. His head exploded in agony, followed by a pitiful groan. Hangovers were a young man's game. He was definitely too old for this shit.

The driver's side door opened and Luanne slid into the driver's seat. "Oh. You're awake."

Even the slight dip her small body caused made his insides bubble and roil. Why did she look so guilty? "Where are we?"

"How are you feeling?"

"Like hell. Where are we?"

"I bought some water. Would you like a bottle?"

"No...yes. Where are we?"

"I know I get terrible cotton mouth when I drink too much." She turned and began rummaging through a plastic bag on the floor behind his seat.

"Luanne." Damn, it hurt to speak above a whisper.

She sat up abruptly with a water bottle in one hand, a pill bottle in the other and an innocent expression so fake she looked like a mannequin. "Yes?"

He eased himself into a sitting position. The alcohol still present in his brain sloshed back and forth like one of those tubes full of liquid. The slightest movement caused a tsunami wave to roll around in his head. "Tell me," he swallowed down some seriously nasty stuff, "Where are we?"

"Not far from Verna."

"Verna?"

She glanced out the driver's side window and bit her bottom lip. "Verna, Mississippi."

"Luanne, I'm hung over, my head is pounding, and I might puke at any moment, so could you kindly tell me why the hell we aren't far from Verna, Mississippi when last I checked we were in Beauchamp, Louisiana?"

"You don't have to yell. I'm sitting right here."

"And yet you aren't giving me any answers." He gripped his forehead with the hand of the arm resting on the door. "Just tell me, please."

She opened the console between them and retrieved a piece of paper. He immediately recognized it. "Where'd you get that?"

"You gave me the first page and I found the second page underneath you when I got you up off the sofa. You're heavy as hell, by the way." Her attempt at levity did nothing for his mood. He gave her a flat-eyed stare that had her looking down at her hands. "Anyway, you told me about you and your dad—"

"My dad!" He started patting his pockets and searching on the floor.

"What are you looking for?"

"My phone. I need to call my dad."

"I have your phone, and I left your father a note."

"You left a note? Who gave you the authority to leave my dad a note? Or drive my car? Or kidnap me and take me to fucking Verna, Mississippi?"

She whipped around to face him. Flames sizzled in her baby blues. "You did, when you got so drunk you couldn't sit up straight, let alone hold a pen to scribble out a note. You put me in the position of coming up with a solution for getting us out of there, especially since you told me your father wanted you gone by morning."

Jack flinched at the words. Fresh heartbreak blasted through his chest. "He didn't mean it." But even he didn't believe his own words.

"I'm sorry. I shouldn't have said that. And I'm sorry for what happened with your dad."

He picked up the papers. Even though there was no way in hell he could focus on the words. Didn't matter. He knew what it said. "Did you read it?"

"I sort of had to. You shoved it in my face and told me to."

"Sorry." He massaged his temples.

"Take these." She handed him the water and shook out two white pills for him to take.

He gratefully took the tablets and threw them back, then chased them with the water.

She unwrapped a packet of gum and gave him a piece. "Here."

"Thanks." He took another pull of water, then leaned his head back and closed his eyes. Sweat broke out on his upper lip and the churning in his stomach worried him. In situations like this concentration was the name of the game. Breath, swallow, will it away, repeat. "Could you turn on the air?"

"Oh, sure. You don't look so good."

With his lids still closed he blew out several puffs of air. "Yeah, well, I don't feel so great. You got any Pepto in your bag of tricks?"

"No. Sorry. We can stop and get some at the next convenience store." She started the car and cranked the air to high.

Something was missing in this conversation. He searched his pickled brain. "I only saw one page of the letter."

She glanced over at him and he didn't like the worried expression on her face. "You did?"

"Yes, what does the rest of the letter say?"

Without looking away from the road she opened the console and withdrew the letter. "See for yourself."

He read but the words on the page wouldn't arrange themselves into a coherent thought. "I can't read this right now. What does it say?"

"Why don't we wait until we get you something for your stomach before we discuss that?"

"Luanne."

"What?"

"Tell me. How much worse can it be than to find out my father isn't a factory worker from Beauchamp, Louisiana, but a gay syrup farmer from Vermont?" He rested his arm on the door and dropped his head in his hand.

She laughed nervously. "I do like syrup."

"Tell me." He hated the defeated tone of his voice, but at the moment it was all he had.

"You have a grandmother and an aunt who live in West Virginia."

Chapter Nine

J ack chewed the inside of his lip. Yesterday his life was pretty
close to perfect. He had money, a kickass career, friends, and
wonderful memories of his mother. So how had he ended up
barreling down the highway with a moody pixie, hung over, and
with a whole new family that he damn well didn't want? "Pull over."

"What?"

"I said, pull over. There's a gas station, pull in there."

She glanced over her shoulder then changed lanes to exit. Once in
the lot she had to maneuver around an eighteen-wheeler to get to a
parking spot. "Are you alright?"

"Dandy."

"Then why did we stop?"

"I'm putting an end to this madness. I am not traveling halfway
across the country to meet a family I never knew existed."

"But—"

"No."

"But—"

"Why is this so important to you, Luanne? I mean why do you even
care about me or my family?" He plunged his fingers into his hair. "We
both know you don't like me."

She drummed her fingers on the steering wheel, not making eye contact with him. "That's not true."

"Really? Name one thing you like about me." When her lips stayed sealed he snorted. "That's what I thought."

"You're funny."

"What?" He couldn't have heard her correctly.

"I mean...sometimes you're kind of funny."

Why did that one statement make him so ridiculously happy? To cover his glee, he gave her his best cocky grin. "Yeah?"

"Stop that. I take it back."

"Uh-uh. You've already said it. It's out there now, and you can't take it back."

She stuck her tongue out at him then laughed. Her laughter curled around his stomach. Dammit. He did not want to have feelings for her, but he knew it was too late for that to be true. He'd liked her from the first day he saw her and she'd threatened to castrate him.

"It's okay, tough girl. I won't tell anyone."

"I'll swear you're lying if you do."

He laughed. "Fair enough."

"Do you feel better?"

Amazingly he did. "Yes."

"Good." She patted his knee, and then went to start the car. "Let's get back on the road."

He put his hand on her arm. "Not until you tell me why this is so important to you."

She sat back in the seat and crossed her arms. Without even opening her mouth, it was obvious that she was fighting some internal battle as to whether she'd tell him or not. "It's my father."

Well, that wasn't what he'd expected her to say. "Your father is why you care if I meet this new family of mine?"

"No."

Her head was down and she was playing with the hem of her shirt. When she looked up, pain had leached the brilliance from her eyes. Her agony was a physical thing. It squeezed the air from the car, and caused his heart to skip a beat.

"My father's the reason I ran."

* * *

There, she said it. It didn't sound any better spoken out loud.

"I don't understand. You said you caught Doug with another woman."

She waved him off. "I did, but that's not why I ran. I wasn't in love with him."

"Why would you agree to marry someone you aren't in love with?"

Yeah, well, that was the million-dollar question. "My father thought it would be good for me. What I said earlier was true. He said he wanted to make sure I was taken care of when he was gone." She sucked in a big breath. "But the bigger answer is, I don't do love."

"You may be the first woman I've ever heard say that."

When she looked at him this time her gaze was deadly serious. "Love makes you weak and stupid. I am neither. Or so I thought until I let my father sell me to the highest bidder."

"Whoa, back up. You've lost me."

"Before I ran, I'd needed a moment away from the wedding hubbub. I found a room off a side hallway in the event center. That's how I overheard Doug and his girlfriend. My father caught them sucking face. He was furious." The pressure building behind her eyes throbbed with every beat of her broken heart. "I was so naïve, I thought he was angry on my behalf. He…" The words got jammed in her throat. She just couldn't say them. "Let's just say my best interest never came into it."

"Lou, you don't have to tell me anymore."

She shook her head. Her father had royally screwed her over, and saying out loud cemented the reality. No more mind games and making excuses for the worst father in the world. "Last night I called my grandmother and he got on the phone. He was all 'Oh, I'm so worried about you', then when I called him on his lie he almost convinced me that I hadn't heard what I heard. That's what he does. He lies so convincingly that you believe you're wrong when you know damn good and well you're right."

Jack's warm finger wiped something from her cheek. Damn it, she was crying. Again. This was third time she'd cried in front of this man.

No. It was one thing to give herself a reality check, but another thing altogether to let someone else see behind the curtain. She wouldn't give into this misery, and she sure as hell wasn't going to give Jack one more ounce of ammunition to use against her.

As quick as she could, she erected the fortress she lived behind. The one she'd begun building when she was four, and her father said she was too sensitive for crying when he left her.

Maybe that's because I didn't know if I'd ever see you again, Dad.

"He's a real son of a bitch."

She flipped down the visor mirror and pretended to inspect her make up, then flicked it back in place. "That's what Scarlett calls him."

"The woman is a genius."

She had to tell him the rest, but she just wanted to be done with this conversation. "There's something else you should know. He knows I left with you and he has people looking for me."

He snorted. "I hope these folks are more competent than that behemoth at your house."

"I'm not going back. No one can tell him no. It's like his superpower. I need time to reinforce my own superpower." She was pleased that her voice had its normal authoritative tone.

"And what is your superpower?"

"Badassery, of course." She pointed one pink-tipped nail at him. "That's why I'll kill you if you tell anyone you've seen me cry."

He held his hands in the air in surrender. "Your secret's safe with me, fireball. Tell you what, I'll take you to an island in the middle of nowhere. I'll call the charter service we use for the record company, and he'll never be able to find you."

She shook her head. "No."

"Why not?"

"Because, Jack, we're going to find your people."

Thunder rolled over his amiable face. "They're not my people." Each word sounded like a chunk of concrete dropping into place.

"Yes they are, and according to that letter they all want to know you. You have two families who love you, Jack. Two. I don't have anyone except my grandmother and she's got her head so far up my father's butt that she can't see what a manipulative jerk he is." She opened the car door. "I'm going to the bathroom and when I get back I expect you to have put on your man-pants and be on board with this plan."

"You can't put that on me, Luanne."

"I can and I am." She got out of the car then poked her head back in. "You're a big boy, Jack. You can handle it."

* * *

Jack was back in the driver's seat, literally at least. Luanne was clearly running this show. He didn't want to be here. This whole road trip was a joke, but he'd play along for a little while longer. He could refuse, of course, but for the first time since her father came back into her life she was back to her bossy self. Even though he'd tried not to, he'd become a student of Luanne Price, and it had made him sick to watch her fade away and wilt before his eyes.

It was like Marcus had killed her mojo. Also, this insane need to keep her safe made him want to keep her happy too. Never mind the fact that he had no intention of meeting any of his long-lost relatives, but she didn't need to know that.

"Do you want some?" She took a huge bite of some kind of pink cupcake thing covered in coconut, and handed him the one left in the package.

He turned down the radio. "I don't actually allow eating in my car." The glare she gave him cracked him up, but he schooled his features. She'd already gotten too much from him. Time to get a little back.

"How is that possible? It's not a road trip without snacks." She picked up the plastic bag from the convenience store and began to dig in. "I've got cheese crackers, Munchos, M&Ms, Snickers, and gummy bears."

The smell of sugar from the pastry did nothing for his already unsteady stomach. "That reminds me, can I have my debit card back?" He held out his hand.

"Oh, sorry." She dug into her pocket. "Here it is."

He tossed it into the console with his wallet. "Now I can rest easy, knowing you're not going to break me buying junk food."

"I'd have to buy a lot of junk food to break you, buddy, if anything Scarlett says is true." She popped the last of the pastry into her mouth.

"What are you talking about?" He changed lanes and rested one hand on top of the steering wheel.

"You're loaded. Don't try to deny it." She cracked open a bottle of Yoo-hoo.

Where did such a tiny woman put so much food? "I'm not denying it. You'll never hear me being falsely modest about my wealth. I worked hard for it, made sacrifices, and make good decisions." He shrugged. "I like having money. It makes life much easier."

She made a scoffing sound. "There's more to life than money, Jack. I mean, there's family and helping others. Life isn't about acquiring all you can."

"I never said money was the only thing that mattered. There are a lot of things more important than money. All I said was that life is easier when you have the funds to pay for the things you want and need. It sounds like you're putting me and your father in the same boat." He took his attention from the road and stared her down. "I am not your father."

She slid her gaze to the window. "Fine. You're right. Sorry."

"Apology accepted."

She'd told him things about her childhood, painful things. He supposed he could give her a little of his. "I grew up very poor. You know that by now."

He felt more than saw her look at him, but she remained silent.

He propped his arm in the window and rested his head in his hand. "Before the house you saw, we lived in a mobile home on the outskirts of town. We were on government assistance for a while, and every stitch of clothing I wore until I was sixteen was someone else's cast offs."

"What happened when you were sixteen?"

"I got a job. The first thing I bought was a black hoodie that had a complete, anatomically correct, upper body skeleton screen printed on it."

"Noooo."

He laughed. "Yep. The best part was the bleeding heart under the ribs." He patted his chest. "I was the shit when I wore that hoodie. I ordered it out of a skater magazine so there wasn't another skeleton hoodie in town."

"Stop. Wait. Are you saying you were a skater too?"

He ran his fingers through his hair. "The only thing I'll say is...I never met a half-pipe I couldn't make my bitch."

They both cracked up. Her laughter ignited every male molecule in his body. It was bad. The color around her pupils turned the most incredible shade of blue when she was happy. And after all the shit she'd told him about her dad he was glad he could make her laugh.

"What about you? What fashion secrets do you have?"

She opened the package of Munchos and offered him one. Why the hell not? He couldn't really feel any worse than he did. He took a few and popped them into his mouth, then thanked the deep-fried gods for the oily, salty deliciousness.

"There were many, trust me. One fall Scarlett and I bought matching neon-green velour tracksuits." She chuckled. "With her red hair, Scarlett looked like a glow-in-the-dark candle."

He laughed. "I bet she did."

"Of course, she wore a conservative tank under hers."

"But not you?"

The wicked grin she gave him went straight to his groin. "No, I wore a hot-pink tube top under mine. I barely had any boobs to hold the thing up, but it caused quite the scandal."

His focus lasered to the boobs in question, which he noted would now hold up a tube top very nicely.

She snapped her fingers. "Hey. Eyes up here, buddy."

"Sorry, Pavlov's dog, you say boobs and I look." He snatched the bag of chips from her lap. "Quit hogging all the Munchos."

Laughter bubbled out of her as she licked the greasy crumbs from her fingers. "My gangsta phase was the worst. For almost a year I wore oversized men's basketball jerseys with skinny jeans. Reebok high tops, unlaced, of course."

"Of course."

"And sweat bands halfway up my forearm, blasting Tupac through my earbuds."

"Tupac?"

"Don't be so surprised, Jack. I'm from the country, but I know good music and true genius when I hear it." She fidgeted in her seat and looked out the window. "Forget it. You probably wouldn't understand."

He pushed a button on the steering wheel. "Play Tupac."

Shocked crossed her face. "Don't be so surprised, Luanne. I'm from the country, but I know good music and true genius when I hear it. Besides, music is my business."

She popped a gummy bear into her mouth. "You think you know a person."

"I cry every time I hear *I Ain't Mad at Cha*. And, by the way, you don't know me, you just think you do."

"Is that right?"

"Yes, that's right, Ms. Price. Would you like to get to know me better? Like, in the biblical sense."

She snorted Yoo-hoo out of her nose. "You're an idiot. Now shut up so I can hear the music."

For the rest of the day, they listened to rap music and ate junk food while the car ate up the miles.

He'd never had a better time.

Chapter Ten

"Two."

"One."

"Two."

"One."

"Jack, I'm not sharing a room with you. Why are you being so bull-headed about this? We need two rooms. Period." Luanne placed both hands on the hood of the car and glared at the most infuriating man alive.

"Damn, Luanne, you sure do like spending my money. My budget for cross-country road trips is pretty tight."

She scowled at him. This. This was why he made her so crazy. He knew she'd sleep in the car before she'd share a room with him, but he was going to push it to the very limit. She reached into her back pocket, withdrew a small red notebook and slapped it down on the roof of the car. "I have written down every penny I've spent of your money, so never fear, you will get back every cent. Also, it was your idea to stay in this hoity-toity hotel, not mine. I would've been just as happy at a road-side inn."

He reached across the car and yanked the book from her hands.

Thumbing through the pages, he shook his head. "This is unbeliev-able." He shot her a look. "And unnecessary."

Oh, he made her so mad. She stormed around the car and snatched the book from his fingers. The plastic bag from the thrift store crackled when she shoved the notepad into it. "It is perfectly neces-sary. I don't want to be in debt to you or anyone else."

"You wouldn't be in debt to me, crazy. I'm helping you because you need help."

"Oh, so now I'm a charity case?" She crossed her arms over her chest.

"For the love of..." He scrubbed his hand down his face. "You are not a charity case, you're my friend." The words were slow and spoken through gritted teeth.

"I don't go into debt with my friends, so there."

"That's not true. You're willing to ask Scarlett for money and help."

"That's different."

"How?"

"It just is." She turned and marched into the hotel.

He quickly caught up to her and matched her stride for stride, even though he had to shorten his considerably to stay with her. "Why are you so difficult?"

"I'm difficult because I want my own room?"

"No. You're difficult because you won't let someone do something nice for you without putting a price tag on it."

"That's not what I'm doing, Jack." They'd made it to the front desk. "Just get me my own room, please."

"Welcome to Birmingham Place, the pride of Alabama. May I help you?" the pretty blonde woman behind the counter asked. Her name tag read *Regina*.

"Yes," Jack said. "Tell me something, Regina. If a man does some-thing nice for you, do you feel the need to pay him back?"

She cocked her head. "You mean like a gift?"

"Sure, or any nice thing he might do out of the goodness of his heart."

"No, I don't think I would."

Jack flipped his hand toward the beauty behind the desk. "See."

"However," Regina cut in, "if the nice thing was a loan, like he was helping me with a problem, I would feel the need to repay him. Like last month, Bill Morrow helped me move into my new apartment and I felt like I needed to repay him in some way, so I made dinner for him. Does that help?"

Luanne reached out and took Regina's hand. "You've been very helpful." Then she flipped out her notebook. "Can you tell me how much a king room is?"

Regina tapped the keys on the computer. "One hundred and fifty a night."

Luanne jotted that number down. "Thanks, we'll take two—"

"We'll take your nicest two-room suite," Jack said.

"Oh...um, let me check if it's available. We only have one." More key clacking. "Yes, it's unoccupied. It's more expensive, though." She nibbled her ruby-red lip.

Jack pulled his wallet from his pocket and slid his black credit card across to her. "That's fine. Price is no object." He grinned down at Luanne. She wanted to slap the smug smile from his face. "Isn't that right, Luanne? You're good for it, aren't you?"

She was going to kill him. Dammit, this was going to be a long night.

* * *

Jack let the hot water pound onto his head and tried to calm down. He had no idea why Luanne wanting to repay him made him so angry. It just did. The woman was maddening, and gorgeous, and even travel-worn and exhausted she made his blood boil. He groaned and leaned his forehead against the tile wall. He may have made a critical error putting her in the same suite with him. Just the thought of her naked and showering in the other room had his blood pounding in his veins.

Way to go, Jack. Now you can spend the next twelve hours with a hard-on.

Then again, maybe not. He slid his hand down his body, but stopped. Somehow it felt wrong to use her like that. Resigned to an evening of sexual frustration, he turned off the water, dried himself, and then wrapped the towel around his waist.

There was a knock at his bedroom door. He opened it to find her freshly showered and her face scrubbed clean of makeup. Beautiful and sexy as hell.

Her gaze dropped to where the towel was connected. When she looked back at him her cheeks were flushed and her pupils dilated.

Interesting.

"Um...hey, are we going out to eat or ordering in?"

He stretched his arm up the door jamb and leaned into it. If she wanted to look, then let her look. He almost took a victory lap when her eyes roamed down his chest and a baby sigh slipped from her lips. "I don't really care. What would you prefer?"

She didn't say anything, but her stare nearly burned the towel from his body. If she didn't stop, the problem he'd had in the shower was going to raise its head again. Literally. "Luanne?"

She blinked. "Huh? What?"

"What do you want to do about dinner?"

She rolled her hands into the hem of her shirt and pulled it away from her body. Was she hiding taut, tight, tantalizing nipples? A man could hope.

"I think I'd rather stay in. I don't want to have to get ready, plus my clothing options are limited."

"Okay, room service it is." He walked into the living room. "Have you seen the menu anywhere?" He went to the desk and flipped through a leather-bound notebook. "Here it is. Mmm, I think I'll have a steak. What would you like?"

"I...um...that sounds good."

"What would you like to drink? Coffee, tea, or me?" The wink he gave her might have been over the top.

She charged at him and grabbed the book from him. "Give me that. Go put some clothes on before you make me sick. I'll order. How do you want your steak?"

He laughed. "Medium rare. I'll be in here." He shot his thumb over his shoulder toward his bedroom. "In case you need me."

She picked up the room phone and pressed the button. "No, I've got it."

He closed the bedroom door and grinned. She might still be on the fence about whether she liked him or not. But one thing was for sure. She wanted him, and he could work with that.

* * *

Luanne put the phone receiver into the cradle.

Damn him, damn him, damn him.

He was only coming on to her to get under her skin. And man, did he ever get under her skin. Her pulse still thrashed around like a toddler having a tantrum. She'd always thought he was handsome—anyone with eyes and ovaries could see that. But he was also a grade-A asshole, and that little trait kept him firmly out of her temptation zone. But now that she'd seen him act very un-asshole-like, his appeal was harder to ignore.

Cripes. When he opened the door in that towel she'd wanted to rip it off with her teeth. Her temperature hadn't spiked like that since... well, never. She'd been with men, but it was more like scratching an itch, nothing like the physical and now emotional reaction she had with Jack.

He was only toying with her, plain and simple. Well, two could play that game. She glanced back at his bedroom door. "You want to play, Jackie-boy? I'll show you I can give as good as I get."

She went to her room and closed the door. She rummaged through the bag with her belongings. Nothing. There wasn't a thing in there that would make a man drool. For a second she regretted not buying the moneymaker shorts and halter top. Oh well, she'd just have to improvise.

The large marble tub in the bathroom was beautiful, and she regretted not being able to take a long relaxing bath with a glass of wine, but she was on a mission. She mussed and fluffed her short hair. A little mascara and lip gloss, and she was ready for battle. It wasn't much, but it would have to do.

As she turned, she saw the perfect piece of armor to win this show-down. Her thrift store clothes puddled on the floor as she wrapped the white, fluffy spa robe around her body. It was big, but she rolled up the sleeves and tied the belt, allowing it to gape at the neck enough to show a little cleavage. She surveyed herself. "Okay, Jack. Let's see how you like to sweat."

"Luanne. Food's here."

"Alright. Be there in a minute."

"Hurry, while the meat's hot."

She chuckled and shook her head. He was relentless.

When she strolled into the living room, she almost tripped. He was putting dishes on the table. Barefoot, in low-slung jeans and an unbuttoned white dress shirt, he looked good enough to eat, his golden-brown chest on display for her viewing pleasure.

"I hope you don't mind but I ordered a bottle of wine too. Nothing's better than steak and a good bottle of wine. Well, I can think of one or two things better—what are you wearing?"

She sashayed to the table. Sashayed, for crying out loud. "It's the hotel's robe." She pouted her lips and batted her lids. "I hope it's okay that I eat in my robe. I'm just so sick of clothes. My skin's overly sensitive for some reason." She picked a carrot from her salad and popped it into her mouth. "Know what I mean?"

He dropped the metal dome that covered the food. The clang seemed to knock him out of his trance. "Yes." His long fingers wrapped around the glass of wine in front of him. "Wine?"

"Yes, thanks." They stared at each other, while the battle lines were drawn.

Well played, Ms. Price. Well played.

I thought so, counselor. Nice shirt.

You're good, darlin', but I'm better.

Prove it.

You're on.

He pulled her chair out for her. Then his lips were at her ear. "Mmm, you smell delicious."

Heat chased goose bumps down her arm. "Thanks, so do you."

He took his seat across from her. His white teeth bit into his plump lower lip, and the look he gave her seared her insides. Damn, he *was* good.

The wine glass came to her lips. "Oops." Without breaking eye contact, she touched her finger to her cleavage then ran it up her chest. "Spilled a drop." His expression darkened and a hiss slipped out when she popped her finger into her mouth.

She bit the inside of her lip when he murmured, "Are you kidding me?"

"Hmm, what? I didn't catch that." Was the eye batting too much? It might be too much.

His chest expanded when he filled his lungs with air. "Nothing. I forgot a call I needed to make."

"Oh. Do you need me to take my meal to my room so you can make a call?"

"No!"

"Alright." She picked up her knife and fork. "This looks delicious." It was hard to cut her food with her hands shaking the way they were. The utensils slipped from her hand when she glanced up. He was sitting back in the chair, his tan chest on full display while he licked the rim of his wine glass. Hoo-lee cow. He was sex on a freakin' stick.

Look away, look away, look away.

She dragged her gaze from him and peered out the window. The lights of Birmingham shone back at her like stars reflecting off a still lake at midnight. Her reflection in the mirror told the story. Flushed skin, glazed eyes, she was completely turned on. Stupid to let this man in enough to do this to her. But there was something about him. If she'd never seen him talk about his mom, or the pain on his face from the revelations from his father, then she might be able to ignore his raw sexuality.

Her gaze drifted to his reflection in the mirror. When she saw the same look on his face, a zing of satisfaction zipped through her. He seemed to sense her watching him and a calculated look of challenge stole over his face.

Yep. There was the Jack she loved to hate. Later she'd have to thank him for throwing ice water onto her desire.

With renewed determination to win this game, she turned back to her meal and began eating. "Mmm, this is yummy. I love a good, thick piece of meat." She let her gaze roam down his chest, to his belly and below. The battle was almost lost when she had to choke down a laugh from the sheer ridiculousness of the over-the-top gesture.

Focus, Luanne.
He would not win.

* * *

Jack was glad the tabletop covered his crotch because this whole thing just got real serious, real quick. She was killing him and he seemed to be having little effect on her. Time to turn up the heat. He took his own bite. "Mouthwatering. I can't decide if I want to take my time and draw out every ounce of deliciousness." He slowly licked his fork. "Or devour it, and go back for more, and more, and more until I get my fill."

She propped her elbow on the table and leaned her shoulder forward, causing the robe to gape and reveal the top swell of her breast. "That's an interesting dilemma." She brought her glass to her mouth, but right before she took a drink she darted her little pink tongue out and touched it to the glass. "We should probably make a list of pros and cons."

Damn. He might've met his match with this woman, and that thrilled him to his core. "Your thoughts?"

Her delicate finger tapped at her *do me, do me now* lips. A filthy reel of things he'd like to do to that mouth scrolled through his brain, and he momentarily lost track of the conversation.

She rested both elbows on the table, and the gap in the robe grew wider. Even though they were playing this flirtatious game, the keen intelligence of her brilliant mind showed in her sapphire eyes.

"Pros for savoring. You can enjoy it longer. It enhances your pleasure. It's more...fulfilling."

He placed both hands on the table. "True, but there's something to be said for devouring the thing you crave. For biting, licking, and sucking until you've had your fill." He dipped his finger into the mashed potatoes on his plate and sucked the creamy, salty goodness from the digit.

The pulse at the base of her neck fluttered. He had her now, and a good thing too—this contest was killing him.

"You've...ah...got some potatoes here." She pointed to the corner of her edible mouth. Then she ran her delicate finger around her criminally sensual lips, and his head exploded.

Sweat broke out at his hairline, his heart bucked like an electrified horse, and all the blood in his body shot to his dick. Daaammmmnnnn. This woman would be the death of him. For a moment, he forgot this was a match of wills, that she didn't like him, and imagined what it would be like to peel back that robe and devour every inch of her creamy skin.

She pulled the straw from her water glass and slid it between her thumb and forefinger, back and forth, back and forth, back and forth.

He couldn't tear his attention from the obscene motion. A mental list of all the ways he'd have her began to formulate in his mind. On the table, against the wall, in the shower...

She cleared her throat, drawing his attention back to her face. She licked the straw from one end to the other. "Also, haste makes waste."

The air between them was so charged it practically sparked. They held each other's stare, and when her lips twitched, so did his.

She snorted and tried to play it off as a sneeze.

His bark of laughter was disguised as a cough. But when he saw the mirth at the edges of her lips, it was all over. He doubled over laughing. "Haste makes waste? Who let my grandma in here?"

"I should've stopped with fulfilling." Her belly laughs were louder than his.

Their shared hilarity was more intoxicating than any of the provocative moves in the last fifteen minutes. "Probably."

She wiped her eyes. "Oh, lordy, that's funny."

"Let's eat. I'm starving."

"Me too."

As he watched her eat, he considered the last twenty-four hours and the life bomb that had rocked his world. The stone of anxiety that usually accompanied those revelations never dropped. For the moment, she'd taken that away. This woman. This smart, sassy, and funny as hell woman. No wonder he wanted her so much. He scrubbed his face.

This was going to be a long trip.

Chapter Eleven

Jack packed his toiletry bag into his suitcase. A quick glance around to make sure he hadn't forgotten anything, then he grabbed his shoes and went to the living room to put them on.

Luanne came out of her room at the same time and gave him a tentative smile. "Oh. Hey."

"Hey."

"I was going to go downstairs and get a coffee for the road. Do you want a cup?"

Momentarily stunned that she'd offer, it took him a second to answer. "Yes, thanks. House blend with a little cream." He reached into his back pocket and handed her some cash.

She slipped it into her pocket. "This is a proud moment for me. I'm leaving a man's hotel room with cash in hand."

"You should be proud, you earned it." He made a gun out of his forefinger and thumb and shot her.

"Har-har. See you downstairs."

He enjoyed the warm bubble of...something that only she evoked. *Careful, Jack. That's a dangerous, dangerous path to go down.*

Shoes on, he checked his pockets for his phone. No calls from his father. He'd hoped he would've heard from him by now. Well, if his dad wasn't going to reach out then he would. He pulled up his dad's contact and dialed.

"Hello." His father didn't sound a whole lot better than he had when Jack was there.

"Dad, it's Jack."

"I know who it is. Your name comes up on this damn phone you insisted I have." The resentment in his tone shocked Jack. That, combined with the fact that the man was slurring his speech, which meant he was already drinking, nearly did him in.

"I wanted you to have something nice and to make sure you could get in touch with someone if there was an emergency." He shouldn't have to defend himself. His mom had been grateful for the phones.

"What do you want, Jack?"

The annoyance and defeat in his father's voice kicked him in the gut. "I was calling to check on you, Dad."

"Don't call me that!"

"Okay, calm down, remember your blood pressure."

"You always think you know so much, boy. But you don't." His father's words assaulted him, blow after blow.

How dare he? He'd been a good son. Hell, he'd been the perfect son, and this was the thanks he got. Kicked to the curb at the first available moment.

"I'm sorry you feel that way."

"I'm sorry you feel that way," his father mocked. "Always so high and mighty. Maybe you should look up that Yankee daddy of yours, he and his people seem to want to know you. They're probably as snooty as you."

Who was this person on the other end of the phone? He'd never heard his father speak this way. "You don't mean that—"

The line went dead. Jack squeezed his lids shut and counted to ten. He wondered if the knife sticking out of his back was visible.

His dad had been so loving, so supportive. But the contents of that letter had changed everything.

That letter.

He still couldn't wrap his mind around the fact that his mother had been engaged to someone else, let alone had a child with that person.

The pain of that revelation was only tempered by his undying love and devotion to his mother. She'd been the one constant in his life. The strength and backbone of their family. So many things made sense now that he knew he wasn't Ray Avery's biological son.

Ray was a passive man, and, if Jack was honest, weak at times. That's why Jack strove to be in control of all things, at all times. Things he'd always denied, excused, or tried to laugh off now became crystal clear.

This was so fucked up. Honestly, he couldn't believe this reality show was his life. He thought of the nosey woman waiting on him downstairs. The one who'd loaded him up in the middle of the night, without his permission, and took off to find his real family. He didn't want to share this latest news with her. She'd be all up in his business, and the last thing he needed was another opinion to sift into this mess.

He gathered his belongings and made his way to the hotel lobby. With each step, he pulled on the armor of arrogance. She hated when he was an arrogant ass. It should keep her out of his business until he had time to figure out his next move.

* * *

Luanne popped the lid off her coffee and inhaled, letting the caffeinated goodness clear the cobwebs from her brain. She considered her interaction with Jack this morning. It was almost sweet, and the ridiculous sexual tension that usually burned between them was at a more manageable level. No doubt because of the way their game had ended the night before.

After they'd stopped trying to one-up each other, the meal had gone smoothly. She'd enjoyed herself more than she ever thought she could in his presence. But that only left her with more questions than answers. Who was the real Jack Avery? Was he the womanizing play-boy, the condescending attorney, the loyal friend, devoted son, or some combination of them all? She didn't like that she seemed to be obsessed with solving the mystery.

Fire and moth, Luanne, fire and moth.

Antsy tingles crawled up her arm and the desire to bolt nearly overwhelmed her. When it came to men like Jack and her father, she couldn't trust her feelings. The younger, better-looking man in question emerged from the hotel carrying his bag and looking absolutely edible in dark jeans, a light blue polo shirt, and designer retro aviator sunglasses, his slightly too-long hair still wet from his shower. Lord, have mercy, but he was a sight. Tendrils of desire wrapped around her body like climbing vines of ivy. She would've run, if her legs weren't as wobbly as a newborn colt.

No way would she let him see how he got to her this morning. "'Bout time you got here. What happened, break a nail?"

"Not now, Luanne." The muscle in his jaw vibrated with tension.

What was wrong with him? He'd been fine ten minutes ago. Just when she thought they'd come to some kind of understanding, he reverted back to jerk-face Jack. "Fine." She got into the car and slammed the door behind her.

He threw his bag in the back storage space, then slid into the car. Without a word, he sped out of the parking lot and maneuvered onto the highway.

"Wanna tell me what's wrong?"

"Nope." No way was he talking about this with her.

"Why not? I'm kind of a neutral party, it might help." There was some satisfaction in throwing his words from the day before back at him.

"Cute." He picked up his Bluetooth earpiece and slipped it into place. "Call Caroline."

"Who's Caroline?"

"My assistant. Not all of us can take a month off from work, Luanne. Some of us have important business."

"I'll have—"

"Yes, yes, you have important business too. I'm sure the folks down at the tractor pull are glad you were there to defend their interest when drunken Scrubs Callie jumped from the stands and ran onto the track, breaking his ankle in the process. And I know Shirley McCoy was grateful when you helped her win custody of her pig when she and JT were getting a divorce."

Wow, low blows even for him. Those were two of her cases, but they weren't quite so simple or ridiculous. Scrubs Callie was suing Johnson tractors for a million dollars because he'd been reckless and stupid. If he'd won it would've bankrupted one of the oldest businesses in the county. And as for the pig, it had belonged to Shirley's daughter, who died in a car accident. JT wasn't the girl's father and was only keeping the pig out of spite. People were shitty sometimes.

Case in point, the dickhead sitting next to her.

"Hello, Caroline, it's Jack." He pointed to his earpiece. "Yes, the awards ceremony went well. It was nice seeing people from Beauchamp again. Listen, I know I said I'd be back in the office by Tuesday, but it looks like it's going to be Thursday or Friday. Why don't you just work half days this week? Check the messages from home and call me if it's anything important, but I know your brother's in town so spend some time with him and have fun."

What? He was only extending his trip a day or two? There wasn't any way they could get to his grandmother's and to Vermont in a few days. Panic raced down her spine. Was he taking her back? Dumping her? Strange as it was, she'd gotten used to the idea of the two of them on this adventure together.

He laughed at something his assistant said. "Yes, it's paid time off. Anything else?" A pause while he listened intently. "Okay. When he calls again, tell him I said he's lost his mind. What's he thinking peddling that shit to me? I don't do business with scum like his client."

Luanne shook her head. He really was the most infuriating man she'd ever met. What had she been thinking? That one night of comfortable conversation and he'd changed.

"Yeah, text me that number. Do you know the story?"

"What kind of trouble?"

"But her agent says she's clean now?"

"Really? She's volunteered to take a weekly drug test? Well that's new. Why do all the good ones have truckloads of baggage? No, I still want to talk to her agent. She's got that scratchy Janice Joplin thing goin' on. She's unique. Good job catching her YouTube video." He laughed again. "You're right about that. She is hot. Okay, talk to you later." He disconnected.

"Who's hot?"

He snapped his gaze to her like he'd forgotten she was there. Really?

"A new artist Caroline saw online. Supposedly, she was some big deal YouTuber."

"Another rock star for you guys?" She turned in her seat.

"No. Country music." He hit a button on the steering wheel and the radio came on.

"I didn't know the record label you and Gavin started was signing country musicians."

"We haven't, yet."

"And you're going to represent her?"

He shook his head. "No. We're also looking to bring on another person, I've got my hands full." The jerk actually winked. "We'll be bringing someone on to handle that side of the business. We want to give new indie artists a platform."

"Interesting. So you want to be a full-service company from representation, to booking, to recording, to distribution? I think it's a great idea. You guys can give individual attention to your artists, not like the big record labels who are nothing more than conglomerates."

His stunned expression almost made her laugh.

Yes Jack, I have a damn brain in my head.

* * *

Jack gulped down a dry swallow. Damn it, was there anything sexier than a smart woman?

What the hell, dumbass? Your plan was to keep her out of your business.

Having a sweet heart-to-heart with her was the fastest way to let down his guard. "Yeah, so?" His insides cringed when she flinched.

"Why are you being such a jerk? Have I done something that I'm not aware of?"

"I don't know, have you?"

"Fuck off, Jack-ass."

If she'd had the capability, acid would've spewed from her eyes. It was a good thing he was driving, or he'd have taken that dirty mouth and devoured it. All of that passion directed in the right place, damn, it'd be a sight to see. He couldn't help continuing to goad her. "Careful, Lulu, or I'll have to spank that fine little ass of yours."

There. It was a tiny spark of interest in her beautiful face, and it was gone faster than she could say, *I'll cut off your balls.*

"I know, let's talk about that night after Scarlett and Gavin's wedding." This was the shittiest thing he could say to her and he knew it. "I want to know more about that fairy dress you said you wanted. And how you wanted to be a beautiful fairy princess."

"Know what, Jack?" She grabbed his phone and tapped the screen.

"What are you doing?"

"I'm looking for the next big city. This was a mistake. I don't need you. I don't need anybody. You can drop me in Chattanooga, I'll call Scarlett and she'll wire me some money, then I'll have her go to my house, get my things and send them to me." She placed his phone into its carrier, turned, wadded up a jacket, and shoved it into a pillow between the door and her head. "I'm done talking to you."

"Sweet dreams, Thumbelina."

When her little hand came up and shot him the finger, he bit back a laugh. He was thinking the exact same thing, but in a totally different context.

The sliver of skin that peeked at him from under her top flashed like a neon sign of desire. The tingle in his hands shot up his arm. He knew how soft her skin was, and seven months later, he could still taste her sassy mouth. That night after Scarlett and Gavin's wedding had been amazing, until it wasn't. Even still, the memory of her small body snuggled up against his kept him company every night.

Her breathing evened out and he knew she'd fallen asleep. Little wisps of her short black hair fluttered as the air-conditioner blew over her head. Melon and lime from her shampoo floated through the car. He sucked it into his lungs like it was the last breath he'd ever take. He'd never been inside her and already parts of her lived inside him.

This was bad.

So freaking bad.

And if that wasn't bad enough, the GPS said Chattanooga was five hours away. But that wasn't his real destination, was it? Honestly, he couldn't avoid this second family forever. He should take her there and get her settled with a plane ticket, a rental car, or hotel room, then be on his way. That's what he should do, but that wasn't going to happen.

His heart bashed into his ribs then slid into cardiac arrest levels when the truth solidified in his brain. Like it or not, he had to see this thing through...and he needed the black-headed troublemaker in the passenger seat with him. She made him laugh when he wanted to rage, and even though they fought about anything and everything, she was on his side. Deep in his gut he knew she was supposed to be on this trip with him, and he always went with his gut.

He inhaled her sweet citrus scent again.

Next task, convince the testy pixie that she wants to continue on this journey with me.

Chapter Twelve

Luanne paced along the sidewalk at the desolate roadside rest stop. She eyed the building where the restrooms were housed and shuddered. No way was she using those facilities without a bucket of bleach and a box of rubber gloves. Evidently Jack didn't have the same hygienic hang-ups as her when it came to bathroom facilities. Why hadn't he gone to one of those convenience stores that advertise clean restrooms? They were everywhere on the interstate.

The bigger question was, where the hell were they? This rest stop was definitely not on the main road. She specifically remembered there was nothing but straight highway from where they were to Chattanooga when she checked his phone.

She wrapped his too-big jacket around her middle, and watched dark clouds gather in the distance. They must be the reason for the chilly air. Hopefully it wouldn't start raining until they got to Chattanooga. That was where he'd leave her, then they'd be on their own… and wouldn't have to deal with each other anymore.

The thought of leaving him alone to complete his task caused her stomach to churn. But her life was falling apart too. She needed time to figure out what to do, and she couldn't do that if she was constantly vacillating between wanting to wring his neck and jump his bones.

The thorn in her side sauntered from the gray stone building. Jack never walked anywhere—he sauntered, or strode, or swaggered. He shot the paper towel he'd dried his hands on into the garbage can and made it, of course. "Hey, hotshot. My jacket looks good on you. If you ignore the fact that you look like you're missing your hands."

It was true. The sleeves hung three inches past her hands.

He knelt to retie his shoe string. "Change your mind about the facilities?"

"No."

He rose, stretched his arms above his head, and yawned. "You sure? I've seen worse."

The lean muscles of his arms nearly made her forget her point, but when he winked at her she remembered what she wanted to know. "Where are we, Jack?"

"At a rest stop," he deadpanned.

"You're like a junior high boy sometimes. You know that, right?" She took a long breath for patience. "I mean, where are we in relation to...anywhere?"

He laughed and ruffled her hair.

She slapped his arm away. "Stop that and answer me."

He slid his sunglasses on. "We're about two hours south of there."

"Har-har. You're hilarious. Why are we on this country road? The last time I looked at the GPS there was nothing but highway between Chattanooga and us. Now we're out in the middle of nowhere without another living soul around."

He straightened and pulled on his lawyer mask. "One, in light of the fact that your father is looking for us, prudence dictates that we take some precautions, namely getting off the main highway. Two, we are not in the middle of nowhere, but even if we were...see my previous point. And, three, there are two living souls in that car right there." He pointed to an older model, baby-blue Cadillac.

The car came to an abrupt stop next to Jack's car when the granny driving it ran into the curb. The other senior woman in the car jerked forward with the impact.

Jack gave a low whistle. "That Caddy's older than the Mayflower and just as big. Looks like something my Uncle Ferris would drive."

"Fascinating." She crossed her arms and gave him her best cross-examination glare. "Tell me the real reason you made this detour."

Her line of questioning was interrupted by the whisper fight the two women were having in front of their car. Oddly, they were both wearing all black from head to toe, including black flat-bill baseball caps and black sunglass, making their lily-white skin and gray hair stand out in sharp contrast. They looked like the Caucasian, geriatric version of Salt n Pepa. That thought made her chuckle. "I wonder if they've had car trouble."

Jack slid his own glasses on top of his head. "I don't know. I better go see if I can help. I'd hate to see anyone stranded out here, especially two defenseless senior citizens."

She shook her head as she followed him down the sidewalk. Not five minutes ago, she would have sworn he was only moments from giving her a wedgie, he was acting so immature, and now Jack the Boy Scout was off to rescue two helpless females.

He was a puzzle.

The women had their backs to them, still arguing, and didn't seem to notice as they approached. "You ladies need any help?" Jake asked.

The women turned at the same time, and Luanne screamed.

* * *

"Hands in the air."

"Holy shit," Jack couldn't believe that one of the helpless grannies had a revolver. The other had a lipstick-sized container of pepper spray, and they were both aimed at them. Jack reached for Luanne and tried to pull her behind him. Of course, she didn't cooperate and stood her ground.

"I'd appreciate it if you'd watch your language. Bobby's in the car and foul language upsets him," the one holding the pepper spray said.

He quickly assessed the situation and knew he could take them, even with Bobby in the car. He turned his charmer's smile to one hundred watts. "Ladies, we don't have to do this. Why don't you get back into your car and drive away, and we'll forget all about this?"

"I don't think so. I want your wallet and that fancy watch of yours in this bag by the time I count to ten." the one with the gun said. "One..."

"Oh, that's good, Pearl, very menacing," the other one said.

"June. We're supposed to be incognito."

"Darn it, I'm sorry. We did talk about this, didn't we?"

Pearl made a *ya think?* face.

"Ah, ladies, if I might interrupt." Jack started to take a step in their direction. "My wallet's in the car, I'll just get—"

"Not so fast, handsome, I'll take the keys," June said, and shoved the tiny canister in his face. He noticed the nozzle was pointed back in her direction.

"Jack, do something," Luanne hissed.

From the corner of his eye he saw his road partner with her hands in the air and his coat sleeves flopped over like dead puppets. It was all he could do not to crack up laughing at the whole crazy situation.

He lowered his hands and straightened to his full height. He had to give it to Bonnie and...Bonnie, they didn't flinch. "I think this has gone on long enough. We all know you're not going to shoot us. That thing's probably not even loaded."

Without taking her glare from his, Pearl pointed the gun toward a tree ten feet away and fired.

Luanne and June screamed, and Jack cussed when wood splinters flew. From the backseat of the car came a plaintive wail, and up popped a little carrot-top head. He must've been three or four.

"Oh, for the love of heaven, Pearl, you woke up Bobby."

"Nana," the boy cried.

"I'm right here, Bobby," June soothed. "Auntie Pearl's only being silly and making a bunch of racket."

"I'm sorry, sweetie. I'll be quieter," Pearl said to the boy in a sing-song voice. Then she growled to Jack, "Hand it over, right now."

This was ridiculous. What was going on here? "Give me a second." His brain churned to put pieces together. There was a kid in the backseat, one armed granny, and the other was about to blind herself if she wasn't careful. Why? There had to be a reason. That was when he noticed the tires on the car were bald and there were rust spots along the side. The sideview mirror hung at a weird angle from the miles of duct tape wrapped around it. Aw, shit. His conscience was about to get the best of him, and Luanne was going to be pissed. "I'm going to reach into my pocket. Keep your finger off that trigger, Pearl."

"Jack?" There was a question in Luanne's voice. Yeah, he didn't know what the hell he was doing either.

"Alright, slow and easy." Pearl did take her finger off the trigger but kept the gun leveled on him.

He unhooked his watch and slipped it into the bag, then handed June his keys. Once she had them in her hot little hands she headed for his baby.

"I bet you've got one of them fancy cell phones too," Pearl said.

"In the car."

Pearl slowly backed away from them and made her way to his most prized possession.

"What about her?" June gestured to Luanne.

Pearl looked Luanne up and down. "Please, his thrift store girlfriend doesn't have anything we want. I bet she ain't got a pot to pee in, or a window to throw it out of."

"Hey, I'll have you know—"

"Let it go," Jack said, and shoved his hands into his pockets.

"Are you kidding me? You could've easily overpowered them."

He shrugged.

She made a disgusted sound. "If you're not going to do something about this, then I will."

He grabbed her arm before she could take a step. "No."

"No? Have you lost your mind? Everything we have is in that car. We can't let them take it."

He glanced at the boy in the back of the car. His spindly arms dangled out of the window, and he was wearing a toddler sized Dallas Cowboys jersey, so old and faded that the numbers on the shoulders were peeling off.

Shit.

Shit.

Shit.

Memories and sympathy sliced through his mind like a serrated blade. "Let 'em have it. It's only stuff and we can get more stuff. It doesn't look like they can."

June walked back to them a little sheepishly. It might've been convincing, but now she carried the gun, and it was aimed at them. "I'm sorry for all the trouble. You seem like nice people, and we don't want to leave you out here with nothin', so..." She handed him a twenty-dollar bill. His twenty-dollar bill.

"Nana, I hungry," Bobby whined.

"In a minute, sweetie," June cooed.

Jack stared at the money, glanced at Luanne's hopeful face, then looked back at the too-skinny boy. "You know what? Keep it."

Chapter Thirteen

Luanne had blisters on her blisters. The little white tennis shoes she'd bought at the thrift store were not made for eating up miles of country road. She wanted to throttle Jack. How could he let two gray-haired grannies drive away with all of their possessions? She probably wasn't being fair to her companion—the women did have a gun pointed at them the whole time. But still.

They hadn't even sped away. Pearl had put on her blinker before she pulled Jack's car onto the road. In fact, if she and Jack picked up their pace she was fairly certain they could catch the bandits on foot.

Jack's whistling cut through her misery.

"What are we going to do, Jack?" She was only a few decibels from full-on panic.

"Calm down, Luanne. When we get to the town we went through a few miles back we'll borrow someone's phone and call for help."

"Oh." She hadn't thought of that. Of course, they would call for help. Scarlett and Gavin would help them, and they had more money than she and Jack put together.

"Yeah, oh." He continued strolling along as if he didn't have a care in the world. "You worry too much. You keep that up and you're going to get wrinkles."

"You worry about your wrinkles and I'll worry about mine."

"Oooh, good one."

She snorted. "Weak, I know. Being robbed at gunpoint has thrown me off my game."

Jack scratched the back of his neck. "I feel sure you'll be back to filleting me with that wit in no time."

"Wonder what made them turn to a life of crime?" She had to take two steps for every one of his.

He tilted his face to the sun. She noticed that he did that a lot when he was outside. "Being poor makes some people do desperate things, Lulu."

"How do you know it's because they're poor? They could just be bored, or crazy."

"Did you notice Pearl's shoes?"

"No."

"There were holes in both of them. And did you see how June kept squinting? Twenty dollars says she needs glasses, but can't afford them."

"You don't have twenty dollars. You gave it to the thieves."

He laughed. "I thought I'd bust a gut when I looked over and saw your hands in the air with the sleeves flopped over your hands like limp limbs.

She flung her arms around and smacked him with the ends of the sleeves. "Watch it, bud. I'll attack you with these limp limbs."

"I have no doubt about that."

"Bobby did look kind of scrawny." She kicked a rock with the toe of her now brown, white tennis shoe.

"I saw a lot of stuff in that backseat. My guess is they're living out of the car."

"You don't really think that, do you?" Bile churned in her stomach at the thought of those three skinny people huddled in that car sleeping together.

He shrugged. "That's what our car looked like when we lived in it."

She skidded to a stop. "You were homeless?"

"Only for a few weeks, then my dad got a job managing a ranch. The job came with a double wide mobile home. It was nice." He picked up a rock and chucked it down the road.

"Jack, I…I don't know what to say."

His sad smile kind of broke her heart.

"It wasn't so bad. My mom tried to make it an adventure. We were like the Swiss Family Robinson, only instead of a tree house, we lived in a car. I was pretty oblivious to the magnitude of the situation. It was only later that the full impact hit me."

"Wow, you've really made something of yourself."

"That was the plan. From the time I was thirteen years old. Get an education, get a job, and get out of poverty."

"Mission accomplished."

"Yes, but now I'm broke, with a thrift store girlfriend, wandering down a backwoods country road in need of money and help. It's a little too déjà vu."

Shame cut through her. What had she made of herself? Done for herself? Sure, she was an attorney and had a successful law practice, but when she hadn't had the seed money for the business and her father had offered to help, she'd accepted. Same with college and law school. She'd taken help from him and fooled herself into believing that he was helping because he loved her. All he'd really wanted was a way to control her.

So while she looked like an independent, successful woman, really she was a weak, sniveling child waiting for her father to give her his next handout.

"Luanne." Jack's words cut through her misery.

"Yes?"

"Can we talk about what happened after Scarlett and Gavin's wedding?"

He wasn't looking at her and somehow that made it easier to talk about. "Sure."

Without missing a step, he scooped up a couple of rocks and shook them in his hand. "I'm sorry I ran off. I just…"

"It's fine. I know I lost it. I'm sure the tears and carrying on freaked you out." Pinpricks of heat and mortification stung her cheeks. She'd gotten drunk and told this man that she wanted to look like a fairy princess when she got married. And if that wasn't bad enough, she'd started crying because she didn't believe that would ever happen.

And somewhere in all of that mess there'd been a proposition for him to be her Prince Charming. Ugh, how humiliating. Who knew it would only be the first in a long line of humiliating things he'd be a witness to?

One of the rocks went sailing down the road. "It caught me off guard, but I shouldn't have run off the way I did."

"I don't blame you. In fact, I'm glad you left. We could've made a huge mistake that night if you hadn't." Jack nodded and frowned at that, but didn't agree or disagree. Some part of her wondered if he thought it would've been a mistake too.

He chucked the second rock at a tree on the side of the road and missed. "Regardless, it's bothered me, and I've wanted to apologize since it happened. But I didn't know how to bring it up."

"Apology accepted. Thanks for clearing the air." She didn't know what surprised her more—the fact that he'd apologized, or how much better she felt now they'd talked about it.

"Looks like we've made it to town."

"What did you say?"

He pointed to an enormous billboard, so out of place on the edge of a cornfield, that read *Quincy, Alabama, The Home of the Fighting Hornets—1978 State Football Champs.*

"Wow, 1978 state champs." Jack chuckled. "The town's had a bit of a dry spell."

She picked up her pace. "I don't care if they're the home of Jack the Ripper, as long as there's a telephone and a place for someone to wire us money."

* * *

Jack held the door to the convenience store open for Luanne. Monday afternoon in Quincy was slower than life in Zachsville, and that was saying something. They were the only customers in the place and they hadn't seen one car on the road on their walk into town. Their only hope now was the Western Union sign in the window.

A reality show blasted from the small TV located behind the counter, where a teenaged boy sat enthralled. He never looked away from the screen when they came in. Clearly, customer service wasn't a priority.

Luanne marched up to the counter. "Excuse me."

No response.

"Pardon me, sir."

Still nothing.

"Sir, we need to use the phone."

Nope, nada.

Oh, this was going to be good. He could see the color creep up Luanne's neck, and when she slammed her hands onto her hips he knew the show was about to begin. He'd been on the receiving end of that attitude more times than he cared to remember.

She waved her hand in the clerk's direction. "Can you believe this guy?"

"Youth today. It's hard to find good help anymore."

"I'm glad you think this is funny. It's not like we're in dire straits or anything."

"You've got a point." He waved his hand in the kid's direction like she had. "Do your worst."

The little flash of evil that sparked in her eyes scared and thrilled him. She stomped around the counter and yanked the TV cord from the wall. Silence. It seemed to take the guy a few seconds to catch on.

"Hey."

"Excuse me. I've been trying to get your attention for five minutes."

"Oh, sorry." He did have the decency to look a little embarrassed. "Don't tell my boss, okay? I need this job."

"That won't be a problem as long as you have a telephone we can use." Luanne walked back around the counter.

"A telephone? Sure, there's one in the office." He chewed his lip ring and glanced toward the door. "But I'm not supposed to let anyone in there."

"Then can we borrow your cell?" Luanne asked.

"No. My parents took my phone because of my grades. It totally blows."

Jack leaned on the counter. "What's your name?"

"Trevor."

"It's okay, Trevor, we're both attorneys. We ran into a little trouble back at the rest stop and need to make a quick call."

When the kid hesitated, Jack realized he'd have to turn up the heat. "Trevor, I'd hate for you to be held in contempt for obstructing justice."

Trevor shifted from one foot to the other. "Obstructing justice. That sounds bad."

Jack glanced at Luanne. "Shame, he seems like a good kid."

"It is a shame, but habeas corpus and all." She shrugged as if to say, *what can you do if folks are too stupid to cooperate?*

Trevor ran his fingers through his stringy hair. "I don't want any trouble."

Luanne placed both hands on the counter and leaned forward. "Well now Trevor, whether you have trouble or not is entirely up to you."

"I guess if y'all are attorneys, then it's alright."

When he turned to lead them to a small office behind the soda machine, they exchanged a fist bump. He mouthed *habeas corpus,* and she stifled a laugh and shrugged. No need for explanation with Luanne. She kept up with him and then some...and he could tell she was enjoying herself. What a woman.

Trevor moved some spreadsheets that looked like they were from the eighties to reveal the phone. "Here you go. Don't touch anything else. My boss is real particular, and he'll know you were in here."

Jack looked around the cluttered, dusty space. "No problem."

Trevor gave them another nervous look before he left the office.

"Yeah, boss man's a real Martha Stewart." Luanne toed a pair of pants that were on the floor and eyed the phone receiver. "I'm glad I've had all my shots."

"No joke."

She lifted the phone with two fingers. "What's Gavin's number?"

"I don't know."

"What do you mean you don't know?"

"I don't know. It's in my phone."

She made a disgusted noise.

"It shouldn't matter, call Scarlett."

"Fine." She punched a few numbers and stopped. "Oh, my gosh. I don't know it either. She changed it after she and Gavin got married, and I never learned it. It's in my phone."

For the first time since Pearl shot the gun he was a tad bit worried. It had never occurred to him that they wouldn't be able to get help. "Whose number do you know?"

"Gigi's, but I'm not calling her. My father would know where we were in a New York minute."

"Even if you asked her not to tell him?"

She snorted. "Her loyalty is to her son, period. She's proven that over and over again in my life."

The bitterness and pain in that one sentence cut him to the core. He decided right then and there that he hated her family.

"Oh, wait. I know the number to Floyd and Honey's house." She quickly punched in the digits and hit the speaker button.

"Hello."

"Honey, it's Luanne."

"Luanne? Lordy, girl, you got the whole town in an uproar."

"I bet I do. Listen, Honey, I'm in a little bit of—"

"Everyone's worried sick about the status of Tank Thompson's testicle. The ladies at the senior center have organized meals for poor Tank. I'm taking my chicken pot pie. Do you know that Sally Pruitt took Swedish meatballs? I find that very insensitive, and I told her so too."

"Insensitive?"

"On account of the fact that he might lose one of his own balls." She whispered the word *balls* like it was the foulest and most delicious of cuss words.

"Yeah, well, Tank tried to—"

"The good news is that there is an experimental treatment the booster club found out about, but it's costly. I've started a fundraiser to try and raise money to help with expenses. I'm callin' it Tots for Tank's Testicle. We're gonna sell 'em at the concession stand at the baseball fields, it ought to go real well."

"His testicles?"

"No! Tater tots. Lord, Luanne, what kind of operation do you think we're runnin' around here?"

"That's nice. Is Scarlett around?"

"No. She and Gavin left for their trip. They won't be back for several days."

"Do you have her cell number?"

"Sure do."

"Oh, good." She gave Jack a thumbs up. "Can I have it?"

"No."

"No? Why?"

"Because my phone's in Floyd's truck and he took his truck to take Joyce to get her car that's been in the shop. Then he's going over to Blade Rock to look at a horse."

"I don't suppose you have either Floyd or Joyce's number?"

"Of course I do."

"Great. Can I have them?"

"I just told you my phone isn't here, Luanne. Are you sure you're feelin' okay?"

"But you said you had them."

"I do. In my phone." She was now speaking to Luanne like she was a few bananas short of a bunch.

"Tell Scarlett I called, and that I'm fine."

"You take care, Luanne."

"I will. Bye, Honey." She disconnected the call and plopped down in the desk chair, oblivious to the pair of tube socks draped across the back. "That was a bust. What about your dad?"

"Yeah, I can call him. I don't want to, but I can." He picked up the receiver and punched in the numbers. No way did he want her hearing this conversation.

"Yeah?" His father slurred over the line.

"Dad, it's Jack."

"For God's sake, can't you leave me alone in my misery?"

"I know, Dad—"

"Just like your mother. Never let me work anything out on my own. Pick, pick, pick."

"I wouldn't have called, but I—Dad? Dad?" The receiver fell into the cradle. "He hung up on me."

"I'm sorry." She placed her hand on his arm.

He didn't acknowledge her. He couldn't. The pain ricocheting around his body might escape and he had to lock that shit down. That was how he got to where he was in life—swallow the humiliation and pain and move forward, all with a cocky grin on his face. Except today, he didn't have it in him. He couldn't pretend that this situation didn't gut him to the core.

"Jack, I'm—"

"Oh, my God. I can call my office." He yanked up the phone. "I don't know why I didn't think about this before."

"Jack, you told your assistant to only work half days, it's nearly six o'clock."

He quickly dialed his office. "She might still be there. Caroline's very dedicated." Even he could hear the edge of panic in his voice. When the answering machine pick up he slammed the receiver down. "We're fucked."

* * *

Luanne tried to hold her panic at bay, but with every step she took it crawled up her spine like a daddy longlegs scaling a wall. They had no money and no way to get any. It seemed crazy that in this day and age they could find themselves in this position. But here they were.

The dark clouds that had been in the distance earlier were now hanging over them, causing the lush greenery of southern Tennessee to look even greener. If she hadn't currently been about to lose her mind, she might find it lovely. But at the moment, it represented the ominous foreboding of their situation.

Jack rubbed his flat stomach. "I'm hungry."

"That's the fifth time you've said that in the fifteen minutes since we left the convenience store. You're worse than a kid." They were on the main street of Quincy walking to...God knew where, and trying to figure out their options, which were pathetically few.

"I can't help it. Once you said it was after six my body immediately realized it hadn't eaten since this morning."

"Get yourself under control. I need you at your best to help me figure out this situation." She glanced around, hoping to see a friendly face. "They roll up the streets early here in Quincy." There wasn't a soul in sight.

"Yeah. I was thinking the same thing. I wonder if there's a park here."

"Why?"

"It's probably the safest place to sleep tonight. Then you can try to call Floyd or Joyce tomorrow."

The panic she'd held at bay roared through her like a locomotive. She grabbed his arm and pulled him to a stop. "What in the hell are you talking about? I can't sleep in a park."

"If you have another idea, then I'm all ears."

She stomped away from him. It was either that or curl up into the fetal position. This was horrible. She had no idea why this was the one thing to send her over the edge, but it was. This was what life with her mother had been like. The desperate vibrations coursing through her body were a little too familiar. Her mama's emotions had always been so all-consuming that they'd seeped into Luanne's soul. Always frantic, always out of control. She'd do just about anything not to revisit that place again. There had to be a way out.

"Luanne, look."

She stopped and spun to face him. "What?" He was smiling like he'd found a million dollars.

He motioned to her. "Come here and look at this."

"What is it?" She rushed back to him. "Have you found something?"

"I sure as hell have. This is our ticket." He tapped a sign hanging on a telephone pole.

It was faded and had mud on it, but she could read *Monday Amateur Night at Rosie's Gentleman's Club, $500 prize.* The rest of the sign was illegible because of the mud. "Oh, hell no. Don't even think about it, Jack."

He held his hands up like he was calming a violent animal. "Before you say no, I want you to consider our situation."

"Our *situation* is your fault. You should've tried to stop those grannies. Now you want me to dance at a strip club? There's not enough money in the world, Jack-ass."

He looked offended. "There's no need to call names. I only thought you'd want to do it for the team. I would do it, but if you're not comfortable, I understand. I'll ask the next person we see the location of the city park. If they don't have a park, I'm sure we can find a shed or field to sleep in." A low rumble of thunder sounded in the distance. Jack looked toward the sky, then back to Luanne. "Shame."

She would not do this. She would not. Another clap of thunder, this time closer than the last. The desperation swimming in her veins spiked.

Damn him. Damn him. Damn him.

"Fine." She poked his chest. "But when this is over, you're a dead man, Jack."

Chapter Fourteen

Rosie's Gentleman's Club was on the outskirts of town. It took a while to walk to the dance hall, and now they were late and, thanks to the sprinkles that had started five minutes before, damp. The contest was supposed to start in fifteen minutes. That was fine. It meant Luanne didn't have much time to think about what she was about to do.

This was a banner day. In only a few minutes she'd be dancing for money. Not only dancing—she'd be expected to remove some of her clothes. Thankfully she'd bought the baby-blue matching bra and panties set. Bile clawed at her throat. No. She could do this. Do what needed to be done to survive.

She wasn't weak. She wasn't like her mother. She could do the hard things to take care of herself.

Bullshit. You've let your daddy step in and take care of you every chance you get, just like your mother.

She shoved that thought aside. The last thing she needed was to bring her screwed up relationship with her parents into this situation.

Jack's warm hands kneaded her shoulders. "You've got this, Luanne. I've seen you dance, you're a natural."

The look she shot him should have burned him to ash.

He held his hand up in surrender. "You're right. We shouldn't talk. You need to get into the zone."

She flipped him off and walked to the door. The big bouncer at the door informed them there wasn't a cover charge. Good thing too, or she would have had to go in on her own. Of course, knowing Jack he'd charm his way in even if there was a cover charge.

They both stopped inside the door to let their sight adjust to the dimness. Rosie's was a classy joint, for Podunk, USA. The walls were covered in red velvet and the booths were black leather. Crystal chandeliers hung from the ceiling along with trapeze bars spread around the club.

I don't even want to know.

There was the obligatory smoky atmosphere, but not as bad as she thought it would be. One thing was for sure—it was packed. The whole county must have been there. Jack put his hand on her lower back and this time she welcomed his touch. Being the shortest person in a crowd could be claustrophobic.

He ushered them to a corner in the back. Lip caught between his teeth, he surveyed the room. When he turned back to her, the fun-loving, charming man she'd grown used to was gone. Deep, furrowed lines of concern creased his brow. "You don't have to do this. We'll figure something out."

Smoky air filled her lungs as she took a deep breath. She looked around too. Not that she could see much. Short people problems. "I appreciate you saying that, but we need this money. I can get it for us... or I can at least try."

"I don't...I'm sorry I ever suggested this."

One statement and all the irritation with him flowed away like a river after a big rain. It was a sweet sentiment. But the bottom line was she could do something about their current situation, and that was what she was going to do. "It's fine, Jack. I can do this."

He caged her body with his. "No. This was a bad idea." His warm breath tickled her ear.

"I appreciate your concern, but I'm a big girl. This is my choice."

His deep amber gaze searched her face like she was a puzzle he couldn't quite figure out. "Okay. I'm going to walk that direction and

see if I can see where you sign up. Stay here. I'll come back and
get you."

His lips brushed across hers once, twice, three times. There wasn't
any heat in the kisses, but somehow that made them more potent. It
took all her willpower not to reach out for his hand when he turned to
go. She slumped against the wall and touched her mouth. This Jack
was far more dangerous to her heart. For the briefest of moments, she
saw right into his soul, and she liked it way more than she should.

A woman squealed to her left. At the same time, a table full of
ladies burst out laughing.

Interesting.

It seemed Alabama men were quite progressive, because everywhere she looked all she saw were other women. She moved from her
spot and climbed onto a chair to get a better look. Yep, there were
women of all ages and sizes at every booth, and in every chair. One
table with a woman in a white veil and a sash that read *Bride* were
particularly rowdy. There wasn't a man in the place. No. Wait. A group
of men sat next to the stage, but they looked like they weren't regulars
at Rosie's Gentlemen's Club. They were perfectly color coordinated
and coiffed.

Suddenly the lights began to flash, and smoke began to flow from
the back of the stage. Shit, it was starting and Jack wasn't back.

A bodacious woman in a red corset and a black flowing skirt, with
four-inch lace-up boots, came striding onto the stage. Her blonde hair
curled down her back and swung from side to side as she walked.
"Ladies! And gentlemen." She bowed to the table of men next to the
stage. "I'm Rosie and I'm here to make all of your dreams come true."

The place erupted into hoots and hollers.

"Bring it on, Rosie!"

"I need my fix, Rosie!"

"Rosie's here to take care of you," she purred into the mic.

"Show us the man flesh!" One of the guys next to the stage yelled
and his friends howled their agreement.

"Rosie's got more man flesh than you can handle, baby. And it's all
for you."

More screams.

Realization hit Luanne like a lightning strike.

Oh. My. God.

Jack.

* * *

Jack mingled with the other dancers at the back of the stage and sized up the competition. As he saw it, Raging Roy, who was currently on stage, was his biggest competitor. For one thing, he had all of his teeth, and it hadn't taken Jack long to realize that good dental hygiene could give a guy a real leg up in this contest.

Karma was truly a bitch. It'd been a real shocker to realize it was he, not Luanne, who had the chance to win the money and save them. He laughed under his breath. How was this shit storm his reality?

He had an amazing life, one where he was in complete control. Nothing happened that he didn't let happen. And now here he was about to take his clothes off for money in a room full of rabid women and a few enthusiastic gentlemen.

"Jack!"

He jerked around to see Luanne barreling through the crowd. Damn, she was beautiful. He'd used every ounce of self-control to not pin her to that wall earlier and have his very naughty way with her. "Hey."

She wiped sweat from her upper lip. "Woo, it's a mad house in here."

His hands went into his pockets. "Yep. These girls and guys like their beefcake."

The corners of her lips twitched. But he had to give her credit. She did try to keep a straight face.

"You're loving this, aren't you?" From the corner of his eye he saw the biggest pair of underwear he'd ever seen fly onto the stage. They caught air and slowly drifted to the ground.

She busted out laughing. "So much."

"Go ahead funny girl, laugh it up. Just remember, paybacks are hell."

She couldn't get herself together enough to answer. All she could do was nod.

"You're ridiculous." He turned away so she wouldn't see him fighting his own laughter.

"Have you come up with a name?"

"How do you know I'm going to do it?"

"Oh, please. It's a chance for you to strut your stuff. I don't see you passing on that."

That wasn't it at all. It was a chance for him to get money and keep her safe, but he'd never tell her that. "You do have a point."

"So, your name?"

"It's a surprise. You'll find out when everyone else does. Now get out of here so I can concentrate and get into character."

"Alright." Before she left, she turned back to him. "Are you sure?"

He was touched that she would ask, but he needed to do this. "I'm sure."

She nodded.

He waved his hand down his body. "I'm sure it'd be a crime to deprive the world of this."

"Break a leg, Jack-ass. I'll be in the back." Her laughter trailed her as she strolled away.

A guy with a headset on tapped him on the shoulder. "You're up next." He peeked down at his clipboard. "What's your stage name?"

He glanced at Luanne's retreating back. "Jack, the Mighty Joystick."

* * *

Luanne jostled her way through the crowd. She got knocked into a table when one of the members of the bridal party jumped up to tuck a dollar bill into the waistband of the guy on stage.

"Hey, bitch, get out of the way," the drunk bridesmaid yelled.

"Actually, you're in my way, but I'll happily move." Luanne tried to sidestep the drunken girl.

"You do that." She was winding up for a fight.

Luanne held up her hands and tried to get past.

"You think you're better than me? Don't cha?" Spittle flew through the air.

Luanne leaned to the side, barely dodging the deluge. "Listen, sister, I'm only trying to find a seat. I haven't given you one thought. Enjoy your night."

The woman grabbed her arm. "Hey, don't you walk away from me."

Luanne glanced down at the woman's hand, then slowly raised her gaze until she met the idiot's bloodshot eyes. "Sweetheart, if you want to keep that hand I'd advise you to remove it from my arm."

"What are you going to do shorty?"

Anger and a little fear danced on Luanne's skin. But she wouldn't let this idiot see it. The advantage she had was that she wasn't drunk, and she planned to use that in her favor. She leaned forward, then wrenched her arm away.

The bridesmaid lost her balance and swung out. Big mistake. The minute the bouncers saw her throw a punch they were all over her. Luanne had to give it to the bouncers, they didn't play. The bridesmaid was escorted from the building before she could say *throw the bouquet.*

The bride reached over and touched her arm. "Are you alright?"

"Yeah, I'm fine." She was pretty sure she was fine. That had been way more intense than she was comfortable with.

"I'm sorry about her, she's an ugly drunk. Would you like to sit down? We have an empty seat now." She pushed the chair out with her stilettoed foot.

Luanne peered through the smoke to the back of the room. It would be hard to see Jack from there. "Sure, thanks. I'm Luanne."

"I'm Alexa, and this is Amanda, Julia, Shayla, Sidney, Julie, Olivia, and Hannah." She pointed in the direction of the delinquent bridesmaid. "And that's Felicia." The girls waved. "Are you here alone?"

"No, my friend is one of the dancers."

"Really! Which one?"

Before she could answer, Rosie returned to the stage in all her glory.

"Ooooh, my darlings, have I got a pretty one for you. And if I'm not mistaken, he's a Rosie's virgin." The cheering hit a new level of enthusiasm. "Without further ado, welcome to the stage Jack, the Mighty Joystick."

All the lights went out, and *I Want It That Way* began to play. Suddenly a huge spot light found Jack. He stood barefoot in his jeans and button-down shirt, and he looked good enough to eat. As the slow beat played he sauntered down the runway-type stage and leisurely unbuttoned his shirt.

Luanne pointed toward the stage. "That one."

"Holy shit, he's hot." Her bride friend fanned herself and took a liberal gulp of her drink.

She glanced back at Jack then back to them. A smile she couldn't control spread across her face. "Yes, he is."

The whole room followed his every move as he grabbed the stripper pole and tenderly guided his fingers up and down it, like the face of a lover. When he began to slowly thrust his hips forward in time with the beat she thought the middle-aged women at the table next to her were going to storm the stage.

The whole time he made love to the pole, he never took his gaze off Luanne. Sweat broke out at her hairline, and blasts of lustful longing danced along the nerves leading to her core, where heat pooled like bubbling lava in a too-long dormant volcano. Hooo-leee crap.

The music changed to a driving beat, and Jack ripped off his shirt, grabbed a water bottle she hadn't noticed before, and poured water over his head and down his chest.

The. Crowd. Went. Ballistic.

Women charged the stage, slipping money in his waistband like he was a sexual slot machine. The group of men were practically crawling on top of each other to get to him.

Chaos reigned around her, but she was helpless to do anything but revel in the heat consuming every atom of her being. He shook his head and drops of water flew in every direction. Time slowed as he dropped to his knees and undulated his hips. It slammed to a stop when his eyes connected with hers. The things he communicated with that look...Lord almighty.

He danced, he teased, he charmed, and he was pretty damn spectacular. One lady grabbed his tight buns, and he turned to wag his finger at the naughty move. All was forgiven though when he laughed and kissed her on the cheek. That gesture earned him another twenty. He worked the crowd, even coming off the stage and giving a few quick lap dances, all the while raking in the cash.

Then he turned in her direction and slowly made his way to their table, each step he took guided by the slow, pulsing rhythm of the music. He was a panther on the hunt. Her new friends nearly fainted.

The bride was the first at the table to be on the receiving end of his panty-melting gyrations. One last *take me to bed or lose me forever* look and he moved to the next girl, and the next, but Luanne knew he was coming for her. He did all the right things to get more bills stuffed into his open jeans, but his smoldering look told her this wasn't just about the cash. The blood scalded her veins the closer he got. She welcomed it.

Burn me alive, Jack. Burn. Me. Alive.

The panther's eyes lit with amber flames when he yanked her out of the chair. Her pulse hammered in her ears, breathing became unnecessary, and the noise from the crowed dropped away. There was nothing but Jack and the music. The beat. The heat. All of it spiraling the tension in her body to breaking point.

He moved behind her and slid his hands down her stomach. Her arms wrapped back around his hips to keep him where she wanted him. She no longer cared that they were in the middle of a large audience. They swayed to the left, then the right, their hips in perfect unison to the throb that vibrated around them. Her lids drifted closed and she relaxed into him, only to come undone when he sank his teeth into the soft flesh of her neck.

He spun her to face him. "This isn't over. Not by a long shot."

With that promise? threat? he danced back through the crowd to the stage.

The little bride grabbed her to yell in her ear. "Damn, girl. I want my man to look at me like that."

Luanne was shaken to the core. Money was sticking out of every one of his pockets, and with each thrust of his hips more was crammed in. It didn't matter if he won or not, there was a couple of hundred dollars bulging in those jeans. She shook her head and pressed a hand to her still-fluttering stomach. That hadn't been the only thing bulging in his jeans.

When the song ended women threw more money and themselves at him. Jack scooped up the cash and winked at the women.

"Marry me, Mighty Joystick!" one of the gay guys yelled.

"I would, but I'm already taken." He pointed to Luanne.

She used the thumb and forefinger of both hands to form a W, then mouthed *whatever*, which made him laugh. But she didn't feel *whatever* about any of this. Her heart still raced like a locomotive on fire. Luckily, there were several performers yet to dance. It gave her time to try to get her lust under control. Good luck. That ship had sailed, sunk, and was sitting at the bottom of the ocean along with her ability to resist Jack Avery.

Finally, Rosie sashayed onto the stage. "Oh, my. It appears we have a real contender in Jack, the Mighty Joystick. Let's hear it for him one more time."

Jack waved to the crowd as a generous-sized bra went flying past his head.

"Can you introduce us?" Julie looked at Luanne like she was asking for a puppy at Christmas.

"Ah...well...I can introduce you, but we're kind of together." What? Where had that come from? She knew exactly where it had come from. The freight train of jealousy chasing her to Lustville.

"I thought you said you were just friends," Hannah said with a pout.

"That's what we usually tell people on the nightclub circuit, but you guys have been so nice to me that I wanted to tell you the truth."

A collective "Awww," came from the table.

"Honey, if you ever get tired of him, give us a call."

"We have a winner, my pretties." Rosie's voice purred through the sound system. "Can I get all of the contestants back on stage, please?"

The men filed out, most of them in some sort of costume. All of them were partially dressed, even Jack. His shirt hung open, and the expanse of smooth brown skin had her wishing everything she'd told these girls about the two of them was true.

"Rodney, can you give me a drum roll?" Rosie struggled to rip open the envelope while she juggled the mic.

Boy Scout Jack reached out and took the microphone from her, and held it to her mouth like a human mic stand. "Thank you, Joystick." She winked.

Jack nodded and scanned the room until he saw Luanne. He smirked and patted the huge roll of cash in his front pocket. Surely there was enough to get a cheap room for the night.

"The winner is...Jack, the Mighty Joystick!"

Screams, cheers, and shouts calling for an encore filled the place. Rosie tried to talk him into another round on stage, but he declined and gave her a big hug. With a pucker of his lips he blew a kiss to the crowd, then bounced down the steps toward Luanne's table. The smile he wore was probably illegal in all fifty states. He didn't stop or slow down until she was wrapped in a fierce hug.

"Congratulations, Joystick." She inhaled his musky scent and her knees went wobbly.

He pulled back and grinned. "I might be changing careers."

She laughed. "I wouldn't quit your day job, but hey, who am I to judge?"

Someone cleared their throat. She glanced around to see the expectant faces of her tablemates. "Jack, these are my new friends Hannah, Julia, and Olivia, and our bride is Alexa."

He took Alexa's hand and kissed her fingers. "Congratulations. Why are all the good ones taken?"

Alexa's face bloomed a pretty shade of pink, and Luanne swore she could hear the poor girl's ovaries begging for mercy. Yep, Jack had that effect on women. Time to break this up. "Where do you get your prize money?"

Jack threw his arm around her shoulder. "Rosie told me to pick it up at the box office."

"Well, we better be going. Thanks for letting me sit with y'all. Best wishes on your marriage."

They wove their way through the crowd, stopping for pictures. When they made it to the box office, Rosie was there giving instructions to her staff. "There's the man of the hour. I could use someone like you on my staff. Are you interested?"

"It's tempting, but sadly, I have to get back to Texas."

Rosie counted out his five hundred dollars. "Our loss."

Jack handed the money to Luanne. "Is there a clean hotel around here?"

"There's a roadside inn about a mile up the road. Take a left out of the parking lot. It's next to the truck stop. Do you want me to call and see if they have a room?"

"I'd appreciate—"

"Two rooms," Luanne said. She needed her own room, especially after his performance.

"Two?" Rosie's artfully drawn-on eyebrows nearly reached her hairline.

"Yes...ah...you see, Jack and I are just friends." It would've been a lot easier to speak with Rosie if Jack hadn't been clucking like a chicken behind her. Damn right she was a scared chicken. No way could she share a room with him after this.

The club owner shook her head while she dialed the phone. "Ooo-kay. If you're sure."

"I am."

"Maria, this is Rose. Do you have a couple of rooms available for tonight? Mm-hmm. Alright, great. I'm sending two friends down right now."

Luanne's eyes filled with unexpected tears. She was exhausted from the events of the day, and her hormones were still recovering from the speedboat ride they'd been on since Jack first stepped on stage. Watching him dance only confirmed what she'd always known.

Jack Avery would be a rock star in bed.

Chapter Fifteen

The travel inn's lobby was clean and quirky, and Jack would have given every penny he'd earned for a bed. But it was the aroma of greasy burgers in the to-go bags he carried that really had him ready to beg.

He glanced over his shoulder to make sure his sassy companion was still with him. She'd been unusually quiet on the walk to the motel. That was fine with him. His body was still on full simmer from the dirty dance they'd shared. Her hips moving beneath his hands had been almost too much. There hadn't been any control when she started rocking in time with him—he'd almost embarrassed himself right then and there. It had been necessary to break it off and spin her around, or his fingers would've gone exploring the soft, warm parts that starred in his dreams. It was good they were getting two rooms, because he'd have a very hard time keeping his hands off her if they were sharing.

"Can I help you?" A small Hispanic woman in a bright blue sweater stood behind the desk. She was barely tall enough to see over the counter.

"Rosie called about two rooms for us." He handed the bags to Luanne so he could get the money from his pocket.

The little woman looked confused. "I tell Rosie that I only have one room. She not tell you that?"

"No, she didn't tell us that." Luanne's voice had taken on a panicked edge.

"One room, two beds." She pulled a key from a cubby in the wall behind her.

Exhaustion yanked on Jack's bones. He didn't care if he had to sleep on a cot, he just needed to sleep. "We'll take it."

"Jack—"

He leveled her with his *don't give me any shit* glare. "We'll take it."

"One night?" The owner was typing things into the computer.

"Yes." They both said in unison.

"Okay, one hundred dollars."

He counted out the money using mostly one-dollar bills from his tips. Rosie had paid him in hundreds, but there was something so satisfying about slipping one bill after another from the stack in his hand to the pile on the counter. This must be how pioneer men felt when they provided for their women. Instead of animal skins he used his stripper earnings. It was close to the same thing.

He noticed a cubby with toiletries behind the counter. "Are those for sale?"

"Yes."

"We'll take two toothbrushes, toothpaste, and two deodorants. One men's and a girly one." He glanced at Luanne. "Anything else?"

"A bottle of lotion, laundry soap, and do you have bottled water?"

"Si. Can I get for you anything else?"

Jack glanced at Luanne.

"Um...extra towels?" she asked.

"Oh, si. I bring them."

Jack slapped money on the counter, and they left the office.

The walk to the room was silent.

"This is us." He slipped the old-fashioned key into the lock and swung the door open. The smell of clean laundry filled his nose and he immediately relaxed. The room was small and the furnishings outdated, but it was clean, and it had a shower and two beds. It would do. "This isn't so bad."

"No, it's actually very nice." She flipped on the bedside lamp and a warm yellow glow filled the room.

"Do you wanna shower first or should I?" He emptied his pockets of the wads of tip money he'd accumulated.

"You've got quite a stash there. Good to see you use that pretty face for good and not evil"

He shrugged. "It's a livin'."

"You must be tired. Your pronunciation has slipped. You take the first shower. I can wait."

"Are you sure?"

She fiddled with the hem of her shirt. "Yeah, I'm sure. You go ahead."

"I'm not gonna argue with you. I can smell myself." He stripped off his shirt and threw it over the only chair in the room. "I'll save you some hot water."

"Thanks. Don't take too long, I might fall asleep on my feet."

He saw her watching him in the mirror, and a thrill of satisfaction shot through him. She may not want to want him, but she did. Lust burned away his exhaustion. He stopped at the bathroom door and peered back at her. "You like what you see?"

"I wasn't looking at you, Jack. I was staring off into space. In case you haven't noticed, I'm exhausted."

"Mm-hmm, you keep telling yourself that, buttercup. You keep telling yourself that."

* * *

Luanne heard the shower come on and wanted to claw her eyeballs out. She'd totally been checking him out and he'd caught her red-handed. Rookie mistake. But seriously. His back was too delicious not to admire.

Get a hold of yourself.

She pulled the plastic bag with all their earthly possessions to her. A quick inventory told her she had what she needed to get as clean as possible. Thank God. She grabbed her toothbrush and made her way to the sink/vanity combo outside the bathroom.

Had brushing her teeth ever felt so good? She didn't think so. She glanced at the room behind her through the mirror. Crazy to think that only a few hours ago she'd thought they might have to sleep outside. Grudgingly, she had to admit that he'd really saved their bacon tonight.

Those women and men loved him. Why wouldn't they? He'd been hot as hell up on that stage, powerful and fun all at the same time. Life with Jack would never be boring, that was for sure.

Where had that come from? She didn't have a life with Jack. He might be fun, but she'd always be waiting for him to get bored and leave. People always left her. Her mother, her father, even Scarlett had left in a way. Her best friend had gone to a place Luanne didn't understand and where she couldn't follow. Luanne Price didn't do love, so while she was happy for Scarlett, she mourned the loss of what their friendship used to be.

When Jack emerged from his shower, she was ready. She'd prepared herself for the sight of him in nothing but a towel. It took her hogtying her hormones, but she was able to keep her gaze on his face.

"It's all yours." He walked to the vanity and grabbed his toothbrush. The man even brushed his teeth with raw sexuality.

"Thanks." She started for the bathroom, then remembered her lotion. When she reached for it her arm brushed against his stomach. And just like that, the monumental effort it had taken to keep her focus above the towel line crumbled. The warm, moist heat of his skin singed her flesh.

His fingers wrapped around her elbow, and as she pulled back his hand slid down her arm until he clasped her hand. God help her. His fingers stroked the inside of her wrist and the sensible, take-no-prisoners Luanne melted. They locked stares, didn't move, didn't breathe.

With his other hand, he looped a stray hair behind her ear, then trailed his fingers down her neck. "Luanne?"

"Yeah."

He bent his head and whispered, "I'm going to kiss you." His lips grazed the sensitive spot below her ear.

A moan curled between them like cigarette smoke in an old speakeasy. His? Hers? She didn't know or care.

Slowly, deliberately, he trailed tiny nips along her jaw to her mouth. Each touch of his lips formed a chain of desire winding its way around her, capturing and holding her where she desperately wanted to be.

"Jack." Her hands roamed his gorgeous back. Desire flooded her body, tightening her nipples to hard peaks wanting to be touched. If something didn't happen soon, she might explode with want. Even so, she grasped for some thread of control.

"What?"

She settled her hands on his fine ass. "I still don't like you."

He tugged one fistful of hair to gain better access to her neck. "Noted and recorded."

"'Cause you're a jerk sometimes." Was that her voice? It sounded like a porn star's.

He nuzzled the place below her ear. "I know, and it's a terrible flaw."

"Alright. As long as we're clear." Every jagged syllable of her words sounded like a plea for more.

He whispered across her neck, "We're clear."

"Now you can kiss me."

His mouth closed over hers and the warm, soft assault of lips and tongue scrambled her brain and sent liquid heat shimmering down her body. Strong arms enveloped her. She thrilled in the shelter his body provided. Usually she didn't like to be so close to...well, anyone, but especially not overly tall people. This was different from anything she'd experienced before. No fear, no hiding. With Jack she was brave and powerful.

Her fingers slid into his thick, wet hair as her head slanted to give him better access. Warm hands gripped her hips and hauled her against his hard body. The contact acted as an accelerant on the blaze racing between them. She needed more, had to have more. What small tendril of control she had snapped and she ground against the bulge nestled between her legs.

"Jesus, Luanne." The words were strangled. In one swift movement he lifted her onto the vanity. Unbidden, her legs circled his waist to pull him to the spot where she had to have him. He stepped into her heat and pushed and pushed again. His body mimicked what she needed, what they both needed to stop the crazy desire tearing through their bodies.

He deepened the kiss, drinking from her like a man dying of thirst, only to rip away in the next beat. "I don't know if I can slow this down." He shuddered as she dragged her nails down his back. "If we go much farther, I won't be able to stop."

"More." The words raced passed her vocal chords and fueled the crazy need to claim him too.

"Luanne, you better not be playing with me, because I'm sure as hell not." He cupped her face as his other hand trailed down to her waist, brushing her top aside, each touch sending showers of sparks behind her closed lids. His fingers danced under her shirt and up her belly until they rested beneath her breast.

Every movement, every touch made her want him more.

"Look at me. I want you right here with me."

He pulled back enough to look her in the face. She couldn't speak, she could barely breathe, but she understood the silent question he asked. Her fingers threaded with his, and raised their joined hands to her lips. A soft kiss across his knuckles and she placed his hand where they both wanted it. "Yes, yes, yes."

His mouth devoured hers, and she loved every conquering moment of it. He easily dealt with the front clasp of her bra and they both gasped when his big hand covered her naked breast. "I can't get enough of you." He licked and kissed down her neck. "I want you naked and sprawled on top of me right—"

Knock, knock, knock. "Senorita, I have extra towels."

They broke apart like a couple of middle schoolers caught in the janitor's closet. Both breathing hard, both a little sweaty, and both a lot dazed and confused.

Jack dragged his hands through his hair and uttered an obscenity that blistered the air.

Luanne slid from the vanity and nearly fell to the floor. Her legs refused to hold her. She gripped the counter for balance. "Um...coming."

When she could stand on her own, she hurried to the door to

retrieve the towels, grabbing a few bills from Jack's wad of cash on the way.

She tipped Maria and took the towels. Reality's cold bite nipped at her ass. She wasn't built to handle a force like Jack.

"Luanne."

She would've given him everything, and where would that have left her? "Not now, Jack. I need a shower."

"Lou."

"I'll try not to wake you when I'm done. Good night." Without so much as a glance in his direction she scurried to the bathroom like the coward she was.

Chapter Sixteen

The honk of a horn brought Jack back to consciousness. He tried to peel his lids open, then decided it wasn't worth the trouble. The bed creaked when he turned to his side. After several minutes of trying to fall back to sleep, he finally opened his eyes.

Luanne's bare back was the first thing he saw. That was a hell of a way to wake up, considering the night before. The case of blue balls he'd sported when he went to bed was world class, but he hadn't been mad at her, still wasn't. Luanne Price was one scarred bunny. He didn't know the whole story, but from the little that Scarlett had let slip, and the morsels of information Luanne had shared, she'd suffered emotionally at the hands of her family.

He wanted her to trust him. That wouldn't be easy to accomplish. He almost laughed. And *that* was the understatement of the century.

His reputation with women wasn't one that inspired confidence. But he could be patient. You didn't get to where he was in his life and career without patience.

From the time he was thirteen he knew the future he wanted, and he worked for years toward that one goal. High school, State University, law school...none had been easy and there'd been many opportunities to lose focus, but he hadn't. Waiting on one woman to trust him was nothing compared to working two jobs to get through college and law school, or staying up nights on end studying for the LSAT, and the bar exam.

Another thing he was good at was identifying what he wanted and implementing a plan to get it. He wanted Luanne Price. He gave his brain a moment to offer opposing arguments to counter that statement. None came. He wanted Luanne and he wanted her bad.

Now that he'd admitted it to himself, he just had to come up with a strategy and put it into action. Oh yeah, and persuade the woman in the other bed that he was who she wanted too.

He jumped out of bed with a new sense of purpose. Her dainty foot was sticking out from underneath the blanket. He grabbed it and tugged. "Get up, sunshine. It's a beautiful day."

A pillow sailed through the air toward his head. "Shut up, Jack, or I'll gut you and hang you with your own intestines." She pulled the covers over her head.

What a delicate flower. If he wasn't careful he'd be madly in love with her before the road trip from hell was over.

"I'll buy you pancakes."

"With bacon?" Her words were muffled but intrigued from beneath the blanket.

"With bacon."

"And coffee? I don't move without coffee."

"Do you even have to ask?"

"Okay, turn around."

"Why?"

"Because I'm naked, Jack."

"Fine." He was naked too, but you didn't see him running and hiding.

The bed creaked and covers rustled. Ah, sleeping beauty emerging from her cocoon.

"Oh, my lord, Jack. When I said I was naked that should've been your prompt to tell me you were too."

"You could always look away."

"I am. Geez, get some clothes on."

She totally wasn't looking away. He could see her in the vanity mirror checking him out. But he wouldn't bring that to her attention. Evidently, Luanne wasn't a morning person, and there wasn't any reason to poke the beast. No matter how fun it would be. Besides, his mouth had gone dry at the quick glimpse of her body he'd gotten when she stood to wrap a sheet around herself and scurry to the bathroom.

"Good news," she said from behind the closed door.

"What is it?"

"Our clothes are dry."

They'd washed their underwear and shirts in the sink the night before, even though it had taken every ounce of effort he had left in his body to perform the task. He was grateful now to have relatively clean clothes to put on.

He brushed his teeth and ran his wet hands through his hair to smooth down a couple cowlicks.

Luanne emerged from the bathroom with her lids down, carrying his boxer briefs and shirt. "Put these on."

"You're such a prude, Ms. Price."

"I'm not a prude. I don't want the sight of your junk ruining my appetite."

He laughed and pulled on his clothes. "You can open your eyes now, I'm decent."

"Now move so I can brush my teeth." She hip-bumped him out of the way. A small kernel of annoyance knocked around his belly. It was like nothing had happened the night before. He quickly squashed it. Getting angry wasn't the way to endear himself to her.

He watched as she performed the same basic tasks as he just had, while he counted up their money. "We've still got almost eight hundred dollars, enough to get breakfast and buy a couple of bus tickets."

"I hope there's a place to catch the bus here." She rubbed lotion on her face.

He loved her naked face. She was as beautiful without makeup as she was with. Time to turn on the charm. "You look pretty."

Her hand froze at her neck. "What?"

"You're pretty."

She gave him a squinty-eye glare. "What are you up to, Jack?"

"Nothing, I just wanted you to know how lovely you are." He gave her his *I'm all you need* smile. It had zero effect on her.

"Um...okay." She continued to moisturize her skin.

He propped his shoulder against the wall and crossed his arms. "It's customary for a person to say thank you after a compliment."

"Fine. Thank you for making things weird, Jack."

He needed to regroup. The moves that worked on other women were ineffective with Luanne. She went to slip on her shoes and it occurred to him that to use his moves on her would be a disservice to her. She deserved better, and he could give that to her. But he had to do it carefully. He opened the door to the room and propped it open with his body. "Pick up the pace, Thumbelina. I'm starved."

* * *

The coffee hit Luanne's bloodstream like jet fuel. Ahhh. She should not be expected to deal with Jack while still caffeine free. He was a lot to take and hard to resist when she was on her A game, but without a cup of Joe? Disastrous.

"Whatcha havin', Luanne?"

She glanced up to see him grinning at her. Lord have mercy. The man sucked the air out of the room. He was so stinkin' handsome.

She wasn't the only one who noticed either. The pretty waitress who'd waddled up to the table was giving him the once over. "What can I get y'all?" But she only looked at Jack.

"The Lumberjack breakfast." No shame. She was starved.

"That's my girl." He closed the menu. "I'll have the same." He glanced at her nametag. "Monica. And can I say, you look beautiful today."

The woman's face bloomed into a rosy shade of red. She had to be twelve months pregnant and ready to pop at any minute. But at Jack's words her tired eyes lit and twinkled like a prom queen.

She curled a stray piece of hair behind her ear. "Oh, my word." She giggled. "Thanks. I really needed that today."

"When are you due?" Jack set his chin in his hand and gave her his complete attention.

"My C-section is scheduled for seven a.m. tomorrow, and I will kill anyone who tries to get between me and the hospital."

Luanne couldn't take her focus off of the women's belly. "Oh. It moved."

"What?" The waitress seemed confused at first, then laughed and rubbed her belly. "They've started doing that all the time. I swear they're gonna come out with black eyes."

"Twins?"

"Yes, my husband's been telling everyone he's got super sperm. He's such an idiot."

"What's his name?" Jack was still giving the woman his absolute attention.

"Connor."

"Well, Monica, idiot or not, Connor is one lucky man."

The dreamy expression on Monica's face told Luanne that she didn't think her husband was an idiot at all, but the best thing since white bread.

She giggled again and practically skipped away to turn in their order.

"You made her day." She watched Monica whispering to another waitress, then they both looked over at them.

He shrugged. "It's true. Pregnant women are beautiful. Besides, my mama used to say there were only two things you should say to an expectant woman: 'You look beautiful' and 'Can I rub your feet?' I didn't think this was the right venue for the latter, so I went with the former."

"You're something else, you know that, right? Such a sweet talker."

He poured them both more coffee from the carafe on the table. "You say that like it's a bad thing. In my experience, you get more with sugary words than venomous words." He eyed her over his coffee mug.

"Point taken. I could temper my words sometimes."

"Ya think?"

She pretended his words didn't bother her by sticking her tongue out at him. He didn't understand that she'd grown the hard shell she hid behind to protect herself from the selfish adults in her life. He didn't know she cried at Olympic athletes' backstories, or was an absolute sucker for puppies. No one but Scarlett knew she had a soft under-belly that she protected with her smart mouth.

Anger fisted into a knot in her chest when she thought of all the people in her life who'd wanted her to be compliant, who didn't want her to rock the boat and call them on their bullshit. Apparently, Jack was just like them. She wasn't going to lie—it hurt.

They sipped their coffee in silence for awhile. She was lost in thought, and if she were honest, licking her wounded ego from Jack's comment, when he set his cup down and took her hand in his. "Honestly, Luanne. I wouldn't change one thing about you. You are one of a kind, and you don't see that every day. It keeps me on my toes."

Monica set platters of food in front of them. Good thing too, because not one word would come out of her mouth.

No one had ever said that to her. No one but Scarlett appreciated all of her—the good, the bad, and the snarky.

She searched his face to see if he was blowing smoke, but she could tell he wasn't. He meant it. Well, crap. This forced her to see him in a different light. He wasn't like her father in any way, shape, or form. That revelation was both exhilarating and terrifying. "Thank you, Jack. That's the nicest thing anyone has ever said to me."

There was an awkward silence as he stared at her. She pointed with her fork and grinned at him. "Stop staring, it's weird. And eat your breakfast. It's getting cold."

One side of his mouth kicked up, and his expression shone with mischief. "Yes, ma'am."

She dug into her own food. "I think we should use some of your winnings to buy a disposable phone, so we can call your office and leave a message for your assistant to call us. Depending on where we are when she calls, we can have her send money."

"Good idea." He checked his watch that wasn't there. "After that I guess we get a couple of bus tickets to Roseman."

"Oh, about that." She needed to tell him she wasn't going any farther on this trip. She'd have him buy her a ticket to the closest big city and figure it out from there. "I'm not going—"

"Son of a bitch. Would you look who just strolled through the door?"

* * *

Jack couldn't believe it. He probably shouldn't be surprised, but even in the crazy town world he'd been living in for the last few days, this was beyond serendipitous. June, Pearl, and Bobby were being led to a table on the other side of the restaurant.

The boy's hair was wet with a precise part down the middle. The women were sporting new dresses. He knew this because June had forgotten to remove the sales tag from her pink floral number and it waved at him with every step she took. Looked like someone had been shopping and found a place to stay last night.

"What are we going to do? Should we call the cops?" Luanne was loaded for bear. He could see it in her moon pie eyes.

"What? No. We're going to handle this like the professionals we are." He stood and offered her his hand. "Ready, counselor?"

With an evil grin firmly in place, she placed her hand in his. "Oh, I'm more than ready...counselor. Wait, am I good cop, or are you?" Luanne said from the corner of her mouth.

"Oh, you're definitely the bad cop, cher. We should all play to our strengths, and you're the badass in this partnership."

"You say the nicest things. You big sweet talker."

He loved it when she seemed to grow three inches at his praise. The woman did love to be the badass, but he was beginning to think that maybe the whole thing was an act.

They were almost on the trio, but the three hadn't noticed them. "Follow my lead." He grabbed a chair from a nearby table and so did she. They pulled them to the end of Pearl and June's booth. "Ladies, how are you this fine morning?"

June squeaked and dropped her menu, while Pearl gave them the hairy eyeball. He had to give it to the ol' girl, she was ballsy.

"I don't believe we had the opportunity to introduce ourselves yesterday. I'm Jack Avery, and this is Luanne Price. We're attorneys over in Zachsville, Texas. Ever heard of it?"

Both women shook their heads.

"And how are you, Bobby?"

The little boy gave them a sheepish chocolate milk grin. "I gettin' waffles."

"What are you doing here?" Pearl hissed.

Luanne clasped her hands together and placed them onto the table. "Now Pearl, that's the same question we wanted to ask you. There was something else, though. Oh yeah, where are our things?"

Jack watched as a kaleidoscope of emotion played across Pearl's face. He had to reign in his own feelings. He was part of the problem in this screwed-up scenario. A lifetime of running from poverty had left him with very little objectivity. Better to let Luanne handle it.

From the corner of his eye, he saw June swipe a tear from her cheek. Fuuuuuck.

"That's none of your business. It's ours now," Pearl declared.

"I beg to differ, Pearl. You do know you can go to jail, right?" Luanne calmly laid out the worst-case scenario for the duo.

June buried her head in her hands and began to cry in earnest.

"Now, look what you've done," Pearl snarled at Luanne. When she looked back at her sister the ferocity melted away and devotion took its place. "It's okay, Junie. Don't cry, I'm going to take care of this."

Pity demanded Jack do something. He reached over to pat her on the back, but Bobby had beat him to it and was patting and cooing, "Nana."

Someone shoot him now. He glanced at Luanne and even she seemed to have lost her anger.

June glanced up, misery seeping from every pore of her face. "Tell them, Pearl. It's wrong. We're wrong. No matter how desperate we are, we can't continue this."

"Alright. Somebody better tell me what's going on, and you better start talking now." He said it more harshly than he intended, but dammit, he wanted answers. And by the mutinous look on Pearl's face, he wasn't getting answers by playing good cop.

"Get waffles?" Bobby said.

"Let me order him some breakfast and I'll tell you everything."

"June."

She leveled Pearl with an *it's over* look. "Everything, Pearl."

The same waitress came to take their order. "Y'all know Pearl and June? Aren't they the sweetest?"

"Sugary sweet," Luanne said.

"I could just squeeze 'em to death. Especially Pearl, here," Jack said through gritted teeth.

"Back at cha," Pearl said, a syrupy smile plastered on her face.

"Pearl," June warned.

The four of them sat in a Mexican stand-off staring at each other. The waitress shuffled uncomfortably from foot to foot. The tension could've been cut and served as slabs of beef.

They might've sat like that all day, but Bobby yelled, "Waffles! Waffles! Waffles!"

"Waffles it is." The waitress laughed and seemed relieved to be able to walk away from the table.

"Okay, spill," Luanne said. "And I swear if I think you're lying, I'll call the sheriff faster than you can say grand theft auto."

June wrung her hands. "Well, it all started a few months ago. My no-good D-A-U-G-H-T-E-R ran off and left B-O-B-B-Y with me. Don't get me wrong, I adore him and truly believed he was better off with me, and for about a month he was. Pearl was so sweet to take him in and not complain at all." She gave her sister a loving look. "We've lived together since my husband died five years ago."

"I love that little squirt, June. You know that." She reached across the table and ruffled Bobby's hair.

Bobby looked up from his coloring page and grinned.

Pearl began to tear up the paper napkin in front of her. "Everything would've been fine too if it weren't for that lousy Marty Franklin."

This made Jack sit up in his seat. "Marty Franklin? Is that Bobby's father?"

"Gawd, no." Pearl said.

June crossed her hands primly in her lap. "We don't exactly know who B-O-B-B-Y's father is."

"Marty Franklin is the scumbag who lives in the duplex next to us. He takes care of the place for the owner. At least he's supposed to take care of things at the place we lived."

"Lived?" Luanne said.

"Yes, lived," Pearl spat out. "He became the manager about the same time June's daughter left. At first it was only June's social security check that went missing. We called the SS office and they assured us the check was mailed, but she never got it."

June picked up the story. "We asked Marty about it. At first he denied knowing anything about it, but then the next month Pearl's check went missing. At that point, we confronted him. He admitted he'd taken them because we had the baby living with us and he's not on the lease." June's voice quivered. "Why would a little boy need to be on the lease?"

"I'm pretty sure they don't have to be, but we'll check that out," Jack said as calmly as possible, but his blood was boiling.

"Then the next month he kept both checks. We told him we'd go to the police, and he told us he'd report us to Child Protective Services and that we'd lose Bobby." June raised her hands helplessly. "What could we do? I can't lose him. As you might imagine, we couldn't pay our bills and three days ago we came home from an errand and all of our things were on the front stoop. Marty said we hadn't paid our rent and evicted us."

"Why would he do that? He can't get your checks if you aren't living there." Luanne looked from one woman to the next.

They both ducked their heads, and before they could answer the waitress returned with their order. Jack had never seen anyone be more excited about a waffle than Bobby.

After the waitress refilled their coffees and left, June said, "Our checks are still going to the address. He said he'll turn us in if we change anything. We've been living out of our car for the last few days. We know what we did was wrong, but we didn't feel like we had another choice."

Fury burned through Jack's body. He kept his shaking hands in his lap, squeezing and releasing a fist over and over. People like Marty were the scum of the earth. They didn't deserve to breathe the same air that decent people did.

"Where's Jack's car?" Luanne asked.

June chewed on her crepe-paper lip. Even Pearl looked a little uncomfortable.

"Ladies?"

Pearl squared her shoulders. "We sold it and got ten thousand dollars for it. That's more money than we've ever seen in one place."

Something close to a sob slipped from Jack's mouth. His baby had been defiled had sold for pennies on the dollar. He scrubbed his hands down his face and breathed through his nose. This could not be happening. That car was the symbol of everything he'd worked for, and now it was gone. Just like that. Poof.

"We still have most of the money. We'll give it back to you. Just don't call the cops." For the first time Pearl lost her belligerent tone. "It would kill June to lose that boy."

"Ladies, will you excuse us a moment?" Luanne took Jack by the hand and led him outside.

He squinted against the bright sun and slumped against the building.

"Are you alright? I know how much you loved that car."

He just waved her off. There wasn't anything he could say.

She patted his arm. "I understand."

And she did. How weird was that? Most women would want him to talk about his feelings and beat the whole thing to death. Not Luanne.

"What do you want to do?"

"Nail that fucking Marty Franklin's ass to the wall. If not for him I'd still have my car."

"I'm with you on that one." She flicked hair from her forehead.

He placed his hand on his stomach. Acid that churned and burned in his gut. "Should we call the police?"

"Let's see who owns the duplex first," she said. "In a small town, you never know. Marty's uncle could be the chief of police. We need all the ammunition we can get first."

"Good plan. The bottom line is this family needs help, and if we can help I won't feel like my car died in vain."

She rubbed his arm. "I am sorry for your loss. She had a good life."

Her lips twitching at the corners made him grin. "Shut up. Let's go use our superpowers to fight crime."

* * *

Luanne did feel bad for Jack. He was the one who'd lost in this deal, so it was only right that she try to fix this. "Ladies, do you know who owns the duplex you live in?" They were all back at the table and had ordered pie. Because why the hell not? Pie made everything better.

"It used to be owned by Carol Flagg, but when she died her kids sold it. I'm not sure who bought it." June pulled out some toys for Bobby to play with. The boy was really one of the best kids Luanne had ever seen.

"We need to find out who the owner is. Can Caroline do that?" she asked Jack. "I'd ask my assistant, but I gave him two weeks off and he's in Mexico."

"Yes, if she's still at the office." He reached for his phone in his pocket and froze. "Would you ladies mind if I borrowed my phone?"

There was an awkward silence. "Um...sure." June gave a awkward giggle and handed it to him.

"Thanks." He pulled up his contacts and selected the one for his office. "Caroline, it's Jack. I'm glad I caught you before you left for the day. Well, it's been interesting. I'll tell you about it when I get back, which probably won't be for a couple of weeks. We'll handle things via email or phone. Right now I need you to check the ownership of a property in Quincy, Alabama?"

Luanne listened to him give his assistant the property details and the info on Marty for a background check. She resisted the urge to do the happy dance. He'd said he wouldn't be back to the office for a couple of weeks, so he planned to continue their adventure.

"I'll wait." He lowered the receiver from his mouth and addressed her. "Don't look so excited, Thumbelina. This trip has disaster written all over it, but I'm willing to see it through if you go with me."

She stifled her grin. "If I have to."

"What in blue blazes are you two talking about?" Pearl snapped. "What are you going to do about our situation?"

Jack licked pie from his fork. "Cool your jets, Pearl. I'm waiting on my assistant to get the info. Why don't you polish your fangs or something?"

Pearl harrumphed.

While they waited, Jack reached over and grabbed one of Bobby's crayons and drew a picture of a cow in a dress. The kid gave him a lopsided grin. Jack asked him how he liked it in a Donald Duck voice, and the boy fell into spastic giggles. When he winked at Luanne she nearly melted out of the seat.

"Yeah, I'm here. Uh-huh. Okay, got it." He scribbled something on a napkin. "Thanks, Caroline. Can you draft a cease and desist order for the owner and cite the fact that Marty Franklin has been stealing Pearl —" He looked at Pearl.

"Moore," Pearl said.

He glanced at June and raised his brows in question.

"Kelso," June said.

"Marty Franklin has been stealing from Pearl Moore and June Kelso for the last four months and has evicted them, threatened them, and is continuing to steal from them. I'm also going to need you to wire me some money. I don't know where to yet. I'll call you back in a bit. Thank you. I owe you." He gave a half laugh. "I'm sure you will."

He hung up. "Okay, ladies, it's time to call the authorities."

"Now wait a cotton-pickin' second," Pearl exploded. "I thought you were helping us, not turning us in."

Luanne put her hand over Pearl's. "Pearl, we are trying to help, but you need to get the chip off your shoulder and let us."

"But why are you wanting to call the police?" June asked.

"You need to report what Marty's done to you."

"But he'll report us to CPS."

"No. He won't. He doesn't have anything to report." Luanne stretched her neck side to side to crack it. "Does he?"

"Absolutely not," Pearl said.

"Then let's give them a call."

And that was how it went. Jack and Luanne advising them what to do, Pearl arguing, and June acquiescing. The police came and took the women's statement. Jack got the name of an attorney from Quincy, who put him in touch with the local senior citizen advocate. They both assured him the sisters would be sorted out by the end of the week. He also told the lawyer to send him the bill.

At one point Bobby got restless, so Luanne took him outside to walk around for a while.

When they came back in she found Jack and the women in an intense conversation.

"We aren't taking charity." Pearl crossed her arms in defiance.

"But you'll steal from me?" Jack asked.

"That's different. Now that it's all out, we can't take your money for nothing."

"I'm not proposing to give you money for nothing. You got ten thousand dollars when you sold my car. You keep that as payment for the clothes you took from Luanne."

"You want to give us ten thousand dollars for a bag of thrift store outfits? Why in the world would you do that?" June asked.

"She's had a tough couple of days, and that bag of clothing is important to her."

"Well, since you put it that way." Pearl stuck her hand out. "You got yourself a deal."

Luanne could hardly believe her ears. Jack was getting her clothes back for her, and helping the sisters in the process. Her vow to hate him for all time grew weaker every day.

The arrow of his words had made a direct hit, and the hard shell around her heart cracked open. All the gooey feelings she kept barricaded away spilled out and there was no calling them back. Tears blurred her vision and a lump the size of a semitruck stuck in her throat.

"I'll go get the clothes." June excused herself from the table. "You've gotcha a good man there," she said as she passed Luanne.

"Oh, he's not—" But her denial fell on deaf ears. June was already out the door. How should she play this? The wall of ice she lived behind had more cracks than the Texas dirt in mid-August. She wasn't sure she could act like this didn't mean everything to her.

"Pearly!" Bobby cried.

Busted. No more hiding behind the wall. She squeezed Jack's shoulder. When he glanced up, she mouthed, *thank you*.

He smiled and gave a half shrug then excused himself from the table.

As she watched him walk away, something very sweet took up residence in her chest.

Pearl held her arms up to Bobby. "Give me that boy before you drop him."

"For some reason this boy thinks you're about the best thing in his world, Pearl." Luanne gave the woman a saccharinely sweet smile and handed her the child. "Clearly you've never held him at gunpoint."

Pearl smoothed down Bobby's orange hair. "Don't listen to her, sweetie pie, she's just mad someone got the best of her."

Luanne dropped into her chair. "The truth is, Pearl, I kinda want to be you when I grow up. You did what you felt like you had to do to protect your family. Granted, it was completely misguided. But go big or go home, right?"

Pearl laughed and so did the boy. Then June returned with Luanne's meager belongings. "Here you are, Luanne. We didn't mess with any of your things."

"Not that we would want any of those thrift store finds," Pearl said.

Luanne sucked down a laugh. The old broad was something else.

Jack came back to the table and ended a phone call as he sat down next to her. "Okay, ladies. You're set up at the extended stay hotel until the authorities get this worked out. If nothing's happened by the end of the week call my assistant." He sat his phone on the table, and wrote his office number on one of Bobby's coloring sheets. "She'll get in touch with me."

He stood and June grabbed his hand. "We will never be able to thank you both for all you've done." A tear slipped down her wrinkled cheek. "Here, we want you to have this." She handed him his phone.

"Um...thanks. Well, we better be going. We have a bus to catch." He kissed June on the cheek and pointed at Pearl. "You ladies stay sassy and unarmed."

When they stepped out onto the sidewalk Jack burst out laughing and leaned against the building. "That was the craziest thing I've ever been involved with. She gave me my own phone as a thank you gift." He could barely finish the sentence, he was laughing so hard.

"I know. Can I see it?"

He dug it out of his pocket. "Sure."

She pulled up Gavin's contact and dialed. "Scarlett, it's Lou. Jack and I have run into a bit of trouble, but we're alright now. We're headed out on the next leg of our journey. I'll call when we get there."

"Good idea," he said. "Let me have it now, so I can call Caroline back and have her wire us money."

This was going to hurt.

But it had to be done.

She dropped the phone and brought her heel down on it as hard as she could.

"Luanne! What the hell?" His shouts ricocheted off the buildings on Main Street.

"I'm sorry, Jack. But hasn't it occurred to you that my father could possibly use your phone to track us?"

"Luanne, this isn't some spy movie. That kind of shit's illegal."

"I can assure you my father's not above illegal activity to get what he wants."

He stared at his broken phone. "Have you forgotten we're broke?"

"We aren't broke. You still have enough money for us to catch a bus, buy a burner phone, and eat for the day. By this evening, we'll be at your family's house and I'm sure they'll put us up. Tomorrow we can borrow their phone and call the people we need to."

"We don't have any numbers." His hands were firmly planted on his hips.

"I imported them to my email. All we need is a computer and a Wi-Fi connection to retrieve them."

She knew he'd taken several blows today, but this was important. Her father was probably already on the move now.

His long fingers threaded through his hair and he took several slow breaths. "Okay. You have a point." He looked up and down the street. "Let's find the bus station, or tonight you'll be the one on the pole."

"You don't have to tell me twice." She looped her arm through his and they set off.

She also ignored how right everything felt.

Chapter Seventeen

The bus wasn't as bad as Luanne had expected. It was clean, and had movies and Wi-Fi, not that the last would help them since they didn't have a smart electronic device to their name. They'd purchased a disposable phone to have in case of an emergency, but it was a flip phone, for crying out loud.

She needed to call her grandmother, who was probably in a complete tizzy by now. Not that she'd really be worried about her welfare, but it always sent the woman over the edge when she didn't fall in line and behave like she was supposed to.

"I guess I should call my grandmother." She set aside the bag of snacks they'd bought and held her hand out for the phone.

"What about your dad?" He dug the device from his pocket.

"He won't be there. He doesn't spend a lot of time with her."

"Gigi, it's Luanne."

"Luanne. Where are you? You need to get home right now. Your daddy is torn up about all of this."

"I'm not coming home, Gigi. I only called to let you know that I'm okay." She picked at a loose thread on her jeans.

"I'm sure you are, since you're gallivantin' all over creation with a man other than your fiancé. Honestly, Luanne, have you given any thought to what people are sayin' about us? I'm not going to be able to show my face in town ever again."

"Gigi, Marcus—"

"Don't you call your daddy by his first name, it's disrespectful."

"Marcus," she ground the word out for emphasis, "made a deal with Doug. He wants Doug's father's company's business, Doug wants to be the CEO and needs a respectable wife to get Mr. Divan's approval. I was the bargaining chip. He sold me to the highest bidder, Gigi."

"Oh."

There was a silent pause. Maybe this was what her grandmother needed to remove the blinders from her sight when it came to her son.

"Please. You're so dramatic, Luanne. Sell you to the highest bidder, indeed."

Then again, maybe not.

"I don't know where you get all of this drama from. It certainly wasn't from me. I guess you're more like your mother than either of us thought you were."

That cut deep. Gigi knew exactly how to bring her in line, and any comparison to her mother was sure to elicit the response she wanted.

But not this time.

"Gigi, he doesn't care about me."

"Luanne, you're a spoiled girl who's been given every opportunity because of the generosity of your father, and you're being horribly ungrateful. All he asked you to do was one little thing, and you couldn't even do that." Her voice quaked with anger.

The part of Luanne that was conditioned to be grateful for any tiny morsel of affection and acceptance from her family wanted to back down from this fight. She pulled on her short black hair.

Not this time. Not this time.

"One little thing? For the love of God, Gigi, he lied to me to get me to marry someone so he could gain a professional advantage. That's not love." She sucked down a lungful of air to offset the threat of tears. "I can't believe you can't see that."

Then it hit her. Her grandmother knew. She knew and had gone along with the plan. "You knew, didn't you Gigi?"

"I certainly did." She could see the woman sit up straighter and jut her chin in the air, like she always did when she got defensive. "It was what was best for all of us, and now you've gone and ruined it. I want you home by tomorrow. Maybe we can still salvage this deal like a real family."

Lies. All lies. *When will I ever fucking learn?* The last remnant of family swirled down the toilet. She was alone.

"When can I expect you back, Luanne? I want to be able to tell your father, he'll be so excited." The manic tone of the woman's voice was confirmation of all that Luanne had just worked out. She'd be able to present Luanne to her father like a prized turkey.

"I'm not coming back, Gigi." She hated the defeated tone of her voice. "And when I do come home, I won't marry Doug, I won't be Marcus's pawn, and I won't see you."

"I have never—"

She couldn't listen anymore. "Goodbye, Gigi."

She handed the phone back to Jack without making eye contact. "Thank you."

"I'm sorry."

His sincerely spoken words were almost her undoing. She waved his comment away and pulled on the mask of indifference. "It doesn't matter. I've always known how it was." That was a lie.

A big, huge lie.

* * *

Jack had wished for a few things in the last couple of minutes. One, that he could've given Luanne some privacy during that conversation, if only to protect her pride. Two, he wanted to pummel Marcus Price, and then do it again. The man was truly a pimple on the butt of humanity. Three, if he could get to her, he'd wring Gigi's neck. The hurt that stained Luanne's face was enough to make him homicidal. And four, he wished Luanne would let him comfort her.

"Do you want to talk about it?" He knew it was a loaded question, but he couldn't pretend he hadn't heard anything. He wasn't that good of an actor.

"Not really."

"I understand." It'd been a long shot, but he had to ask.

She turned her sad sapphire gaze to his. "What's wrong with me, Jack?"

"Absolutely nothing," he said with as much confidence as he could muster.

"Sure seems like there's something wrong with me. I can't ever seem to do enough for my family."

He couldn't take it anymore. She might bite his arm off, but he had to try. Cautiously, so as not to spook her, he slipped his arm around her shoulder. When she didn't try to gut him, he drew her to him and kissed the top of her head. She smelled like fresh rain and a lifetime of disappointment. "Tell me about it, Luanne. We've got a long bus ride together and I'm already bored."

She gave a sad laugh into his chest. "Well, by all means, let me ease your boredom with stories of my sad childhood."

"Was it all sad?"

She sucked in a huge gulp of air, and he thought that maybe he should've started with a more benign question.

"Not when I was with Scarlett and her family."

"I'm sorry."

That seemed to be all the comfort she could stand, because she pulled away from him and scrubbed her face with her hands, shook back her hair, and almost, but not quite, succeeded in pulling on the mask of badassness she wore all of the time.

"Nothing for you to be sorry about. It was my messed-up universe, and at the center of the whole screwed-up thing is Marcus Price." She threaded her fingers together in her lap. "My mother and Marcus started dating right after she graduated from high school. He was five years older than her and she worshipped the ground he walked on. When I say dating, I use that word loosely. They snuck around and hooked up for a while. My mother wasn't acceptable dating material for someone like Marcus Price."

"Was he still living in Zachsville?"

"No. He'd just graduated from college and was living in Austin, so they didn't see each other that often. To hear my mother tell it, it was exciting and adventurous. He'd sweep into town, pick her up, and off they'd go to some motel. It's sad really, that she could call something like that a real relationship." Luanne wiped at her eyes. "Anyway, they'd been together about six months when she got pregnant. I have no idea if it was an accident or she did it intentionally. Either way, he freaked when she told him, and broke it off immediately."

"Dick."

She laughed, but there wasn't an ounce of humor in it. "Yes, well, he can be that, but he can also be persuasive and charming. He wanted her to get an abortion, but—"

"She told you that?"

She picked at the label on her water bottle. "No. He told me when I was eight, and Gigi insisted he take me to the circus. It's one of the few memories I have of us doing anything together. Evidently, he had to change some important plans to be able to go, and he felt I needed to know that if he'd had his way, I would've never been born."

"I'm so sorry." What do you say to counter growing up with a monster like that?

"The thing is, he has this way of saying terrible things and you think he's being nice until later when you replay the conversation in your head. It screws with you. I didn't even know what an abortion was. I had to look it up when I got home."

Horror raced through his veins. He tried as hard as he could to keep it off his face—she would hate his pity. "What kind of sick bastard says that to a kid?"

She continued like she hadn't even heard him. "When I told my mother, she swore he was lying. But when I pressed her about it, she actually defended him. He'd left her pregnant, penniless, and humiliated for years, and she still defended him." She snorted. "Then she asked if he'd said anything about her."

This was all kinds of fucked up, and his heart broke for her. "Some people's capacity for narcissism is unbelievable."

"She asked me that every time I saw him, which wasn't often, and he never came to the house to get me. Gigi always picked me up, and you should've seen the two of them, Mama and Gigi, clucking over me, making sure my dress was cute, my hair was combed, and my hands were clean." She pulled her legs into the seat and snuggled into the corner. "I'd get a lecture from my mother to be sweet and pleasant, to not make trouble and do what my daddy said. Then I'd get the same lecture from Gigi. They'd both tell me how much my daddy loved me and how glad he was going to be to see me, but when I was with him it always felt off. Oh, he said all the right things, but he wasn't like they said he would be. It was...what's the word?"

"Abusive."

"No. I was never abused. No one ever laid a hand on me." She snapped her fingers. "Mixed signals. Those kinds of mixed signals mess with your head."

"And you don't call that abuse?"

"No, don't be ridiculous, Jack. I was cared for, no one hurt me or left me alone for days on end like poor Gavin."

Not true, if what she'd told him was accurate. A million statements ran through his head, but he stayed silent, and let her talk.

"My mom was young and desperate. And Gigi, well, he's her son." She shrugged. "I don't think they could help it."

Bullshit. But he wouldn't say it out loud. Somehow he knew she wasn't ready to hear that yet. "What happened to your mom?"

She glanced out the window. "She died of a broken heart. For years she hung onto the hope that Marcus would come back, then we heard he was engaged, and she couldn't take it."

"She committed suicide?"

"Not outright. But she wasted away to nothing and died in her sleep one night. I was nine. After that, I went to live with Gigi."

"That's horrible, Luanne."

"Yeah, it is. Loving Marcus Price sucked the life out of her."

"I don't really get the dynamic between you, your grandmother, and Marcus." He adjusted his long legs to try to make them fit better in the small space.

"It's not that complicated. As you know, Marcus's treatment of women is abysmal, and that includes his mother. But it's candy-coated cruelty. He leaves you in a haze of false adoration. Like I said, you don't know you've been conned, charmed, or lied to until he's long gone."

"He must be really good, because you see straight through my bullshit."

"Oh, I'm probably the biggest sucker around when it comes to him." She rubbed her temples like she could dislodge some memory. "I was never in love with Doug."

"Thank God. Otherwise I'd have to have your head examined."

She gave a mirthless laugh. "Yeah, well. I didn't lie to you about why I was marrying him though. My dad convinced me that he wanted me taken care of when he was gone. That it was good for me to have someone like Doug, who could provide for me. I bought every ounce of his bullshit. Lapped it up with a spoon. It's humiliating to think a few crumbs of affection could make me lose my mind."

Jack shrugged. "He's your dad. I'm sure on some level he meant what he said."

She picked at a loose piece of leather on the armrest. "I told you the reason I ran from the wedding was that I saw Doug with another woman."

"Yes."

"That was true—I did see him with his girlfriend—but I ran because of what Marcus did."

He nodded. "I heard." Was there more to this sick, sad story?

Her hands clenched then unclenched in her lap. "Not only had he given me to Doug, he told my fiancé he could have all the girlfriends he wanted after we were married."

"Are you kidding me?" Rage crackled within him. He'd find a way to make Marcus Price pay for what he'd done to this beautiful woman.

"When I confronted him about it, he denied it. Said there's no way he would've done that. He was so sweet and caring, I began to believe I was mistaken. I know what I heard, Jack. But for a minute I questioned my memory. That's why I can't go back right now. I'm afraid I won't be able to tell him no. Not yet. I'm getting stronger though— there's no way I would've spoken to Gigi like that a week ago."

He squeezed her knee. "Progress."

She gave a half laugh. "Yeah. Anyway, he can barely be around Gigi or me for longer than a day. But she's always believed him and hoped we'd be a real family someday. And if I'm honest, so have I." She looked up at him and the pain written on her face nearly knocked him out of his seat. "Pretty sad, right?"

He took her face in his hands and looked her square in the eye. "They're the losers in this tale, Luanne. In spite of everything, you are loyal, kind, and brilliant. It's them I feel sorry for, because they're so blinded by their own selfishness that they can't see the amazing person you are."

She tried to dip her head, but he wouldn't let her. "I mean it, Luanne."

"Thank you." Her dark lashes fluttered.

This time when she tried to look away, he let her. He knew how hard it was for someone like her to admit this stuff to him.

"Scarlett says the same thing to me. If it hadn't been for her and her family there's no telling where I would've ended up. The only real love I've ever known is from Scarlett, and my only example of how a family should treat each other is from her family."

He made a mental note to hug Scarlett the next time he saw her. "You spent a lot of time with them?"

"Every chance I could, especially after I went to live with Gigi." She pulled two long Twizzlers from the pack and handed one to him. Then she gave him a look of disbelief. "I can't believe I told you all of that."

"Frankly, I can't either, but I'm glad you did. I swear it stays between us." He held up his Twizzler.

She smiled and tapped her candy to his. Something warm and luscious rippled under his ribs, and it made him happier than he'd ever been.

Chapter Eighteen

Jack paced the lobby of the Porter County bus station. Being cooped up in a bus seat for two hours had taken its toll on his back. His long legs weren't made to fit into such a small space. Did Mitch Rawlings have long legs? He glanced at his hands. Long fingers and toes? He'd always known he didn't look like the father he'd grown up with, but he looked enough like his mother that the question of having another father had never even crossed his mind.

How was he supposed to process this? How many hours on a therapist's couch would it take to make peace with the fact that his mother, the only person in the world who he'd ever truly trusted, had lied to him his whole life? An unexpected fury roared through him, and on the heels of the fury came a bone-crushing guilt. He loved his mother, and he'd find a way to forgive her.

He was distracted from his personal crisis when Luanne came strolling out of the bathroom. She was talking to a mother and her little girl. Something the little girl said made her laugh and the sound chased away his misery. How someone who'd been treated so badly as a child could've grown into such an amazing woman was beyond him.

She waved to the little girl and her mother and made her way to him.

"Making friends?"

"Yeah, they're headed to see the little girl's father at Fort Benning. He's coming home from a nine-month deployment, and they've been living with family while he was gone." She watched the mother and child make their way to the ticket line. "She showed me pictures her daddy drew and sent to her while he's been away. They're very sweet."

They sat in a couple of seats next to the window to wait for their bus. "Sounds like a good guy."

"The mom said this was his third deployment in four years. I can't imagine the kind of stress she must live with every day." She took a deep breath and blew it out. "The good news is, this is his last trip ever. He's out after this. Lucy, the little girl, said they're getting a house and she's getting a puppy."

"Did you ever have any pets?"

"No. Mama wouldn't let me, and Gigi's allergic to almost everything. You?"

"A blue tick coonhound named Sis. After we got settled my dad came home with this puppy and I just about peed my pants. Cutest little speckled thing you ever did see, she and I were inseparable. My mother originally said she couldn't stay in the house, but after I kept sneaking her in to sleep with me, she finally gave up that fight."

"Sis, huh?"

"Yeah, I loved that dawg. She passed after I left for college. Mom said she was only waitin' for me to get settled and then she let go. I cried like a baby. Here I was, this eighteen-year-old boy, hidin' under his covers cryin' over a dawg."

She laughed. "Your accent comes out when you talk about your life in Louisiana. Did you know that?"

"Really? I never noticed, but then again I don't usually talk about my life there." And wasn't that a little sad? He wasn't that poor kid wearing hand-me-down clothes anymore. He was successful, intelligent, and had everything he ever wanted. Maybe it was time to make some peace with his past.

She leaned to one side then the other to stretch out her neck and back. "The bus was nice enough, but I feel all stove up, as Honey would say."

"Me too. I had to take a couple of laps around the lobby to work out the kinks."

She grabbed her left elbow with her right hand, and stretched her arm across her body. A glare flashed, nearly blinding him. "Hey. Put your hand down."

"What?"

"The sun reflecting off that rock on your hand damn near blinded me."

"Oh, it's my engagement ring."

They both froze. They looked at the ring, then at each other, then back at the ring.

"Are you telling me that I took my clothes off for money in order for us to survive, when you had that three-carat monstrosity on your finger the whole time? Mother—" His hands went to his waist and his fingers flared across his hip bones. "I can't believe this."

Her hand flew to her mouth and the ring mocked him.

"Oh, my lord, I don't even notice it's there most of the time."

"How can you not notice that rock?"

She held her hand with the other and gazed at the ring. "The setting's flat. It never snags on my clothes or anything...I forget I have it on most of the time."

"How did Pearl and June miss that thing when they robbed us?"

"I had your jacket on and it covered my hands. They never asked me to take it off and I was so freaked out I never thought of it. And by the way, you only took your shirt off."

He stood and took her hand. "Come on."

"Where are we going?"

"To pawn that sucker."

* * *

"Fake? *Fake?*" Luanne fumed, stomping down the street. She couldn't remember the last time she'd been this angry. "I'm going to kill that lying piece of horse shit."

"Wait up, Luanne." Jack jogged to catch up with her.

"No."

His big hand wrapped around her upper arm and he pulled her to a halt. "Stop. Think about what you want to do. Take a deep breath and calm down a minute."

Anger sizzled through her whole body. Even the tips of her ears burned. "Don't you tell me to calm down, Jack Avery."

"All I'm saying is you don't want to go off half-cocked. Let's get a plan together, then I'll help you hang the guy."

She sucked in a lungful of cool, crisp West Virginian air, letting it calm her fury long enough to think. "Alright, a plan is good. You're right. We need the perfect plan so that I may relieve my ex-fiancé of his balls."

Jack's eyes crinkled at the corners, and she knew he was trying not to laugh. "It is not funny, Jack Avery. My fiancé bought me a fake engagement ring."

"Would it make any difference if I told you it was an excellent fake?"

"No! I'm going to pinch his nipple off."

That must've been all Jack could take because he doubled over laughing. "You looked like he'd slapped you with his dirty underwear when he said it was cubic zirconia."

She shoved him away. "I repeat. It. Is not. Funny. The little weasel lied to me. He said it was a family heirloom. He teared up when I put the fucking thing on. I actually felt sorry for him." She kicked the air. "I'm such a fool."

He lifted her face to his. "No, you're not. You just didn't care enough to get it checked out."

She stopped her fit and looked at him. "You're right."

That one admission was enough to calm her down. She shook her fist at the sky. "Well played, Doug Divan, well played," she said with mock admiration.

He wrapped his arm around her shoulders. "Don't worry, killer. You'll get him next time."

Oddly, that made her feel better. "Okay, where to? I've got an extra hundred dollars burning a hole in my pocket." A hundred dollars. Doug had made her think the ring was worth thousands of dollars. Dick. If she was honest, it wasn't that Doug had given her a fake ring, it was that he'd pulled one over on her. She hated that. In all likelihood, her father had been in on the joke. She'd get them back one way or the other.

"What devious plan are you cooking up?" He pulled a lock of her hair. "No time for that. We both need some clothes and to find a way to rent a car. I am not getting back on that bus."

Good thing too, because the bus had left them far behind. After they'd realized she had her engagement ring, Jack had got a refund for their tickets and bought the mom and little girl's fare to see their soldier.

He was like that—generous and kind. Luanne knew that now. He would tell you he was no one's champion. In fact, he'd told her that very thing. But, like it or not, Jack Avery was a hero. A reluctant hero to be sure, but a hero all the same.

Why was he so determined to not show that side of himself in his normal life? She remembered the arrogant, condescending jerk who'd showed up on Scarlett's doorstep eighteen months ago. If he'd shown even an ounce of this kind of chivalry toward Scarlett, their whole relationship would be different. Instead, he'd bullied his way onto Scarlett's land, and home, all the while pouring on that fake charm. Not that his sweet talker ways weren't genuine. They were, but now that she knew him better, they seemed...not his true nature.

"Where should we go first?" His red-velvet voice cut through her thoughts.

That dimple in his chin nearly did her in. Good lord, he was handsome, and that combined with his heroic ways was a combo she could barely resist. Not to mention his kindness toward her. He'd been sincerely furious about how she was treated as a child. Only Scarlett had ever been so mad about all of that.

Granted, he'd been a little overly dramatic by saying she'd been abused. She hadn't been abused. No one had ever hit her or screamed at her. She was given nearly everything she wanted, especially after she'd gone to live with Gigi. Okay, maybe she hadn't had the attention of the adults in her life until it suited them, but you could hardly call that abuse. It was just bad parenting.

Jack snapped his fingers in front of her face. "Hey. Where'd you go?"

"What?"

"You kind of checked out on me. You okay?"

"Oh, sorry." She could feel the prickly heat of embarrassment creep up her neck. "Let's get clothes and—thank you, Jesus—new underwear, first."

"What? Wearing two-day old undies isn't your idea of fun?"

"Oh, I ditched my undies back at the hotel room. It's been commando all the way today."

A low growl rumbled up from his chest. "Woman."

It was a warning, and it sent little zings of pleasure zipping around her body.

She patted his arm. "Not now, Jackie. We've got shopping to do."

"Alright. But no thrift store clothes for you this time. I know how to treat a lady. It's Wally World all the way."

"You're too kind."

"Nothing's too good for my dumplin'."

She laughed and shoved him aside. "Shut up, you idiot."

Chapter Nineteen

J ack steered the car down a country road. The snack mix he'd
eaten slithered around his belly like snakes on a hot rock.
Renting the car had been his biggest coup. Honestly, he hadn't
thought he could pull it off, since he hadn't had an ID or credit
card, but he'd turned on the charm and out the door they went with a
four-door sedan.

"You will arrive at 2354 Amethyst Lane in five minutes," the voice
from the GPS said.

Damn it. He didn't want to do this. In fact, he wasn't going to do
this. He had no obligation to anyone to put himself through this shit.

"Jack, I'm so proud of you for going through with the plan to meet
your family. I don't know if I could do it. It's very brave of you, and you
know how it pains me to say that." Luanne lowered the visor and
checked her hair in the rearview mirror.

Damn it. What was he supposed to do now? No way could he turn
tail and run now that she'd said that. He tried to laugh it off, but was
pretty sure he sounded like a donkey in severe pain. "Um, thanks."

His fingers flexed around the steering wheel and the tension from
his hands crept up his arms as he followed the winding country lane.
The headlights cast an ominous glow, illuminating big trees on either

side of the road. It looked like the climactic scene of every B-movie slasher film he'd ever watched. The one where the hero and heroine march to their doom. The irony wasn't lost on him.

What was he doing here? This was a harebrained idea, based on a letter from a total stranger, about an anonymous father he never knew existed. This was the most out-of-control stunt he'd pulled since he and his high school buddies streaked naked down Main Street at three in the morning.

"You okay, Jack?" Luanne shifted in her seat to face him.

He couldn't lie to her concerned face, so he focused on the road and pulled to a stop at the end of the drive. He rested his forearms on the steering wheel and let his hands drape over the top. "Not really. I don't think I can do it, Lou."

She rubbed little circles on his shoulder. "You can, I know you can."

When he couldn't stand it anymore he turned to her. Her little gasp proved he wasn't hiding his emotions very well at all. "I know I can do it. But why am I doing it? Seriously, a letter from the partner of a man I don't know who, allegedly, is my biological father. This man probably wouldn't recognize me if I walked up and slapped him. And his family? I'm pulling up to their house at eight o'clock at night to what? Say hi?"

"It sounded like they knew about you, so it probably won't be a huge surprise. But it's up to you. If you can't handle it, then you can tell me."

The silence in the car pressed in on them. He knew what she was doing, daring him, putting him on the spot to make him squirm. She also knew he wouldn't back down from a challenge. Damn her. He couldn't decide whether to kiss her or kick her out of the car. "No, we're going in, but let me do the talking. They'll probably have no idea who I am."

"Alright. If you're sure." She wiped a hand over her mouth, no doubt trying to hide her victorious grin.

Whatever.

They'd come this far—what was another twenty feet? He unfolded his long body from the car and smoothed back his hair while he surveyed the property. It looked like a typical country house—two stories, with steepled windows and a big wraparound porch. He noticed some outbuildings to the side of the house, but they were hard to see in the dark. A cat rose and stretched on the front steps of the house. The rhythmic hooting of a nearby owl matched the thrumming of his heart. What would he find on the other side of that door?

"Man, it's downright chilly out here. It's got to be thirty degrees cooler here than at home."

He tore his gaze from the front of the house to look at her. "What?"

"Nothing. I was trying to distract you. It obviously didn't work, sorry." She took his hand and squeezed it. "I'm with you, Jack."

He squeezed back. "Alright, Thumbelina. Let's do this thing."

They climbed the steps together. The musky, sweet smell of the flower bushes lining the porch did nothing to calm his nerves. The cat ran for cover under the stairs. All the while she never let go of his hand. It wasn't a couple kind of thing or sexual in any way, it was purely for moral support. He almost laughed. Of all the people he'd expect to have his back in this situation, Luanne Price wasn't even on the list. But here she was, ready to go to battle with, and for, him.

The old screen door squeaked when she opened it. He took a big breath—*now or never*—and knocked. A feminine voice scolded the yapping dog from the other side of the door, then a tall, dark-haired woman with the same dimple in her chin and the same brown eyes as his opened the door.

"Hello, you don't know me, but—"

"Jack." Her hand went to her chest. "Mama, come quick. Jack's here."

If Luanne hadn't been standing slightly behind him he would've fallen.

From somewhere in the house another female said, "Jack? Jack Avery is here?"

"Yes, Mama, and he is a sight to behold." The lady at the door beamed at him.

An older woman with a long gray braid came to the door and before Jack could speak she threw herself at him. Her arms went around his waist and she pressed her face to his chest. "Oh, my word, boy, you are a sight. I knew the good Lord would bring you to us one day, I just knew it."

If these people had opened the door naked and juggling pigs he wouldn't have been more flummoxed. How had they recognized him? Where had they ever seen him before?

"Mama, let the boy in the house," the younger woman said.

She stepped back and wiped tears from her face with the sleeve of her housedress. "Where are my manners? Come in, come in."

They stepped out of the way so he and Luanne could cross the threshold. His partner in crime pulled him along, and he followed like a lost child. It was all he could do since his brain had short-circuited the minute *mama* started crying on his chest.

The living room was open, with hardwood floors, comfortable furniture, and smelled of fresh laundry.

"Sit, sit." The younger woman removed a book and an afghan from the sofa. "Sorry, I was reading. Can I get you something to drink?"

He knew she was waiting for an answer, but he couldn't form words. Thankfully, Luanne jumped in. "Sure. Some water?"

"Okay. I'll be right back. Don't start talking until I get back."

What was his grandmother's name? He'd seen it in the letter, but for the life of him he couldn't remember what it was. He barely remembered his and Luanne's name.

The younger woman came back into the room. "Here you are." She handed them the water and sat on the love seat with her mother.

They all stared at each other for several long moments. Again, Luanne came to the rescue. "I'm Luanne Price."

"Oh, my word. I'm Leslie, Jack's aunt, and this is Mimi." She smiled at Jack.

He finally found his voice, but it sounded like it had been shot full of holes. "It's nice to meet you both."

"Well, it's nice to finally meet you too," Mimi said. She grabbed Leslie's hand. "I can't believe you're actually sittin' in my living room."

Frankly, neither could he. Surreal didn't even begin to cover this bizarre scene. How had they known him? It was time he got some answers. "Mimi, Leslie, how did you know—"

"Jack." Luanne had walked over to a side table with photos on them.

"What?"

"Come here." Her voice was barely above a whisper.

He almost said no. Something about her tone made him want to run for the door. But he wasn't a pussy and he needed to see what she was looking at.

The walk to Luanne was the longest of his life. Vertigo made it hard to stay upright when he got to her side and saw what she was seeing. It was his high school graduation picture. How? Why? Where had they gotten it?

He spun to the women, who were both crying. "Where did you get this?" Before they could answer he spotted the far wall, where there were three rows of photos, each row with six pictures. The first two rows were of children he'd never seen before, but the first six years of his life hung in the last row.

His hands went to his hips and he stared at the pictures. He turned back to his grandmother and aunt. "Ladies, I don't mean to be rude, but somebody needs to tell me what the hell is going on."

"Jack, we need—"

He put his hand up to silence her. "I need some answers, Luanne. My face is plastered all over the goddamned walls."

"Jack." Luanne's tone was reprimanding.

The women glanced at each other, and Mimi nodded.

Leslie came to stand by him. "Your mother sent the photos to your father, and he shared them with us. I guess we didn't think about how shocking this would be for you. I'm sorry."

He waved off her apology as he examined the room and saw his whole life played out before him. "Why?"

Leslie put her hand on his shoulder. "Why what, Jack?"

"Why..." He swallowed. "Why all the secrecy? Why don't I know him? Why don't I know you?"

"Come sit down, boy," Mimi said. "Leslie, get the good whiskey. This talk calls for more than water."

Luanne was back at his side and holding his hand. "I got you," she whispered, and led him back to the sofa.

Leslie came back from the kitchen with four glasses and a bottle of Maker's Mark whiskey. She poured them all two fingers and passed the drinks around. Once she'd reclaimed her spot next to Mimi the older woman began to speak.

"I want you to know that I'm only telling you this because I got your daddy's permission if you ever came calling. I don't talk out of turn, even about my own children."

"Is he...is he...dead?" The way she was talking he couldn't tell, and he needed to know.

Leslie's hand flew to her mouth, and Mimi shook her head. "No. He's been very sick, but thank the good Lord, he's doing better."

"Okay. Good." Jack let the burn of the whiskey ground him in the moment.

"Mitch was always a sweet, gentle boy, and he grew into a kind and gentle man. Lord, he was handsome. Every girl in his high school was after him. We were livin' in Louisiana back then and that's where he met your mama. She was the prettiest little thing, we all loved her, including Mitch, and she was crazy about him. Lookin' back I think Mitch was tryin' so hard to fit in, to do the right thing, and to be who we all expected him to be." She sipped her drink, then wiped her mouth with the back of her hand holding the glass. "So, he and your mama got engaged. We were so excited. Your mama...well. You know how special she was."

"Yes, ma'am. She was something." The knot of emotion filling his chest made it hard to get the words out of his throat.

"Anyway, as we started to plan the wedding I could see Mitch become more and more withdrawn, and so did your mama. Finally, I cornered him and made him tell me what was the matter. Looking back, when he told me he was gay I don't think I was surprised. And I'll tell you something else, I love my son, and I don't care if he loves men, women, or little blue aliens. He's mine, end of story."

Leslie snaked her arm around Mimi's shoulder and squeezed. "You're like that with all of your kids, Mom. That's what makes you so incredible."

Mimi swiped a lone tear from her round cheek. "I hated it for Robin. She did love your daddy somethin' powerful. But I'm the one who told him that he owed it to that sweet girl to tell her the truth and to not marry her. She would've come to hate him, and she deserved someone who could give her everything, and my Mitch wasn't that person."

She sipped her whiskey and then stared into the glass. "When she told him she was pregnant, it was the saddest day of their lives." Her head jerked up and she looked into Jack's eyes. "Not because they weren't happy about you, but because they knew they wouldn't be able to raise you together."

"Mitch said he would marry her anyway, but she said no, and it was the right decision. Within a month, she'd married Ray Avery. Ray always had a thing for Robin, and they even dated a few months when she and Mitch broke up the summer before she got pregnant. Mitch wanted to be a part of your life, but he knew how hard it would be for you. He didn't want to put that on you, and neither did Robin."

Jack sat forward and rested his arms on his knees. "So she sent him pictures of me every year?"

"Yes, along with a letter of what you were doing. He lived for those letters and pictures. They made him happier than anything else in the world, but they also made him sad. He'd be lower than a snake's belly for a month after they arrived."

He didn't know what to say to that. This whole situation was the last thing he'd expected. He'd thought he could waltz in here, charm his way around these people, and get the answers he wanted. Not to be met at the door with all of...this, and to be stripped bare in front of these strangers. He had to find his equilibrium, now.

He pulled on the casual mask he wore most of the time, but somehow it felt all wrong. Didn't matter. He would walk out of here and no one would know how devastated he was by these revelations. "Ladies, you've given me a lot to think about. Do you mind if we table this discussion until tomorrow? We've come a long way, and we still have to find a place to stay tonight." He rose to leave.

Mimi stood too. "Sit yourself down, Jack Avery. You're not staying anywhere but here tonight."

"We couldn't possibly impose." He would not sleep here. He would not sleep here. He would not—"

"We'd love to," Luanne piped up.

What had the woman done? He squeezed her hand, but not in a *thanks for helping* kind of way, more like a *sleep with one eye open* way.

"Good. Come on Leslie, let's get their rooms ready."

"Room." He slipped his arm around Luanne and looked adoringly into her stunned face. "I can't spend even one night away from my girl." A sick satisfaction settled over him at being able to get her back so quickly.

Mimi looked like she might protest, but Leslie steered her from the room.

"What in the hell, Jack," Luanne whisper yelled when the pair were gone.

He tightened his hold on her. "If I have to be miserable tonight, so do you, darlin'." He bopped her on her nose.

She nearly slipped off the sofa trying to wriggle out of his hold. "Get off me. I can't believe you."

"I can't believe you. How dare you accept an invitation to stay here? You were out of line. Besides, you said you were here for me."

She jumped up and straightened her clothes. "I meant I was there for moral support, not to warm your bed. And didn't you see Mimi's face fall when you said we couldn't impose? How are you, by the way?"

He rested his ankle on his knee and stretched his arm across the back of the sofa. He wouldn't let her see the shit storm brewing inside him. "Right as rain."

She shook her head. "Liar."

"I can tell you all about it while we're cuddled up together tonight."

* * *

Luanne climbed the stairs to their room like a woman being led to the gallows, while Leslie pointed out more photos of Jack that lined the staircase. She'd done this to herself.

Suck it up, buttercup.

When would she stop trying to run other people's lives? Hell, she couldn't even run her own. What made her think she could run Jack's?

Jack. What a jerk. She actually owed him, because if he hadn't been so blasé about the whole situation she would've wanted to comfort him, and that was a recipe made for disaster. He had to be hurting. However, in true Jack fashion, he hid behind the devil-may-care attitude that was so fake and infuriating.

"Here you go." They followed Leslie into the room. She looked between the two of them. "Do you all have luggage?"

Luanne felt, and probably looked, like a beggar standing there with her meager belongings in plastic bags. Why had she talked Jack out of buying the overnight bag to put their things in? Oh, yeah, she was scared of running out of money.

"Unfortunately, Leslie, we were robbed on our way here, so this is all we have." Jack held up his own plastic bag.

Leslie's delicate hand went to her chest. "Oh no, you poor things. You weren't hurt were you?"

His warm arm went around Luanne's waist. "No. We're fine. Luanne tried to fight 'em off, but they still took my wallet and car."

His fingers massaged her waist, sending quivers rippling all the way down to her toes. This crap had to stop. She spun out of his hold. "Somebody had to."

Leslie laughed. "You two crack me up. This is the old master so there's a bathroom through that door, and there's also another bath down the hall. Mitch and Kyle built mom and me our own master suites on the bottom floor. The stairs are too much for Mom most days, and we all thought I should be close to her." She walked to the door. "You have the second floor all to yourselves, so you can go crazy." She winked at them before leaving them alone.

The silence was a living, breathing thing that stalked between them like a big cat up to no good. "I'll take the bathroom at the end of the hall." Luanne scurried out of the room. She hated when she scurried, and she'd done it more in the last week than she had in her whole life.

The hot water in the shower released the too-tight muscles in her shoulders. She and her common sense had a little talk, and with every minute that passed her defenses grew stronger.

I don't have anything to worry about. Jack is his least attractive self when he's playing Mr. Suave, and right now he's going for Mr. Suave Universe.

His arrogance set off all of her triggers. She hated that side of him, or any man, because she'd been burned by it a few too many times. Memories of her father sauntering into Gigi's house like he owned the whole place, acting like there wasn't a thing wrong, like it hadn't been three months since they saw him. Or like he hadn't sold a piece of Gigi's property because he needed extra capital for a business deal. Or like he hadn't missed her graduation to go to Vegas with a potential business partner.

That was why, when he came back into her life nine months ago, begging for forgiveness and pledging to be the father he should've always been, she'd bought it hook, line, and fiancé.

The scrape of the shower rings on the metal rod echoed off the walls when she threw the shower curtain aside and stepped out. The bathroom could've been something off Scarlett's 'Dream Home' Pinterest page. Tall ceilings, bead board wrapping the space, with creamy yellow paint covering the walls. The big, fluffy towels felt soft against her skin and smelled like lavender. This was a home, and a lot of love was woven in every room.

She pulled the tags from her new undies, sleep shirt and shorts. How slowly could one person dress for bed? The pep talk she'd given herself in the shower was a distant memory. Hopefully Jack would already be asleep when she returned to the bedroom.

He wasn't.

He was sitting on the the love seat on the far side of the room, in a pair of athletic shorts, with his elbows on his knees and his head in his hands. The misery that poured off him was like a magnet. She made her way to him and ran the fingers of one hand through his damp, spiked hair.

He raised his head and pinned her with his tortured expression. Pain turned his beautiful eyes to pools of dark chocolate.

"Oh, Jack."

"Lou. I..."

She gripped his shoulders and before she could talk herself out of it, she climbed into his lap. Damn the rational, self-preservation argument for staying away from this man. He'd been gutted tonight.

His big hands slid under her shirt and around to her back. "I need you."

She ran her thumb over the dimple in his chin then took his face in her hands. "I know."

He took her mouth in a crash of lips and tongue, kissing her like a man clinging to the side of a cliff. Desperate, anxious, and completely sure she could save him.

Panic tried to claw its way through the passion. She wasn't the solution to his problems. She couldn't save herself, let alone another person.

Air. She needed air.

When she broke the kiss to breathe, he kissed up the column of her neck to her ear. "You are the best thing I've ever tasted."

Passion kicked panic in the ass, and why wouldn't it with the way he clung to her?

The noise she made was all about sex. Great sex. Sex with this man.

He chuckled and nipped her neck. "Listen to you." His tongue lapped at her ear lobe right before he bit down. "I want you too."

"Are you going to talk me to death, counselor, or take me to bed?"

She closed her lids and let the rumble of his growl turn her desire into a throbbing need between her legs. With his big hands around her butt, nipping kisses on her neck, and rough licks on her hand that clung to his shoulder, she could barely think.

Wait.

Rough licks on her hand?

She opened her eyes and screamed, "Cat!" Before she knew it, she was across the room and leaning on the bed.

The confused look on his face almost made her laugh. But her heart was pounding too hard. Her hand shook as she pointed to the frightened feline who'd jumped to the windowsill. "There's a cat. I don't like cats."

He turned and retrieved the scared kitty. "Hello, girl." The cat curled into Jack's chest. "Did that mean girl scare you? Take it from me, buddy, she's all bark and no bite."

She scowled, and he laughed.

"Why are you afraid of cats? They're just cats. Are you allergic?"

"No." She started to give him the laundry list of reasons she didn't like the creatures and realized she didn't actually have one of her own. "I have no idea."

He looked more than confused. "Marcus doesn't like cats." She shrugged. "I guess I picked up his prejudice."

Geez, she hated admitting that. But wasn't that the first step in any recovery, admit you have a problem? And when it came to her father she had a serious problem. The same one all the women in her family had—desperation for his attention and approval.

"Do you want to pet her?"

Did she? The cat was sort of cute. She chewed her lip, because while she didn't personally have anything against cats, she'd heard Marcus rail against them for years. So what? Just because he didn't like them had nothing to do with her. His hold over her stopped right now. "Sure."

Cautiously, tentatively, she stretched her hand toward the cat. The fur behind her ears was soft and warm. Purrs coming from the thing sounded like a tiny jet engine. "Her purring is so loud."

"She likes you. That's what they do when they're content."

A gorgeous man holding a cat was way more of a turn-on than she could've ever guessed. "She's probably content because you're holding her against your naked chest. It's a spectacular chest. Isn't that right, girl?"

The immediate change in his demeanor was palpable. His hot stare devoured any control she'd gained from jumping away. Damn. She wanted to purr too when she let her gaze travel from his face down those sculpted abs to the obvious bulge still tenting his shorts.

An insistent knock on the door interrupted their eye foreplay. "Jack? Luanne? I'm sorry to bother you." It was Leslie. "But you haven't seen my cat, have you?"

Luanne dropped her head with a sigh and went to open the door. Was she grateful for the reprieve or not? "Yes, Leslie, the little hussy has attached herself to Jack's chest."

"There you are. You bad girl." She took the cat from Jack, who'd strategically placed a throw pillow over his groin. "Tallulah, I thought you'd gotten outside." She buried her face in the feline's fur. Pretty pink stains bloomed on her cheeks when she gave Luanne and Jack her attention. "Sorry, my husband gave her to me before he was deployed the last time."

Jack leaned against the footboard of the bed. "Is he..."

A sad smile ghosted across her face. "He didn't make it back. That was five years ago. He was career military. Anyway, our kids were out of the house, living their lives, and he didn't want me to be alone, so he gave me Tallulah. And now I can't sleep without her in the bed with me." She smoothed her long black hair from her face. "Silly, really, but..." She shook her head. "I'll let you all get some sleep now."

The click of the door rang through the quiet room like a gunshot. What was supposed to happen now? Luanne glanced at the bed then to Jack. He was impossible to read, but she thought she saw the same uncertainty in his expression that was knocking inside her.

"I'm—"

"We—"

They started at the same time.

He held his hand out to her. "You first."

Thank God for that little feline furball, for keeping her from making a big mistake. "I'm going to sleep on the love seat." She slid a fuzzy blanket from the foot of the bed and headed for the small sofa.

"No. I'll sleep there. You take the bed."

Echoes of his touch still rang through her body, and sexual tension still crackled between them. She had to break it or crawl back into his lap. She made a production of eyeing his long, tall body and then the love seat, then raised a brow.

He chuckled. "Point made. I'll take the bed."

She noticed that they both ignored the pink, panting, horny elephant in the room. Nothing had changed between them. He was still Jack, and she was still Luanne, and they were both in emotional crisis. That was definitely not the time to make life-altering decisions. All she knew was that she liked this man. Really liked him. But that wasn't a good enough reason to have sex.

Sigh.

She was so freaking confused.

He climbed into bed, while she nestled into the couch.

He flicked the light off and the silence was ear piercing. "I'm sorry, Luanne. That won't happen again."

"It won't?" She squeezed the words past the dry glob of regret caught in her throat.

"Well, actually, I hope it will happen again, but not like that. I won't be another person who uses you, Luanne. You deserve so much more than that."

"Oh." What else could she say? The confusion swirling around her heart intensified into a tornado. No one had ever worried about her feelings.

"Good night, trouble."

"Night."

He was wrong, so very wrong. She wasn't trouble. He was.

Chapter Twenty

J ack's legs churned, eating up the road that led to Mimi's house.
The rays of dawn flicked through the trees, making the asphalt
glitter in the early morning light. Luanne was right, it had to be
thirty degrees cooler here. It was considerably more pleasant to
run under these conditions than the sweltering Texas heat. The brisk
air heightened the dopamine coursing through his brain. Thankfully,
he had his running shoes on when they'd been robbed, because the
only thing that would calm his mind today was to run as far and as fast
as he could.

His brain ached with the information it was trying to process.
People he never knew existed had pictures of him plastered all over
their walls. They loved him. How was that possible? His mother and
Mitch had done this for him. Both had sacrificed their own happiness
for his sake. What was he supposed to do with that?

Then there was Luanne. God, he'd wanted her more than air last
night, but it would've been wrong to take her like that. He needed to
buy Tallulah a can of tuna for stopping what he couldn't. And that
confused the hell out of him. He'd been out of control. He couldn't
have stopped the raging need for her any more than he could stop the
next beat of his heart.

The feel of her still clung to his hands, the smell of her still filled his head, and the taste of her still tingled on his tongue. It had ruined him for the rest of his life. But he wouldn't use her.

Fury chased him even now at how close he'd come to being no better than her horrible family. He pushed his body faster. Harder. His tough girl would've given herself to put light in the darkness of his heart. The next time would be when they were both on even footing, when it was her idea and not because he was about to fall apart.

The next time.

Would there even be a next time? She was skittish and afraid and oblivious to the abuse she'd suffered. Her family had fucked with her head and heart until she trusted no one except Scarlett. He wanted to pound the shit out of her father for the crap he'd dished out over the years. Until she could recognize what had been done to her and see he was nothing like that, they wouldn't have a future She'd always wonder what his end game was.

"You're my end game, Thumbelina," he panted. Saying the words out loud gave him absolute clarity about his objective. No matter how his family's lies, sacrifices, and secrets shook out for him, Luanne Price was going to be part of his future.

As the house came into view his chest refused to hold the cool morning air. He and Luanne had time to figure out their stuff. But his time with these people was limited, and he still had questions. Their answers would determine whether he continued this crazy road trip or not.

Mimi was sitting in a rocker on the porch with a cup of coffee. "You're up with the chickens."

He grabbed the porch rail and stretched the quads of his right leg. "I'm an early riser, even when I don't have anywhere to be."

"Mornin's when I get my thinkin' done." She sipped from her cup.

He switched legs. "Me too."

"I expect you've got a lot to think on." The rocker creaked as she pushed off with her slippered foot.

He snorted. "Ya think?"

"Watch your smart mouth, boy. I missed a lot of years of washing your mouth out with soap that I could make up for right now."

He watched her rocking with her eyes closed and a soft smile playing on her lips. "Yes, ma'am. My apologies."

She nodded. "That's better. So tell me what you're trying to outrun."

He sat on the step, then bent forward to stretch his hamstrings. "I'm not sure I can even put it all into words."

"I'd say to start with the hardest part."

"I get that he stayed away while I was growing up. It would've been hard on me. But why didn't he ever try to help us?" Here it was, the down and dirty part of this reunion, and it pissed him off to discover how important her answer was to him. "Mimi, we lived in our car for a time. We never had anything. My dad tried, but he was a blue-collar worker doing the best he could. We were on government assistance. My mom had to take me to the free clinic when I was sick, for God's sake."

She picked at the rocking chair arm, and continued to rock. "Some of these questions you'll have to ask him, but I can tell you that Robin wouldn't take a dime from him. She respected your daddy too much to take another man's handouts. Plus, by the time things got so bad she was in love with your papa. How would she have explained the money?"

Several stuttered breaths jumped around his chest and eased the ache there. However, with every answer came ten more questions. He followed the line of ants climbing up the porch rail. "How do you know so much about her? She never told me any of these things."

"Of course she didn't. This was grown-up stuff, not kid stuff. We exchanged letters until you were about six or seven. After that she said she couldn't do it anymore."

He tried to engage the logical part of his brain to help sort through all that she was saying. Tried to find the part that had helped him navigate the treacherous social waters of high school, the part that knew exactly how much he could party in college without losing his 4.0 GPA, the part that he evoked when he was slogging away in law school, and the part that helped him separate emotion from fact when he struck out to represent clients on his own.

Logic failed him now. He was too raw, too hurt to understand how his mother could deceive him his whole life. "I'm sorry, Mimi, but I think they were both selfish, and did this whole secret thing to protect themselves."

The rocking stopped and her lids snapped open. "Shame on you. You have no idea what it was like back then for gay men. Folks saying they carried the plague, that they were evil, degenerates who should be burned at the stake. Do you think either one of them wanted that for you? Selfish? Boy, you don't know what you're talking about. How do you think you got into and paid for that fancy college and law school?"

"What are you talking about? I got in because of my grades and I paid for it through scholarships, and what they didn't cover, my parents paid with money they'd set aside for school..."

She gave him what he imagined was her steeliest stare.

Clink. Clink. Clink. The pieces snapped into place. He'd never really thought about how they had paid for all the extras. He'd assumed they'd saved up so he wouldn't have to work extra jobs. He'd accepted the scholarship he hadn't applied for but believed he deserved. He'd never thought to question a single thing. *Clink, clink, clink.*

"I didn't know." He could barely hear his own voice. "I never thought about it."

"Of course you didn't. You weren't supposed to know. It was his gift to you. His way of showing his love for you, the only way he could. Were your parents perfect? No. But everything they did, they did because they loved you. Still love you."

The revelations were coming too fast.

"Are you going to see him?" she asked quietly.

"I don't know." That was as honest an answer he could give.

She rocked, and neither of them spoke. He stared into the morning mist. In the distance someone started a tractor, a rooster crowed, and a critter rustled in the bushes. The hum of the country was all around them. It would've been nice if the explosion of his world going super-nova wasn't distracting him.

An old tom rubbed against his leg. He reached down and scratched its head. "I'm not sure what I'm going to do, Mimi. Do you mind if we stay here a couple of days until I figure it out?"

"Don't wait too long to decide, Jack. He's sick, really sick, and while we're all praying he'll get better there's no guarantee he will." She wiped a tear from her face. "You've come this far, shouldn't you see it through to the end?"

He wanted to say something to make her feel better, but couldn't. He didn't have a clue what he was going to do.

"And you and your girl are welcome here as long as you like."

He laughed. "She isn't my girl." Though after last night he was more determined than ever to make her want him for more than sex. "She's only a friend."

"Really? Then why did you say you only needed one room? Y'all aren't those friends with benefits they talk about on those reality TV shows, are you?"

He nearly choked. "No. I was upset with her for butting into my business. She likes to do that a lot, so it was my way of getting her back. She slept on the sofa in the room."

"That little thing? She must've been so uncomfortable."

"I tried to get her to let me sleep there, but she's stubborn."

Mimi's laugh filled the morning air. "Good, that's probably just what you need."

He laughed with her and thought of the feisty woman still asleep in his room. "I think you're right, Mimi. I think you're right."

"Mama." Leslie was standing behind the screen door.

"Yes, baby."

"It's all arranged. Everybody's really excited Jack's here."

Everybody? Who the hell was everybody? An uneasy, itchy feeling began to gnaw at the back of his neck. "What's going on?"

Mimi smiled, closed her eyes and began to rock again. "We're havin' a party, boy, and you're the guest of honor."

* * *

Luanne finger-combed her hair, and deemed it good enough. She'd been glad Jack was gone when she woke. She wasn't ready to face him.

She'd fallen asleep on the wave of his words that rocked her to her core. *I won't be another person who uses you.* How had he known that was her secret pain? It was part of his voodoo power. Somehow, he could see and slip past her defenses.

Case in point, what almost happened last night. Incredible didn't begin to describe it, but to have gone any farther would've been disastrous because she still didn't know if she knew the real Jack. Was he the charming sweet talker, the arrogant ass, or the good guy who'd let two senior citizens steal his prized car because he knew they were in trouble?

She smeared on the lip stick she'd bought at the drugstore. She hadn't worn drugstore lipstick since she was in junior high. She'd grown up with the finer things in life, for sure, but everything she'd ever been given came with a price. The first thing she ever remembered getting was a pretty pink dress when she was about four. But her mother made sure she knew that it was for when her daddy visited.

You can have this pretty thing, but only when your daddy comes to see you.

She wore it once. By the time it her daddy came back to see her again, the dress was two sizes too small.

When she got braces at twelve, it was because Gigi thought her daddy would like her better if she didn't have "that god-awful overbite." She started getting cosmetics from department stores because Gigi said her daddy didn't like the smell of cheap makeup.

The best education money could buy was hers, if she went to Marcus's alma mater. He'd even pay for graduate school, but only if she went to law school.

Her father would love her and show his care as long as she married a man he picked. The list went on and on. And on. And on.

Shame crawled over her like a big black centipede. Who would complain about such a pampered life? She was spoiled and ungrateful, like Gigi and her father always said.

She examined her reflection in the mirror. No. She wasn't spoiled. She would've traded every gift she'd ever received, worn hand-me-down clothes, and gone to junior college for one lousy day with her father where there was no other reason for him to be there except that he loved her.

Jack's phone rang. The display said Gavin. "Hey, Scarlett."

"Don't you *hey* me. I've been worried sick. Where are you?" Her friend's voice was approaching a decibel that only dogs could hear.

"Calm down. I'm fine. I'm still with Jack and we're in West Virginia visiting some of his...um...relatives."

"What? Luanne, none of this makes any sense. I get home from our trip and Honey says you called, but didn't leave a message, then nothin'."

"Jack and I got robbed and I needed some help, but it's all fine now."

"Robbed! Good Lord, Lou. What have you gotten yourself into?"

Luanne chuckled and went back into the bathroom to put her meager belongings away. "Can you do me a huge favor?"

"Of course."

"I need you to go to my house and get my purse and my phone and send them to me. Hang on, let me get the address." She retrieved the letter with Mimi's address on it, and gave Scarlett the information.

"Okay, I'll go today."

"Great. I knew I could count on you." She chewed on her thumbnail and glanced at herself in the mirror. "Um, what's happening with Tank's nether regions?"

Scarlett snorted. "He's fine and unfortunately for the rest of humanity, he'll be able to procreate."

A weight rolled off Luanne's shoulders. Doing permanent harm had never been her intent. She ran her little finger under her eye to get rid of a mascara smudge. "Well, that's good. So what's going to happen to Honey's Tots for Tank's Testicles campaign?"

"Oh, good gosh. Can you believe that? She's of course heartbroken that he's going to be fine. When we got home she'd already hand-made some signs to put up around town. Can you imagine the faces of the Baptist women's group if they ever got a load of those posters?"

They both laughed, and it was the release Luanne needed to let go of some of the tension between her shoulder blades. "Thanks again."

"You're welcome. How are things with Jack?" Scarlett asked the question casually, but Luanne knew there was nothing casual about her interest.

Luanne paced around the bathroom. "Things are...interesting and kind of screwed up. I'll tell you about it when I get home."

"Interesting and screwed up, sounds about right for anything to do with Jack."

"Don't say that. He's going through a bad time right now."

"Oh, really? So bad that you're defending him. This must be the screwed-up part."

She rested a hip against the counter. "Yeah, well..."

"Never mind, I'll let you off the hook for now. Oh, my gosh, I almost forgot to tell you. Charlotte Kline is back in town."

Luanne held the phone between her cheek and shoulder while she folded the hand towel on the counter and affected an announcer's voice. "Star of TV and film, Charlie Kay?"

Scarlett laughed. "The one and only."

"Really?" An errant hair refused to lay down, and she twisted it back in place. "Why is she in town?"

"Her grandfather had a car accident, and she's come to take care of him."

That damn hair would not cooperate. She wet a comb under the faucet and ran it over the stubborn spot. "Wow. What was she, three years younger than us?"

"Four. I used to babysit her before she and her mother went to Hollywood."

"If half the things they say she's done are true, it ought to be interesting having her among the citizens of Zachsville again."

"I know. Hey, gotta go. Aiden just dragged Gavin's guitar into the living room. If I don't save Patsy, my husband will never speak to me again. Oh, my gosh, he's strumming it and singing. It's the cutest thing I've ever seen. I'll send a video."

"Alright—" But her friend was already gone. A few minutes later the phone dinged with an incoming text. It was the video of Aiden, and she had to admit it was the cutest thing she'd ever seen too.

Fast, heavy footsteps pounded across the bedroom floor, letting her know Jack was back about a nanosecond before he burst into the bathroom. "Luanne." He was white as a sheet and looked like he wanted to jump out of his skin.

She dropped the comb. "What is it?"

He swiped his hand across his mouth. "Shit. Shit. Shit."

"Tell me what is going on."

"They've invited the family to a party...in my honor. They'll be here in a few hours."

She would've laughed at the horror on his face if he hadn't been so serious. "I'm sure it will be fine, Jack. They're excited you're here."

He ran both hands through his hair and began to pace. "This is more than I counted on, Lou." He pointed to the door. "Those people think they know me, and I don't know any of them and don't know if I want to. What the fuck have you gotten me into?"

"Me?" Her attempt at indignation fell flat when he gave her a *yeah, you* look. "Fine, but how was I to know they'd have a big family reunion once you showed up?"

The color drained from his face. "A family reunion? You think that's what this is?"

She took his arm and led him to the chair in front of the vanity. "Sit."

He sat.

"Breathe."

He breathed.

"Relax."

He re—well, he tried to relax.

She got behind him and rubbed his shoulders like a coach with his fighter who was losing the round. "Listen to me. You're Jack Avery. You can handle anything and charm the skin off a snake."

He nodded as she spoke, absorbing her words.

"Now, repeat after me. I'm the shit. Say it."

"Luanne, I really—"

"Say it!"

"I'm the shit."

"I'm Jack Badass Avery."

"I'm Jack Badass Avery."

"Who's sometimes a pussy-man."

"Who's sometimes a—hey."

She dug her nails into the flesh she was kneading. "Say it."

"Sometimes I'm a pussy-man."

She slapped his head. "Now get over yourself and get ready to meet your family. They clearly love you, or at least the idea of you. That's more than most people get in their whole lives."

"Fuuuuuuuck, I feel like the guest star on the Jerry Springer Show."

She laughed. "Don't be so dramatic."

He let out three quick breaths. "You're right."

"I'm going to see if Leslie and Mimi need any help with the party prep. You take a shower. You have a few hours to get your mind right, join us when you're ready." She made him look her in the eye. "Alright."

"Alright. I can do this. But you'll be with me, right?"

"Right beside you."

He nodded and went into the bathroom.

He was about to meet a family he never knew, but who couldn't wait to meet him. She wasn't sure she'd ever been so jealous of another person in her whole life.

Chapter Twenty-One

Jack lost count of all the people about an hour into the shindig. There were aunts, uncles, cousins, and second and third cousins. There was more food than anyone could eat, and the beer and moonshine flowed freely.

"Jack Avery, get over here and give me some sugar." Harley, his cousin by marriage, stood with her young nubile arms stretched into the air, opening and closing her hands. He had a sneaking suspicion that Harley didn't have familial intentions when she hugged him and grabbed his ass.

"Ow!" she squealed.

He turned to see Luanne with his cousin's fingers bent backward.

"Hands off, Hurley," his personal bulldog said.

"It's Harley." The I-have-no-boundries woman rubbed her fingers.

Luanne plastered on the fakest smile he'd ever seen. "Hands off, Harley, he's taken."

Harley slid her purse higher on her shoulder. "I was only being friendly." She gave him a coquettish wink.

"Okay, you've been friendly, time to move along." Luanne made a shooing motion with her hands.

He bit back a laugh. She was taking her duty as his guardian very seriously. He slung his arm around her shoulders. "Thanks, Thumbelina, she was a bit handsy."

"Sadly, I don't think she knows that the concept of kissing cousins is wildly inappropriate."

He laughed. "Come on, let's see if we can get some food."

"Yes. I'm starved. Was that a pig they were roasting? How did they throw all this together so fast?"

"Leslie said they get together like this once a month. This was supposed to happen next weekend, so they moved it up." They dodged a couple of boys fighting over a football.

"How many people do you think are here?" She took a plate and handed him one.

"No idea. Maybe forty?"

They filled their plates with barbeque brisket, roasted ham, potato salad, baked beans, and coleslaw. Once filled, they made their way to the table where Mimi sat. His heart squeezed and flipped when she smiled like the entire solar system revolved around him. How had he grown up without this woman in his life? It seemed very unfair.

"Did you come to sit with me, Jack Avery?" She sipped something from a mason jar.

"Yes ma'am." He looked around the table at the faces he didn't know, but all similar to the one he saw in the mirror every day. "If there's room."

"Of course. Luanne hardly takes up any space. Clyde, scoot." Mimi made a shooing motion to an older man with gray hair that stuck up all over his head. "Jack, have you met my brother, Clyde?"

"I don't think I have." He went to shake the man's hand, but realized his hands were full of food. "Nice to meet you."

"It's good to finally meet you. Sit, sit."

They took their seats on the bench and dug into the food. It was the best thing he'd tasted in forever. "This is fantastic."

Luanne said something around a mouthful of food and nodded in agreement. He ran a thumb along the side of her mouth and caught a drip of barbeque sauce. When he slowly licked the spicy goodness from the digit, her face flushed and her pupils dilated.

"Damn, son, get a room." Clyde laughed.

"Uncle Clyde, leave them alone." Leslie said and sat next to Jack.

"All's I'm sayin' is those are bedroom eyes if I ever saw 'em." He smiled, revealing that he was missing a tooth.

"You dirty ol' coot," Mimi chastised, but there wasn't any heat in the words.

"Hehe. That I am." He swigged something from his own mason jar. "So Jack, Mimi tells me you're in the music business."

Jack wiped his mouth with his napkin. "Yes, sir. I'm a talent manager, and Gavin Bain and I have our own recording label."

"Mm-hmm. I'd heard that. You need to hear my boy Beau sing. He's about the best singer I ever heard."

Great. Now his relatives were going to line up their 'young 'uns' and make him listen to them all sing. "Well, I'm not sure I'll be in town long enough to hear him."

"Oh, he'll be here in a bit," Clyde said. "He wouldn't miss one of Mimi's get-togethers."

Mimi nodded while she swatted a fly. "Beau is always part of the entertainment."

"Entertainment?" Luanne took a sip of her drink.

Leslie pushed her plate away and wiped her hands. "Oh, yes. We have music and dancing. You city folk only think you know how to party."

"I'm not a city girl. I grew up in Zachsville, Texas. You don't get much more Podunk than that."

Clyde shoved a toothpick into the corner of his mouth. "So anyway, what I was sayin', Jack, you need to listen to my Beau and give him one of them record deals."

"Well...I...um—"

"Jack, do you still play the guitar?" Mimi asked.

Thanks for the save, Mimi.

Luanne's head whipped around so fast he was worried she might fall off the bench. "You play guitar?"

"As I understand it he sings too. Or at least he used to." Mimi beamed with pride.

He took a minute to digest the fact that this woman knew of his secret talent. If his mother was alive they'd be having one serious conversation. "Yes, Mimi, I still play, and I can sing a little."

"What? Why haven't I ever heard you sing?" Luanne had forgotten about her food.

"You probably have. I sang backup on Gavin's last record. Our backup singer got strep throat and I had to fill in." He shrugged and continued eating. He didn't like talking about this subject.

Mimi clapped her hands. "When Beau gets here you two should do a duet."

"Oh, I don't know about that."

"Yeah, Jack. You and Beau should definitely do a duet." Luanne's cat-like smirk told him she was loving his discomfort.

"We'll have to ask Beau." He pushed his plate away.

"Ask Beau what?" A guy a few years younger than Jack walked up to the table and squeezed Clyde's shoulders. He extended his hand to Jack. "Beau Callen."

"Jack Avery. And this is—"

"Luanne Price." Luanne reached for Beau's hand, and be damned if she wasn't wearing the goofiest grin he'd ever seen. Sure the guy was pretty, but come on. Have some pride.

"Oh, Beau, you're here." Mimi smiled.

Beau bent and kissed Mimi's cheek. "Hey, Aunt Beulah."

Everyone at the table laughed, except Jack, Luanne, and Mimi.

Jack's grandmother gave her great-nephew a squinty glare. "Boy, if I've told you once I've told you a thousand times. You can call me Mimi, sweetie, or good-lookin', but if you call me Beulah one more time I'm gonna jerk a knot in your tail."

The table erupted in laughter again.

"This is the oldest-running feud in our family," Leslie said. "She's threatened to jerk a knot in his tail since he was nine years old and found out her real name. It hasn't done one bit of good."

Beau nuzzled Mimi's cheek. "I'm still your favorite, though, aren't I, Mimi?"

"Go get on that stage and sing for your supper, before I change my mind about allowing you to live. Unless you're hungry now?"

"Nah, I'll eat later. Let me go set up."

Clyde began cleaning his teeth in earnest with a toothpick. "You'll listen to my boy sing and then we'll talk."

"Sure." Jack wasn't sure what he was answering. His attention was on Luanne, who was following Beau's progress from their table to the makeshift stage. "Really?"

The dreamy and unrepentant look she gave him caused an unfamiliar feeling to take root below his breastbone, and it wasn't at all pleasant. If he had to name it, he'd have to call it jealousy. But that was ridiculous. He didn't get jealous. Other men were jealous of him.

"He's pretty," she said with a giggle.

"Get a hold of yourself, it's embarrassing."

Leslie leaned into their space. "He is the best-looking of us all." She glanced at Jack. "Present company excluded."

"Whatever." He did his best to pretend he didn't care.

Leslie and Luanne laughed.

* * *

She'd been busted ogling Beau Callen, but come on. The guy was *hot damn* on a stick. Tall like Jack, and wiry, he had that long, confident walk of a man who knew his own sex appeal and would use it at will. His eyes, aged whiskey in sunlight, were the same color as Jack's, and they had the same jaw, but that was where the similarities ended. Beau's hair was blonde and the longish curls that stuck out under his cowboy hat did nothing to soften his strong, masculine face. He was rougher somehow, like life had ridden him hard and put him up wet. Sure, he joked with Mimi, but whereas Jack's charm was an extension of him and flowed off him in waves, Beau's was a mask he pulled on and took off at will. Maybe. Hell, what did she know?

Clyde was telling Jack that he was Beau's manager, and he'd be negotiating his son's contract with Jack. She took pity on the guy. "Walk with me, Jack. You don't mind, do you Clyde?" She gave him her best Miss Corn Harvest smile.

"Um..." For a moment she worried that she might've poured it on a little too thick—the old guy seemed to have trouble forming words,

But then he rallied. "No, that's fine. You should get closer to the stage anyway, so you can get a good look at Beau."

"We'll do that. My new goal in life is to get a good look at Beau." She winked and everyone laughed. Everyone except Jack, who pinched her arm. "Ouch."

He took her by the hand and led her behind an old garage. Once they were out of sight he put her back to the worn boards of the building, anchored her with his body, and kissed the ever-lovin' shit out of her. "So you want to get a better look at Beau?"

"Yes—ahhh..."

His warm fingers traced the skin above the v-neck of her tank. Goosebumps danced along the swell of her breast. His soft lips were at her ear. "I can think of better things for you to do with your time, Luanne."

"Oh, really?" She'd meant the words to sound sassy, but they came out on a needy moan as, one torturously slow kiss after another, he made his way along her jaw to her mouth. The fragrance of the azaleas and rhododendrons that circled Mimi's yard, combined with his wicked tongue, made it hard to think, let alone be sassy.

His hand moved to cradle her face, and his mouth hovered just above hers. "Want me to show you?"

Control. She needed to wrestle back control. Her hand went to the back of his head and she grabbed a handful of his hair with the intent of guiding his mouth to hers. He resisted her attempts to pull him closer, lingering a hair's breadth away from her lips. With each stroke of his thumb on her cheek she found she didn't much care who was in charge as long as he kissed her. "Yes."

"Now, who do you want to get a better look at?"

She tilted her head up to try to reach his lips. "I don't know. I think I need to be taught a lesson."

He pulled back with a triumphant look. "I think you do too, but one of these eighty-nine kids will probably be running around that corner any minute. So later."

"You're an ass. You only wanted to get me all hot and bothered to show me you could." He didn't deny it. "You're the worst."

He flashed that grin that turned her insides to goo. "And the best. Never forget it."

Instead of anger, lust slammed into her like a bull on a rampage. "Stop saying things like that. This isn't the time or the place."

"You're right, sorry."

His quick admission of wrongdoing threw her off. "Okay, what's up? This is about more than that good-looking cousin of yours."

He rested his forehead against hers. A sigh slipped through his lips. "Mitch paid for most of my college and some of law school. My mother told me the money for college was from a teacher fund she'd set up when she went to work for the district, and I had no reason to question her." He straightened and stared out at the large oak trees dotting the yard. "I had scholarships that covered a lot of my school, but not all of it, not to mention my living expenses after I moved out of the dorm. That all came from him."

"Really?"

"That's what Mimi said. I can't get my head around any of it. Am I just being a...pussy-man?"

She gave a half-hearted laugh, but she couldn't get her head around it either. His father had contributed thousands of dollars to his education, anonymously. Asking for nothing in return. In fact, except for a weird twist of fate, Jack would've never have found out.

Who did that? What kind of love must you have to make that kind of sacrifice? Before she could spend too much time pondering those questions the music fired up, and a voice like she'd never heard before filled the air. "Oh, my."

* * *

Jack stood there with his lids lowered and let the sound sink into his pores. Raw and gritty with a dirty southern rock vibe, Beau's voice punched him in the gut, made him want to cry and grab Luanne and kiss her until she didn't know her name. "Damn. He's good." He looked at her and grinned. "I want him."

She grinned back and winked. "So do I."

His arm went around her neck and he growled into her ear. "Not a chance. Come on, let's go see my next client."

While they'd been behind the shed, Mimi's backyard had filled up with half the town. Some were dancing, some were in lawn chairs, and some were milling around by the food tables. White carnival lights strung in the trees had been turned on and fireflies flickered on the edge of the yard. The whole scene looked like a Mumford & Sons music video.

Beau was set up on a flatbed trailer with his guitar, a mic, a bass player, and a drummer. And good Lord, could he sing, but more than that he had the crowd eating out of his hands. His stage presence was like a seasoned pro. His interaction with the women standing in front of the stage was what most entertainers work their whole careers to cultivate. In fact the only other person he'd ever seen as good with a crowd was Gavin, and this guy might be able to teach his best client some tricks.

Luanne elbowed him. "Somebody's trying to get your attention."

She nodded to the other side of the yard, where Clyde stood alternately waving at him and pointing to Beau.

"This is going to be painful."

"Yep."

"I'll pay you to go deal with him." He reached into his pocket for his wallet and pulled out a hundred-dollar bill.

She held up her hand to stop him. "Your money's no good here, mister."

"So you'll do it?"

"Not on your life. This is your family. You may as well learn to deal with them now. I'm going to stand next to the stage with the rest of the groupies."

"You're going to throw yourself at him, aren't you?"

"No comment. But if you see a pair of underwear sail through the air, know that I tried but failed to control myself."

"You're embarrassing."

"True, but I feel good about it."

He laughed. "You'll be back."

She gave him a finger wave without turning around.

She'd be back.

Chapter Twenty-Two

"What the hell do you mean you're not interested?" Jack resisted the urge to shake his head. He'd offered Beau the chance of a lifetime and the guy had turned him down.

"Beau, is there anything we could say to make you change your mind?" Luanne leaned forward in her chair.

At some point in the conversation they'd become a team, doing everything they could to sign the best country and western singer he'd heard in a long time.

"No. I do appreciate the offer, though." Beau took a swig of beer from a long-neck bottle.

"Do you mind telling me why?"

He glanced around. "I can't leave Clyde."

"Your father is all for this. In fact, he's the one who told us about you."

Beau tipped his chair onto the back legs and picked at the label on his beer bottle. "Clyde's not my daddy, he's my granddad."

"Oh."

"My parents died in a car accident, when I was a kid. I don't remember 'em at all. We were livin' in New Orleans at the time." The chair rocked down on four legs. "It took 'em a while to find Pops. He was a musician out on the road touring. When he found out what happened he quit the road, came and got me, and brought me back here. He gave up his dream of stardom to give me a home. I can't leave him now."

Jack pinched the bridge of his nose. "What's so special about now?"

"He's dying, Jack. Mimi didn't tell you?"

"No, man. I'm sorry."

Beau shrugged. "It's life. He's got cancer. They haven't given him much time, but the ol' coot refuses to believe it's as bad as they say. It's probably why he's doin' as well as he is." He glanced over to where Clyde was telling some story and grinned. "He's the best. I'm a lucky bastard. I'd do anything he wanted me to, but this. I won't leave him now."

Jack could wait until the guy was ready. "I don't have a card right now, but I'll give you my number, because this is an open-ended offer."

"I'll get a pen and a piece of paper." Luanne's smile was bright enough to light up the backyard.

Jack watched her walk away, then noticed Beau was checking her out too. "Don't make me hurt you, cuz."

Beau laughed. "Sorry, but she's...somethin'. You're a lucky man."

Jack grinned. No way was he telling this pretty boy they weren't a couple. "Listen, Beau, you take care of your grandfather, and anytime you want to take me up on the offer, you call me."

"I'll do that, Jack. Thanks for understanding. If you'd asked me six months ago, I'd have jumped on the offer like a duck on a June bug, but now..."

"I get it." Uncomfortable with how personal this conversation had gotten, he tried to change the subject. "So are you making your living with your music?"

"Yes and no. I was rodeoing professionally before Clyde got sick. The diagnosis, plus a jacked-up knee, meant it was time to come home. I've been playing honky-tonks around here to make a little scratch."

Jack peeled the label on his beer. "Professional rodeoing? Were you any good?"

"I was alright."

"Is there any money in it?"

Beau grinned. "Some."

Jack thought it was a lot more than some, judging by how cagey Beau was being. "Well, that's definitely an angle we can use in marketing."

"I doubt anyone will care much about a broke-down cowboy."

Jack tipped his bottle in Beau's direction. "You'd be surprised."

Beau took a pull of his beer and glanced around at the people in the yard. "This must be pretty overwhelming for you, huh? You didn't know about any of this or us until a few days ago?"

"Not a thing."

"Really?"

Yes, really. A whole truckload of my life is *really* circling the toilet. But he would never let that show. He shrugged, grinned, and made sure his façade of affability was firmly in place. "What did you say? It's life."

Beau raised his beer in salute. "I don't know if I'd have the courage to make this trip. Where'd you get the guts to do it?"

He pointed in the direction of the house. "Luanne. She looks all sweet and tiny, like you might want to pick her up and put her in your pocket. But she's really a militant pixie, and you don't argue with her if you know what's good for you." He laughed. "At least that's what she says."

Luanne returned with the pen and paper. "Here you go."

Jack scribbled down his number, gave it to Beau, and then extended his hand. "You call me...for anything."

"I appreciate it. I better get going. We're playing the last set at Crazy Joe's tonight."

Luanne rested her chin in her hand and sighed as she watched him walk away.

"Damn woman, you're killing my self-confidence."

She grabbed his face and kissed him fast and hard. "I think you can handle it. I'm going to see if Leslie needs help cleaning up."

She made him feel like superman.

Too bad she was his kryptonite.

* * *

Luanne snuck up the stairs to their bedroom. She hadn't gone to find Leslie like she'd told Jack. She needed time alone to deal with the tidal surge of emotion threatening to breach the walls she'd built around herself.

The revelations about Jack's dad had rocked her. The man gave up his son, a son he clearly loved, because of the pain his lifestyle would cause. Then he paid for Jack's college knowing Jack would never know what he'd done. Then tonight, listening to Beau tell his story about how Clyde had given up what he loved to raise his grandson, and now Beau was doing the same to see his grandfather through the end of his life. She had no frame of reference for that kind of self-sacrifice.

She made her way to the window. Jack was dancing with Mimi. He twirled her and then dipped the older woman as she laughed. It was too much. Fresh, ugly tears spilled over her lashes. This woman held her grandson in her heart for thirty-three years, knowing she might never meet him, but hoping against hope that one day she would. That, combined with the blind acceptance and love Jack's surprise family showered him with, all pointed a glaring, harsh, ugly light on the reality of her own family.

A mother who couldn't get over herself and her own pain long enough to love and care for her daughter. A woman who tried and failed to use that daughter to get the attention of a man, who never loved her, back into her life. A child who bore the brunt of the resentment when her mother's harebrained schemes didn't work.

I wasn't responsible for your choices, Mama.

The clarity of that thought gave her courage to look honestly at the grandmother who should've protected her and given her safe haven, instead of using her as bait to try to lure her son back into her life. A son who couldn't care less about her, who treated her horribly, and who used her when he needed money.

You should've protected me, Gigi.

The common denominator in her childhood of neglect? Marcus Price. She'd known her whole life that Marcus wasn't a good father—all she had to do was look at Floyd Kelly and his relationship with Scarlett to see that. Over the years she'd justified his behavior with the same excuses that her mother and Gigi used.

He's so busy.

She should be grateful she had a father.

He can't show his emotions, but he loves me in his own way.

Lies. All lies.

He'd never sacrificed one thing for her.

"My father is a misogynist and a narcissist," she whispered to the room. Tears washed down her face, unbidden. Grief bloomed like a bloody wound in her chest.

It hurt like hell, but the truth made her stronger.

"My father is a misogynist and a narcissist, and he never cared about me." She grabbed the disappointed ideas of being daddy's little girl and threw them onto the burning pyre of unfulfilled dreams.

Which made her stronger still.

"My father is a misogynist and a narcissist, he never loved me, and isn't worthy of my loyalty." The shouted truth grabbed the last hope for the father that never was and would never be, and yanked it out by the root.

The room was a dark, quiet place to hide. But her heart and mind wouldn't let her get away from the blinding truth. A truth that Jack had been trying to get her to see for days. She'd been neglected and abused by the family that should've loved and treasured her, and she deserved more. A whole hell of a lot more.

The heavy weight of grief for all she'd never have crashed over her. But she wouldn't crumble under the weight. She would stand against the tide and let it roll over her, making her stronger and more vulnerable with each surge of reality.

Stronger because she knew she should've been given more love and attention than she'd received from her family.

Vulnerable because now she knew she needed those things, but to have them she'd have to find them elsewhere and make a new family for herself.

The isolation of the dark room was too much. She didn't want to be alone anymore. She'd been alone enough. There were a ton of people outside. She only wanted one.

Beau and his band were gone, but there was still music, coming from an old boom box. Couples danced and the older family members were sitting at long tables, talking.

She surveyed the crowd and spotted Jack with a group of men she hadn't met. She didn't think about it, she didn't consider the consequences. She leaped from the porch and ran straight to him.

He saw her coming and took several steps toward her, opening his arms. With no thought about what anyone else would say, she jumped into his arms and buried her face in his neck. "Jack."

* * *

Jack carried her back to the house and up the stairs to their room, all the while rubbing little circles on her back and trying not to lose his shit. What had happened? Was she hurt? Had someone died?

When he reached to turn on the light she grabbed his arm. "Don't."

"Can I turn on the small lamp?" He had to see her face to make sure she was alright.

"Okay."

He flicked on the light, sat on the love seat, and adjusted her so he held her across his lap. She was so small in his arms. "Tell me."

"I never cry."

One side of his mouth kicked up. "I know."

"I never cry unless I'm around you. You've seen me cry more than any person in my whole life. Why do you think that is, Jack?"

"I don't know, Lou." He wiped the tears from one cheek with his thumb. "What's wrong, darlin'?"

"It's just..." she hiccupped. "I have a shitty family."

Finally. "Yeah, you do."

"I think I've always known it, but I've always made excuses for them. I can't do that anymore. You're right, Jack, about all of it. About my mom, Gigi, and my dad. It was neglectful and abusive. What do I do with all of that?"

It broke his heart to see this fierce, capable woman doubt herself. "What do you want to do with it?"

She wiped her face and climbed off his lap. "I'm not taking it anymore."

"Damn straight."

"I'm not taking responsibility for my mother's actions ever again."

He sat back and stretched his arms across the back of the sofa. "Anything else?"

"I will never let my father manipulate me."

"Yes!"

She stopped pacing and stared at him for several long seconds. "You knew I'd get here, didn't you?"

He shrugged. "You're a brilliant woman, Luanne. I knew you'd figure it out somehow. What brought about these huge revelations?"

"Your family. There's so much love going on here. It's not perfect or pretty, but it's the real deal." She crawled onto the sofa, sitting sideways with her legs crossed. "You're so lucky."

Lucky? Was she watching the same shit show he was? His whole life had become a joke, exactly like it had been all those years ago, when he wore hand-me-down clothes and was on the free-lunch plan in school. He wasn't lucky, he was laughable. The whole damn situation was laughable.

Anxiety pricked his skin like vultures pecking at road kill. A sensation, so foreign and yet so familiar, pressed in on him. Fear and paranoia had been his sadistic sidekicks growing up, and sometimes they'd bring along their old buddy panic to the party. It was unfortunate that they chose now to stage a reunion.

He was prepared to handle her issues, wanted to be her hero, but he hadn't counted on her turning the tables on him and his screwed-up family. He plastered on his most charming grin. "If you say so."

Guilt punched him in the gut when he saw confusion on her tearstained face. "I do say so. They're wonderful. Surely you can see that."

"Yeah, they're great." Sugar coated the words, but sweat gathered in his palms. His heart vibrated in his chest, and the air in his lungs turned to concrete. Damn it. It was coming. He knew the signs all too well. With all of his strength he wrapped himself in the last ounce of charisma he possessed. "Listen, if you're alright, then I need to go take care of something downstairs."

She held her hand out to him. "Jack...stay."

Her whispered words shot a hole all the way through him. He wanted to take the comfort she offered, but his pride wouldn't let him. He hooked his thumb over his shoulder. "I really should..."

She drew her knees to her chest, closing herself off to him. Her disappointment about killed him, but he couldn't stay. Jack Avery didn't do public breakdowns.

He coolly strolled from the room, closing the door behind him. One stumbling step after another got him to the bathroom, where he concentrated on even breathing and calming his revved-up heart. All he wanted to do was retreat into the counterfeit affability that had seen him through his life.

Unfortunately, he wasn't sure he could ever get to that place again.

Chapter Twenty-Three

Jack relaxed at Mimi's kitchen table and watched Luanne shovel a bite of French toast into her mouth. He loved watching her eat. Was that weird? If it was he didn't care. He pretty much loved everything about her. In fact...he loved her. He was in love with Luanne.

Well, damn it.

Just what this situation needed, love. Talk about terrible timing. He waited for the panic, but it didn't come. He probably knew he loved her last night, but was too scared and freaked out to admit it. Still, this was the worst possible time for this to happen. His life was unraveling at the seams, and now he was in love.

Awesome.

After he fled the room last night, he hid in the bathroom for a while then went for a long drive, hoping to get some clarity. It hadn't worked. He was split in two and unable to merge the pieces together. The only real conclusion he'd come to was that he needed to apologize to Luanne.

For her part, Luanne had been pleasant and cordial to him and he hated every minute of it. And now he was in love with her, he really hated it. Her unhappiness with him was a living thing, but she pretended she wasn't upset. He didn't want her to hide from him. Yes, that was hypocritical, but he'd deal with that later. For right now he wanted to knock down her barriers.

He slid his arm around the back of her chair. "You sure have pretty eyes, Luanne."

She eyed him suspiciously. "Thank you." The words were wrapped around a mouthful of French toast, so it sounded like *Hank ewww*.

He winked at her the way he knew she hated.

"What are you up to, Jack?"

"Not a thing. Can't I tell a pretty girl she has nice eyes?" He dabbed at her milk mustache with his napkin.

She slapped his hand away. "Stop it, or I'll shove that napkin down your throat."

Ah, there she was, his fierce little blossom. The sweet smell of jasmine shampoo filled his nose when he put his mouth to her ear. "I'm sorry for leaving last night. Will you forgive me?"

Her surprised gaze softened, and she gave him the sweetest smile he'd ever seen. "Yes."

"Just like that?"

She shrugged. "I know you're going through a tough time. I can understand that."

"I should've stayed. It's just—"

"Y'all eat up. There's more where that came from." Mimi placed another piece of egg-coated bread on the griddle.

"These are delicious, Mimi," Luanne said.

Or he assumed that's what she said. It was hard to tell with her mouth as full as it was. "You might want to slow down there, champ. I'd hate for you to choke and I'd have to give you mouth-to-mouth. On second thought..."

"You wish." She flipped him the bird. Covertly, of course, since Mimi and Leslie were in the room.

He did indeed wish. Thoughts of her straddling him, with her hands in his hair and her lips on his, were all he could think about these days. He reached over and wiped a bit of syrup from her lower lip with his thumb. The sticky goodness was sweet on his tongue as he licked it off, while never looking away from her. "This syrup's delicious, Mimi."

"Your daddy and Kyle made it."

The bites he'd eaten coagulated into a ball of confusion, disappointment, and anger in his belly. He pushed his plate away and picked up his coffee.

"Are you going to eat those?" Luanne asked.

He slid his plate her direction. "Be my guest."

His *daddy*. He needed to decide what he was going to do about that situation. Mimi had stressed several times that Mitch was sick. But he wasn't ready to confront him. And besides, what was there to confront? It sounded like the man had done all he could to protect Jack. He just wasn't ready to see him yet.

The sound of the front door opening and closing came from the other room.

"Clyde, is that you?" Mimi called.

"No Mimi, it's us." Two men appeared in the entry to the kitchen. Both were tall, but one was blonde and fit, while the other leaned on a cane.

Even without anyone saying a thing, Jack knew this was his father.

Mimi dropped the spatula and gasped. "Mitch, Kyle, what in heaven's name are you doing here?"

Mitch's partner came into the room and kissed Leslie and Mimi on the cheek. "You know him, Mimi, stubborn as a mule. Once he found out Jack was here, nothing would stop him from coming."

A hand appeared in Jack's face. "I'm Kyle Harris-Rawlings. You must be Jack."

Jack never took his eyes off Mitch and Mitch never took his eyes off him.

"I'm Luanne Price, Kyle. It's nice to meet you."

Kyle didn't seem the least bit flustered by Jack's rudeness. He switched his focus to Luanne. "Oh, my word, if you aren't the cutest thing I've ever seen."

If Jack hadn't been having an out-of-body experience, he would've laughed at that. Luanne was a lot of things, but cute wasn't one of them. Fierce, fiery, spectacular, but not cute. However, he was in the middle of his own existential crisis, because the father he'd never known existed was standing six feet away from him.

"Mitch, honey, sit down, before you fall down." Leslie went to him and tried to lead him to a chair.

He waved her off and stood staring at Jack.

"Mitch, why in the world would you risk your health by getting on a plane?" Mimi went to him and fluttered her hands over his body.

"Because my son is here." His voice cracked on the word son, and Jack had to fight the urge to run from the room.

"Don't be a doodle, Mitch. Sit down," Kyle said.

Mimi walked beside Mitch as he made his way to the chair opposite Jack. He vaguely wondered what she thought she would do if Mitch went down.

He extended his hand to Jack. "I'm Mitch Rawlings."

Never let 'em see you sweat.

Jack leaned across the table and took his hand. "Jack Avery."

Luanne squeezed his leg under the table. He ignored it, no matter how bad he wanted to hold on for dear life.

"Kyle, Mitch, are you hungry?" Mimi wiped her hands on her apron.

"Starvin', Mimi," Kyle said.

"I'm fine," Mitch said.

"No you're not." Kyle sounded snappy, but even Jack could see the worry in the man's face. "He'll have a piece of French toast and a glass of milk." He tried and failed to give Mitch a stern look. "You know what the doctor said."

Mimi stopped and whirled around. "What did the doctor say?"

For the first time since he walked into the room Mitch looked away from his son and smiled at Mimi. "That my scans and blood work came back clear. But Dr. Travis says I'm too thin. He wants me to gain some weight." His voice shook with emotion. "I'm cancer free, Mama. We just found out."

Mimi dropped the spatula, then grabbed the bottom of her apron and buried her face in it, crying silently.

Mitch rose from the table and went to her, wrapping her in a hug. "It's alright, Mama. It's alright."

She lowered the apron and took a huge breath. "Thank you, Jesus."

Leslie and Kyle wiped their own tears and laughed. Mitch made his way back to his seat. On the way, he squeezed Leslie's shoulder. She leaned her head to his arm, love radiating from her face. He dropped into his chair and put his arm around a crying Kyle, who immediately crumbled into his embrace.

Mitch glanced at Jack and Luanne. "He hasn't broken down at all since we got the news. I think being here with the family he feels like he can finally let down his guard."

Kyle sat up and wiped his face. "Stop talkin' about me like I'm not here."

The sweetest expression swept across Mitch's face, and he wiped a tear from Kyle's cheek. "I could never forget you're here."

Jack's skin felt itchy. Not because of the poignant scene across the table from him, but because he felt like an interloper. He didn't know these people, and it seemed wrong to be sharing in their pain and joy.

He took Luanne's elbow and stood. "We're going to run an errand."

He had to give Luanne credit, she didn't hesitate or balk. "Yes, I need a few things from the drug store."

Everyone looked at him like he was crazy, and a little heartless. Everyone but Mitch, who'd started eating the food Mimi set in front of him. "Okay, I'll see you when you get back." And even though he didn't want to, Jack's estimation of the man grew exponentially.

"We'll be back." He escaped with Luanne in tow.

As soon as they were out the front door he dropped her arm and walked down the steps and into the yard, leaving her on the porch. At the edge of the yard he stumbled and caught himself against a tree. This was so embarrassing. It had taken all of his strength not to blow chunks in the kitchen, and now he almost fell to the ground.

A water bottle appeared in front of his face. "Here."

He grabbed it and chugged. "Where'd you get that?"

"I had it in my purse." She took the bottle back and replaced the lid. "You alright?"

"Yeah, yeah." He waved her off. "I must've gotten too hot."

"Uh-huh."

It was evident she didn't believe a word he said. He took her hand

and led her through the trees. "Come on, I want to show you something."

She stumbled along behind him. "Hey, slow down. Short legs here."

"Oh, sorry." He slowed his pace to match hers.

"Where are we going?"

He tightened his grip on her hand in case she decided to bolt. "To a place Leslie showed me yesterday."

They walked maybe a quarter of a mile until they came to a clearing. There was a stream that opened into a small swimming hole, with a wooden structure next to the water. He dropped her hand and filled his lungs for the first time since seeing Mitch Rawlings walk into Mimi's kitchen. Then he bent over with his hands on his knees and squeezed his lids shut.

"Jack?"

Shit. For a moment, he forgot she was there. Without opening his eyes, he said, "Yeah."

"Do you want to talk about it?"

"No."

"What do you want to do?"

Forget this whole freakin' mess. Not look pitiful. Take back some fucking control. He peeked up at her and gave her his most convincing I-don't-give-a-shit-that-my-life-is-falling-apart smile. "Let's go skinny-dipping."

* * *

Luanne's heart broke a little bit for Jack at that moment. He was trying so hard to hold it together and pretend like nothing happened that he was now talking like a crazy man. "You want to go skinny dipping? Now?"

He began undoing the buttons of his shirt with jerky movements. "Yes. It's hot as hell out here. We should jump in and cool off. Don't ya think?"

His words came out so fast she could hardly understand him. "Skinny-dipping isn't exactly what I had planned today. Why don't we sit and talk?"

He worked at toeing one shoe off while still unbuttoning his shirt. "What's the matter Lulu, you chicken?"

His movements were choppy and manic, not at all like the sleek, smooth-talking Jack Avery she'd come to know, and lov—no, she didn't do love. But she did care about him, and the idiot couldn't get out of his own way long enough to realize that he didn't have to hide from her. After all, hadn't she told him things and opened up to him in a way that she never had to anyone else?

There was no help for it. She'd have to do something drastic to snap him out of this fight or flight episode. He was way past reason. And because she cared about him, she'd do this for him.

She grabbed the hem of her Charity Mart green sundress and began inching it up her legs.

Jack stopped moving. "What are you doing?"

"I'm getting undressed."

"I can see that." He sounded downright peevish.

She bit the inside of her cheek to keep from laughing. "You said we were going skinny-dipping."

"I...um...I didn't think..."

Her dress inched up a little more.

He stilled her hand. "Stop that."

She smoothed down the material. "Then stop acting like an idiot and talk to me."

There was a long beat of silence then he exploded. "Gaaaaaaah!" He stomped away then stomped back to her. "This is so fucked up!"

"I know." It was all she could say until he calmed down. She held her ground as hurricane Jack whirled around her.

"Look at my hands." Both shook like puppies in a thunderstorm. "I don't do this." He hid the evidence of his freak-out by crossing his arms over his chest, the shaking appendages shoved into his armpits. "I do not lose it."

"I know." It was a strain to keep her voice steady and even. It was so hard watching him suffer this way.

He jabbed his finger in the direction of Mimi's house. "Did you see what happened in there? Why is he here? I wasn't ready to see him." He laced his fingers on top of his head and took several shaky breaths.

"I know." The breathing seemed to be working. When he opened his lids, the wildness was gone, but the torture was still front and center. Seeing him in this much pain hurt her heart and caused a strange, powerful sensation to seep between her ribs and fill her chest.

He stalked around for a bit more, mumbling and muttering to himself, then finally seemed to run out of steam. "What do I do, Lu?"

"Come with me." She took his hand and led him to the wooden structure by the pond. He followed along wordlessly, which worried her more than his ranting.

The little shack wasn't a shack at all, but a bird observatory. Comfy chairs and a chaise lounge filled the space. A glass wall revealed the pond's bank, the beautiful green meadow dotted with wild flowers beyond, and an electronic bird feeder like the one Gigi had in her yard hanging in a tree. Birds of all shapes and sizes loitered around waiting for the bounty. She led Jack to the chaise. "Sit."

He did, then rested his elbows on his knees, clasped his hands between his legs, and dropped his head. The scrape of the chair she pulled in front of him seemed to get his attention.

"I'm sorry." His handsome face was drawn and flushed from his outburst.

His leg was warm and strong under her fingers. "You have nothing to be sorry for. That was a hell of a blow. I get it. This is a lot to take in."

With his elbows still on his knees, one hand over his mouth, he stared out the window. She could see his emotions and his brilliant brain fighting for control. The silence almost killed her, but she waited him out.

"Do you think I'm a shit for running out of there?"

She pushed back a lock of hair that had fallen over his forehead. He still wasn't looking at her. "No."

"I'm...hell, I don't know what I am."

"You're not wrong for being freaked out. I'd be freaked out too."

"Really?"

It leveled her to see him so unsure of himself, but she could tell he wasn't ready or able to talk about it. She was grateful for the honest emotions he had shown her, though. Baby steps. She could wait. "No. But, let's face it, you're wimpier than me."

He snorted a laugh. "Thanks."

Satisfaction unfurled in her when he turned back to her and grinned. A real grin, not one of the fake, counterfeit, plastic things he gave when he was hiding from her. She shrugged. "If a friend can't kick you when you're down, then who can?"

His laughter was a victory. Winning a gold medal couldn't possibly be better than knowing she'd made things better for him. Especially when she considered how much he'd done for her. "Feel better?"

He looked at her like he'd discovered the answer to a calculation he'd been working on his whole life. "I do." He took her face in his hands and stroked her cheeks with his thumbs. "Thank you."

The drugging kiss he gave her twisted her mind until she couldn't tell up from down, right from wrong. This man did it for her, and all he'd ever done was kiss her. She stroked the scruff on his face. "I like this."

He licked the side of her bottom lip. "I want to make *you* feel good, Luanne. Will you let me?"

"Yes." She'd been craving his body for far too long with no relief. Her fingers grasped his shoulders as his hands slid to her butt.

"Hold on." It was a command not a request. He picked her up and carried her out of the shelter.

She had no intention of letting go. "Where are we going?"

"I think I still want to go skinny-dipping."

She laughed. "Jack, that water's going to be cold."

"I don't care. I want you wet and naked."

The flash of white teeth in his wicked smile convinced her that naked and wet was a spectacular idea. Somewhere along the way, she'd lost her flip-flops, and the grass tickled her feet when he lowered her to the ground. Faster than she could blink, he pulled her sundress over her head and her thong down her legs.

He stood back, his hungry gaze devouring her. "Beautiful."

The softly spoken word knocked the breath from her body. It was the craziest thing. Bared to the world, the most exposed she'd ever been in her life, and yet she'd never felt more powerful under his worshipful stare.

She moved to the water's edge, and kept walking until she was waist-deep in the pond, taking short breaths to try to adjust to the cold temperature. But even the chilly water couldn't tame the inferno burning inside when she turned to face him.

Holy hell.

The only thing more edible than Jack Avery in a custom-tailored suit was Jack Avery in nothing at all. He was spectacular, all long bones, muscle and sinew. A craving to roam every inch of his body with her eyes, fingers, and mouth gripped her and refused to let go. Her hands skimmed along the top of the pond. "Come on in, Jack. The water's fine."

He barely made a ripple as he sliced through the water, eating up the distance with long, purposeful steps to get to her. His wet hands cupped her cheeks and he tilted her face to his. "Luanne." The whisper blew across her face.

"Yes?"

He took her mouth in a kiss that burned away the memory of every other kiss in her life. He may not have been able to open up and share his feelings, but he more than made up for it with his body. His kisses grew wild and out of control. He plundered her mouth, stealing any thoughts other than how much she needed him inside her.

She couldn't hold back the moan when he slid his hands to her bottom and picked her up again. Her legs wrapped around his waist, and she felt the hard heat of him there pressing, insisting, promising.

He adjusted her weight so that he held her with one arm. With his free hand, he traced each vertebra of her spine, banding her flesh with his wet fingers. Pleasure seeped through her skin at every point of contact. "The things I want to do to you..." His voice was hoarse and guttural.

"Jack." She tilted her head to the side as he skimmed the tip of his tongue along her neck.

He chuckled. "Do you like that?"

"Yes." It was desperate and needy and she didn't give a damn.

He nipped her earlobe, then licked and kissed the sting away.

"Mmm, you taste good." He cupped one breast, his thumb circling the nipple until she cried out in frustration.

"I wonder if you taste as sweet here?" Without any warning, he yanked her higher and latched his mouth onto the stiff peak.

She wove her fingers through this thick hair and held him in place. His tongue swirled across the tip, then he sucked it in deeper. The fire obliterated her will to think and consumed her body with a desperate hunger.

Unable to take the building fire another moment, she lowered her head and kissed him hard. Her pelvis ground against him. Her mouth, her hips were both imitating what she wanted the rest of her body to do. "Make love to me, Jack."

"Hang on, baby, I've got you."

His panted words were dry and gritty. They clawed their way through her body, increasing the desperate need building at her core. Without warning, he slid two fingers between her legs and pushed into her. "Jack." She rocked against his hand. He withdrew far enough to rub the sensitive nub until she bucked in his arms. This time he pushed his fingers deep into her, sending showers of light cascading behind her closed lids. "It's too much. It's too—"

"Let go. Trust me."

For one brief moment, her rational brain understood that his plea meant so much more than what they were doing in the lake. Her mouth opened to answer, but his fingers filled her again and again and again until she couldn't hold on anymore. Pleasure spiraled through her body and she threw her head back and cried out his name.

This man destroyed her. She nestled into the crook of his neck while she waited for her heart to slow down its punishing pace. She placed tiny kisses on his neck until enough strength returned to lift her head. "I do, you know. Trust you."

He smiled like he'd won the lottery and pulled her in for another sweet kiss.

"That was..." She had trouble choosing the right words for what they'd just done.

"Something I've wanted to do for a very long time." His triumphant expression did something to her heart.

"Do you have a condom?"

"Yes, but we don't need it. This was for you, Luanne."

"But—"

"I'm good. Promise."

She searched his face and realized he was completely sincere. For some unknown reason that made tears sting the corners of her eyes. He'd given her something amazing without asking for anything in return. Her forehead rested on his. "Thank you."

"Thank you."

"For what?" She was truly baffled.

"Being here today. Talking me down from the edge."

Her fingers roamed over his shoulders, his chest. She couldn't stop touching him. "That was nothing. But this was...wow."

He chuckled. "Anytime, Lulu, anytime. Now hold your breath."

"What?"

Faster than she could blink, he tossed her into the air. She screamed, then closed her mouth right before she hit the water. When she surfaced he was laughing, and it was so unguarded and genuine she didn't have the heart to be mad at him.

She used both hands to splash him in the face. When he sputtered and choked she laughed too.

They spent the next hour, playing, kissing, and having fun. Their problems were a million miles away. At some point, she knew they'd have to talk about what had happened. But, for now, it was only the two of them in this beautiful, secluded place, making each other happy.

Chapter Twenty-Four

Jack and Luanne stumbled back into Mimi's yard, both laughing so hard they had to cling to each other to stay upright. The weight he'd worn around his neck since he'd found out about his parentage seemed lighter and more manageable since he'd spent the last hour loving and fooling around with Luanne.

Damn, but she'd been a sight to behold when she came apart in his arms. He'd known she would be, but his many fantasies of the woman hadn't done her justice. It'd taken all of his self-control not to bury himself inside her. When the time was right, he'd take her until they were both oblivious to the outside world, come up for air, then do it again. And then he'd tell her he'd fallen completely and utterly in love with her.

Her grip tightened on his hand. "Jack."

"Yeah?"

She tilted her chin toward the house. "I think someone is waiting on you."

The bottom dropped out of his mood, and the carefree vibe he'd been enjoying drained away at the sight of Mitch sitting on the porch looking their direction. Crap. It wasn't that he was angry with the guy.

It was messy and awkward and he didn't want to deal with that shit right now. Or ever.

Luanne's arms went around his waist. "Hey. Are you going to be okay?"

He winked at her. "Yeah. I'm golden."

A flash of disappointment streaked across her face. She blew out a breath and patted his chest. "Okay, go get 'em, tiger."

After saying hello to Mitch, Luanne disappeared into the house. Jack followed her to the porch and took a seat next to his father. He sat forward in his chair, holding his cane below the crook. He let it slip through his fingers until it lightly tapped the porch three times, then he picked it up and did it again.

"Mitch."

"Jack."

They sat in silence for several long, uncomfortable minutes.

Tap, tap, tap.

Tap, tap, tap.

Tap, tap, tap.

Finally, Jack couldn't take it anymore. "So, a syrup farmer, huh?"

Mitch didn't look at him, but smiled. "Yep."

Jack sat back in his chair and placed the ankle of one leg on the knee of the other. "How'd you get into that?"

The cane kept tapping and Mitch looked out over the yard. "Kyle and I were both in the tech industry and worked for the same company. After we got together we started our own company, and five years later sold it for...well, a lot. We were sick of the city and decided to move to Vermont. It all kind of happened from there."

"Is there much money in *syrup*?" Jack cursed himself. He hadn't meant for that to come out as snarky as it had. He did not want this man to know how badly this shit got to him.

Mitch chuckled. "Some. Though not nearly as much as in tech."

Jack couldn't trust himself to speak, so he gave a noncommittal grunt. Then they were back to silence.

Tap, tap, tap.

Tap, tap, tap.

Tap, tap, tap.

This was ridiculous. Jack slapped his hands on his knees and started to rise. "Well, I better go check on Luanne."

"I was very sad to hear about your mother's death."

He collapsed back into the chair. "Thank you."

Mitch picked the cane up and rested it across his lap. "I loved Robin, had loved her my whole life, and it killed me to break her heart."

"Yeah, Mimi told me." Jack tried to modulate his voice to a casual tone. He had no idea if he accomplished it.

Mitch's Adam's apple bobbed several times, and tears swam just beyond his lashes. "But the hardest thing I've ever done was let her take you away from me." He finally looked at Jack, and the agony there nearly laid Jack out flat. "It's just...it was a different time then, and we knew how hard it would be for you."

"Yeah, yeah. No, I get it." He picked at an imaginary piece of lint on his pants leg. "You did what you thought was best. I understand." Bullshit. He didn't understand any of this. None of it. Sweat beaded at his temples and the thud of his heart grew harder and faster like a demented, pissed-off giant running at full speed.

With every ounce of will he had, he held Mitch Rawlings' stare and grinned. "You don't have to worry. Mimi explained everything to me. I'll admit it was a little surprising, but I totally understand your reasoning. I'm not angry and I hope we can be friends." There, that sounded mature and reasonable. He extended his hand. "I'd also like to thank you for the help you evidently gave me in college and law school. I truly appreciate it."

Mitch shook his hand. Sorrow and disappointment showed in his gaze. Jack hadn't fooled anyone. "It was my pleasure. Friends would be nice."

"Excellent. That's...excellent." Jack chuckled. "Luanne and I went swimming in the pond, so I better jump in the shower before dinner. Thanks for talking to me, Mitch."

"You're welcome, Jack." The man still had the same sad look and his voice was even sadder. What the hell? He'd just absolved the guy of any wrongdoing. What more did he want?

"I guess I'll see you inside." Jack made his way into the house.

Luanne and Kyle were sitting on the sofa looking through a photo album. He gave them a jaunty two-finger salute.

Nothing to see here, folks. I'm just fine. See how fine I am? I'm waving in a casual manner.

He made his way up the stairs—*he was fine, damn it, just fine*—to the bedroom—*still fine*—then into bathroom.

Where he promptly threw up.

* * *

The crack in the hard shell around Luanne's heart deepened when she saw the asinine two-finger salute from Jack. She wanted to go to him, to comfort him, but she knew he wouldn't let her.

The funny, open, and giving man she'd been playing with an hour before was gone. She'd watched him retreat as soon as he saw Mitch sitting on the porch. It made her sad that he didn't trust her enough to be honest with her.

Trust is a two-way street, girl.

She ignored that little voice. She trusted Jack...to a point, at least with her body. On any other level, she didn't wholly trust anyone but Scarlett, and she'd known her forever. She'd known Jack about six minutes.

"What was that all about?" Kyle opened an envelope and withdrew a handful of photos.

"Um...Jack is working through some stuff." She wasn't going to share Jack's secrets with Mitch's partner or anyone else. They weren't hers to tell.

He chuckled. "Yes, Mitch is working through some stuff too."

"Should you check on him? I left him and Jack talking on the porch."

"No. Mitch is a thinker. He needs to sort things out, then he'll talk to me about them. I've learned to be patient and wait him out."

He began organizing the pictures into piles. Luanne noticed they were of Mitch and Kyle, backdropped with lush greenery. She picked up a few and flipped through them. "Is this where you live?"

"Yes, that's Lillie Belle's Sugar House Farm." The pride in his voice loud and clear.

"Lillie Belle?"

Kyle's face lit up. "My grandmother. She taught me to make syrup and everything else I know how to cook or bake."

Luanne replaced the photo then curled into the corner of the sofa. "You cook? Marry me."

Kyle raised his left hand and wiggled his ring finger. The sun glinted off the gold band there. "Sorry, doll. I'm already taken."

"All the good ones are."

"True."

"Shame."

He began slipping the photos into the sleeves of a photo album on the coffee table. "So you don't cook?"

She shrugged. "I can cook the basics—scrambled eggs, grilled cheese, ramen noodles. But we had a cook when I was growing up, so I never learned."

"Well, la-te-da." He gave her a playful slap on the leg. "You had a cook."

Heat burned her cheeks. Why had she said that? She hated drawing attention to her family's wealth. "I didn't mean...it wasn't like *I* had a cook...my grandmother—"

"Hey." He placed his hand over hers. "I was only joking." He squeezed her fingers. "Sore subject?"

"Sort of." She tried to arrange her expression like she didn't care, but didn't think she quite pulled it off when his brows knit together.

"Want to talk about it?"

"Not really."

He stood and held out his hand. "Come with me then."

She looked at his hand and then at his face. "To where?"

"The kitchen. I'm making chicken and dumplings for dinner. They're Mimi's favorite, and I could use some help."

"I'm not sure how much help I'll be, but I'll come with you."

His smile was brighter than a Texas sunrise. "Fabulous."

* * *

"Now that you have the flour in a nice pile, stick your fingers into the top and make a little well."

Luanne did as Kyle instructed. "Like this?"

"Exactly like that, clever girl." Kyle praised her like she'd figured out the solution to world peace instead of making a hole in a pile of flour with her two fingers.

"Kyle, it doesn't take a genius to do this."

"I beg to differ. Anyone can make dumplings, but under my tutelage you're on your way to making world-famous dumplings."

It hadn't taken long to realize that Kyle had a flair for the dramatic.

"Listen to him, Luanne. He makes the best I've ever tasted." Mimi was slicing vegetables from her garden for a salad.

She placed her palms together like she was praying and bent at the waist. "Then teach me, Obi Wan. I'm yours to mold."

They laughed. "That's right, missy," he said. "And don't you forget it." He handed her an egg to put into the well she'd made.

"So, Luanne, where're your people from?" Mimi asked.

"I grew up in Zachsville, Texas. The only people I have are my grandmother and my father."

Mimi stopped chopping. "Just the three of you? Lord, I wouldn't know what to do if there were only three of us."

"You'd do what you've already done and adopt every stray in the county." Kyle went to her and kissed the top of her head.

"Don't make me clean your plow, boy. You know I will." Even as she made the threat she leaned into his hip when he hugged her.

"How exactly do you clean someone's plow?" Luanne asked. It sounded like something Scarlett's aunt Honey would say.

"I've always wondered that myself." Kyle wiped down the counter with a cup towel.

Mimi pointed the knife at him. "Slowly and painfully."

They laughed and Luanne realized she felt more at home with this family she barely knew than she ever had with her own family. Sadness over what could have been enveloped her like a wet wool sweater.

"Where are Mitch and Jack?" Mimi asked.

"They're working through some stuff." Luanne and Kyle said at the same time.

"Together?" The hopeful tone in Mimi's voice kind of broke Luanne's heart.

She shook her head. "No, Jack went upstairs, and Mitch was on the porch when we came in here."

"Oh." Mimi chopped with a little less enthusiasm.

"Luanne, what's your story?" Kyle must've felt Mimi's disappointment too because he jumped in with that question rather quickly.

She rubbed her face with the back of her hand. "Oh, it's lengthy and boring. How long do the dumplings cook?"

"Until they're done." Kyle slapped the cup towel he was holding on the table. "Spill it, sister. Lengthy and boring stories are mine and Mimi's favorite kind. Am I right, Mimi?"

"You bet cha." She looked at Luanne and said, "You may as well talk. He won't leave you alone until you do. He's worrisome that way."

"And you love it." Kyle blew her a kiss from across the room.

Mimi tittered like a ninth grader crushing on the captain of the varsity football team.

"I'm not sure where to start."

"I've always found that it's best to start at the beginning." Kyle opened the fridge and pulled out a pitcher of iced tea and retrieved three glasses from the cupboard. Evidently, they were settling in for a good, long story.

So she told them everything, about her sad mother, Gigi's indifference, her father's manipulation, and the whole wedding debacle. "I know it seems ridiculous that a grown, educated woman would let her father pick the person she was going to marry, but you'd have to know my father to understand."

Kyle stirred the chicken broth on the stove. "I don't think I have to know him. You're a daughter who wanted to believe that her father loved her and wanted the best for her. Unfortunately, you put your trust in the wrong person."

"Thankfully you came to your senses before the wedding and Jack was around to get you out of there," Mimi said.

She smiled at the memory. "Yeah, I owe Jack—" Then she realized she didn't owe Jack, because he would never hold that over her head.

He would never make her pay for his kindness. "Yes, thank goodness he was there."

Kyle flipped the faucet on and spoke over the spray of the water. "What are you going to do about your father?"

"I...I don't know."

He grabbed a cup towel and dried his hands. "Can I give you some advice?"

She shrugged. "Sure."

"You can't keep running. You need to deal with him. The longer you avoid this the longer he has a hold on you. You need to cut ties with him or try to work things out, but either way, you can't keep running from your problems."

"The only way to work things out with him is to do what he wants." She ran her finger through some of the excess flour on the counter.

Kyle refilled his glass of tea. "You don't know that. Deal with him like the capable woman you are and draw your boundaries. Then the ball's in his court. He can either have a relationship with his beautiful, intelligent daughter on her terms or he can't. It's his choice."

The *whack, whack, whack* of Mimi's knife stopped. "He sounds like a bully to me, and the only way to deal with a bully is to stand up to them and don't back down."

She dusted the remnants of the flour from her hands. "You're right. I know you're right. It's just..."

"He's your father and you think even a screwed-up relationship with him is better than no relationship at all." Kyle folded his arms across his chest. "And I'm here to tell you that you deserve more than that."

A smile spread across her face, unbidden. "Thank you." Exactly what she'd told herself last night. If she needed more validation of her decisions, she'd gotten it hand-delivered with chicken and dumplings. "Do you mind if we talk about something else?"

He carefully removed the chicken from the boiling pot. "Alright. Why don't you tell us how long you've been in love with Jack?"

She dropped the fork she was beating the egg with and flipped flour into the air. "What? I'm not in love with Jack. We're barely friends."

"Really? Because the looks you two have been giving each other don't look all that friendly," Mimi said, and popped a piece of carrot in her mouth.

"With all due respect you two, you're wrong. I'm not in love with Jack. I don't do love."

"Why on earth would you say that?" Mimi asked.

Luanne's hands moved in jerky motions as she tried to follow the directions of the recipe. "I'd think after what I've told you, that would be obvious. Love makes you weak and stupid, and I'm neither."

Warm hands cupped her cheeks and Kyle turned her face to his. "I'm sorry that your family taught you that. But they're wrong, and so are you. Love with the right person makes you brave and fearless. It gives you strength to get through the worst days of your life and makes the best days that much sweeter. I hope you find that someday."

It wasn't a reprimand but a blessing, and it caused tears to gather in her eyes. "Thank you." She had no idea why she was thanking him, but it seemed appropriate and important that she recognize his words for what they were.

He kissed her forehead and went back to his task.

Even though she disagreed with him, the power of his statement burrowed into the hopeful places in her heart. It expanded, pulsated, and became a living breathing thing in her soul.

Chapter Twenty-Five

J ack rinsed toothpaste from his mouth, grabbed a towel, and
wiped. The three-day stubble that he never let grow covered his
face. But Luanne said she liked it, so maybe he'd keep it. Who
the hell knew?

He glided his hand over his jaw. The man in the mirror was a
stranger to him. Along with the facial scruff, his hair was too long, and
he wore a Gladiola High School t-shirt he'd picked up at the Gladiola
Walmart. It was wrinkled and had a grease stain that hadn't come out
in the wash.

But mostly it was his eyes. They looked...well, not like his own. His
always had the glint of a winner, someone who had the world by the
tail and knew how to make it submit to his will. This guy staring back
at him looked like life had punched him in the balls and wasn't done
kicking his ass yet.

Self-doubt wasn't something he suffered from, not as an adult
anyway, but he sure had a bad case of it right now. He had no idea how
to feel about Mitch, except that he wished he'd never found out about
him. Guilt swam in his stomach. The man seemed sincere and like a
genuinely nice guy. A father who'd made the ultimate sacrifice for his

son. But none of that was enough to crush the desire to run far, far away.

He punched the mirror, then grabbed it as it shuddered from the blow. When had he become so shallow that he couldn't even give Mitch a chance? His mother would be ashamed of him. She'd loved Mitch, and for that reason alone, he'd somehow find it in him to be kind.

Suddenly, he desperately needed Luanne. It'd taken all of his willpower not to try and seduce her the last several nights, but something about her body language—or maybe it was the fact that she bedded down on the sofa—told him she wouldn't be open to his advances. But that hadn't stopped him from having plenty of dirty dreams about her blazing blue eyes and willing body every damn night.

He heard her before he saw her. She was on the porch talking to Beau.

Son of a bitch.

What the hell was that pretty boy doing spending a private moment with his woman? Okay, true, she didn't know she was his woman yet, and they weren't exactly having a clandestine meeting, but that hardly mattered to the caveman who apparently lived inside him.

"I'm so sorry, Beau. I can't imagine how painful that is." Luanne's voice was full of compassion.

"Thanks, Luanne. It's really hard, you know? He's all I've ever had. It guts me to think of him being so damn sick." Beau's voice vibrated with emotion.

"I'm sure it does."

"And if I'm honest, it messes with my head to think about being alone in the world. Damn. I can't believe I'm unloading all of this on you."

Jack couldn't believe it either. Did the guy have no pride? Beau had emotionally thrown up in front of a beautiful woman. What in the hell did he think would happen? Jack almost felt sorry for the guy.

"Oh, Beau." Luanne's voice was so gentle that it made Jack want to go to her.

He peeked through the front window and saw Beau with his head bowed and Luanne holding his hand. He nearly went through the window when she rubbed her hand up his cousin's arm. Confusion, jealousy, and fear smashed into each other in his brain. What was happening?

Beau looked away from Luanne while taking several shuddering breaths. "Sorry."

Luanne sat back in her chair. "You never have to be sorry for being honest about your feelings. Besides, chicks dig it."

Beau chuckled and scrubbed his face with his hands. "How about you? Do you dig it?"

"I do. A man who can be vulnerable in front of a woman is sexy."

Is that what she wanted from him? Jack knew the answer—yes. But he'd not wanted to appear weak in front of her. Maybe he'd been playing this whole thing the wrong way.

"Sooooo, you and me..." Beau grinned and let the question hang in the air between them.

Luanne grinned back. "No, I'm afraid not. I'm kind of...well, I'm not available."

Jack let out the breath he'd been holding. Thank goodness.

"I'm not surprised you're already taken. You're so nice, Luanne. Jack's a lucky guy."

Luanne snorted, and Jack had a hard time holding back a belly laugh.

"What?" Beau asked.

"Many would strongly disagree with you, your cousin for one."

"But I thought y'all were together."

She pushed off the porch with her toes, rocking the chair she was in. "It's complicated."

"Ah, I've had a few of those relationships."

"I don't want to date you, Beau, but I do want to speak to you about your career."

Jack's ears perked up at that. What the hell was she talking about?

"What about it?"

"I know Jack spoke with you the other night, but I couldn't tell how seriously you were taking him. I can assure you he's quite serious about signing you. You have an incredible voice, and amazing stage presence, and I could see you crossing over from country to southern rock very easily." She picked up her coffee cup and sipped, then replaced it on the table next to her. "You'll need a good manager, someone who won't take any crap, and who will look out for your best interests. You won't find anyone better than Jack. And if you tell him I said that, I'll swear you're lying."

They both laughed and Jack's heart nearly swelled out of his chest.

"Yeah, I knew he was serious, and I'm interested. It's all I've ever wanted, but to tell the truth, I've never really played for anybody who doesn't know me. I play fairs and honky-tonks around here and the next county over, but I'm not sure if I'm big-time star material like Gavin Bain. And I think I'd like you to represent me."

"Me?" The shock in Luanne's voice rang through the morning air.

Her? Jack had to admit it had merit. She was smart and she fought for the people she cared about. He'd need to work with her, and she had things to learn about entertainment law, and client representation, but they were all things she was capable of doing.

Beau chuckled. "Yeah, you."

"I'm flattered, but it's my duty as an attorney to tell you that I'm not the best person for the job. I don't practice entertainment law."

Jack decided it was time to join the conversation. The screen door squeaked when he opened it and they both turned to him. "Beau, you might be onto something."

* * *

Luanne stared at Jack like he'd lost his mind. "Have you lost your mind?"

Jack unfolded a lawn chair and sat between Luanne and Beau. "I think it is something you should consider."

Beau grinned. "See, I told you."

Jack held his hand up. "Back off, pretty boy. You won't be her first client. She has a lot to learn before she can handle the likes of you."

"Oh, I think she could handle me just fine." The challenge in his cousin's voice was undeniable.

"I swear, I will set you both on fire if you don't stop talkin' like I'm not here." Barbed wire wrapped around every one of her words.

"She means it, cuz. I've seen her in action. She is a force to be reckoned with, our Luanne." Jack picked up her coffee and took a sip.

She grabbed the cup from him and ignored the warm fuzzy feeling his words caused. "Give me that and quit talking crazy."

"It's not crazy. You'd be great. I think you should seriously think about it. You could come to work with Gavin and me. I'll teach you about entertainment law—you'll learn the job from the inside out."

"Are you forgetting I already have a law practice?"

"No."

"Then why are we even talking about this?"

Beau's head swiveled back and forth between them. "I see what you mean by complicated."

Luanne laughed. "Yeah, well..."

"I better get going. I need to take Clyde to the feed store." He rose and kissed Luanne on the cheek. "Thank you."

"You're welcome." He was pretty, but she felt nothing at all at his nearness. All her attention was on the brooding man sitting next to her.

They watched him get into his truck and drive away, then sat in silence for several minutes. "I'll think about it," she finally said.

Jack's flash of white teeth could've lit up three counties. "That's all I ask."

"I don't want to talk about it anymore."

"That's fine. What do you want to talk about?"

"You." She wondered what he'd say. He'd probably find some excuse to run away.

"Okay. What do you want to know?"

She almost fell out of her chair. That was the last thing she'd expected him to say. "Um...how are you doing? I mean, with Mitch being here?"

He glanced out over the lawn. "It's hard. There's a part of me that's so fuckin' angry that I have to deal with this whole thing. Then I feel guilty because the guy made this huge sacrifice for me, and I just want him to go away. And then there's my mom." He turned back to her. "Hell, I don't even know..."

The brokenness in his voice caused her to get up and crawl into his lap. He was lost and confused and she could help. She wrapped her arms around his neck. "You can only do what you can do. You don't have to have all the answers today, or even tomorrow. You and Mitch have time to figure things out." She stroked the hair away from his handsome face. "I do think you would like him if you got to know him, but that's up to you. There's not a playbook for this kind of thing."

"Thank you." His warm arms wrapped around her and she snuggled closer to him. He dotted kisses down her neck while a ripple of desire rolled down her back. She arched into him like a cat. "I'm glad you shared that with me, Jack. I...um...want you to know I'm here if you need to talk."

"Luanne." His big hand flattened on her back.

"Yes."

"I don't want to talk anymore."

The kiss was tender, slow, and deep. It quickly escalated faster than a brush fire in the desert. Tongues, hands, and moans of desire punctuated the warm summer day. Would it always be like this between them? Being wrapped in his arms was the missing piece to something she didn't know she'd lost.

"Luanne!" Kyle yelled from somewhere inside the house. "It's time!"

They slowly disentangled. "Time for what?" Jack rested his head on the back of the chair.

She ran her fingers around her swollen lips. "Kyle's teaching me to cook. Today we're making blackberry jam."

Jack chuckled and arched an eyebrow. "Really?"

She grinned. "He says my education was sorely lacking and he's here to remedy that. He told me that I'm his calling in life. Isn't that ridiculous?" She didn't want to tell Jack how it tickled her to her toes to hear Kyle say that to her. Or how grateful she was that he'd take the time to teach her something so basic.

Jack picked her up and stood her on her feet. "Never let it be said that I stopped a man from his true calling."

She laughed. "He's kind of dramatic."

He followed her into the house. "Ya think?"

"I like him." She glanced over her shoulder. "Where are you going?"

"With you. I wouldn't miss this for the world."

Chapter Twenty-Six

Jack repeated his kindness mantra even as he wanted to run from the room. It was like one big unconventional, screwed-up, happy family. Mitch sat at the kitchen table working a jigsaw puzzle, and Kyle, Mimi, and Luanne scuttled around the kitchen, while he loitered in the background.

"Jack, we could always use an extra pair of hands." Mimi said as she arranged small jelly jars in a row on the counter.

Jack leaned a hip against the hutch in the connected breakfast nook. "Actually, Mimi, I'm only here for the show."

"The show?" Mimi sounded confused.

"He's talking about me, Mimi. He thinks I'm going to create some kind of kitchen disaster, and he wants to be here to see it," Luanne said.

"Nonsense," Kyle said. "Luanne's a natural in the kitchen. She just needs a little practice."

Luanne stuck her tongue out at Jack and he laughed. He couldn't help it. She was so stinkin' cute with her apron on. Something was already smeared on her cheek, and they hadn't even started. "If you say so."

Kyle gave him a withering look. "I think we'll punish you by not letting you have any of this delicious jam."

"You're right, Kyle. Jack needs to be punished." She licked sticky syrup from a spoon with a slow sweep of her bubble-gum pink tongue. The kitchen temperature shot through the roof and Jack didn't give a damn about jam or watching Luanne cook unless she was doing it naked.

"Focus, Luanne," Kyle reprimanded.

"Sorry." She didn't sound very sorry, and Jack was glad.

"Careful, Jack. Kyle doesn't have a sense of humor when it comes to food prep," Mitch said.

Kyle pointed a wooden spoon at Mitch. "I've never heard you complain, Mitch Rawlings."

"And you never will."

"Dang right, if you ever want to eat again." Kyle's air kiss caused his threat to fall apart.

Jack noticed the puzzle Mitch was working on. The picture on the box was a winter scene of Aspen trees all covered in snow. Every piece of the puzzle looked exactly the same. Jack loved puzzles. It was how he spent weekends when he needed to unwind. No one knew that about him, except his mother.

When he was a kid, the two of them would work puzzles all the time. It was one of her best ways of distracting him if he was anxious, or bored. Grief grabbed him. He missed her so much. Even as confused as he was by her actions, he'd give anything for one more day with her.

He tapped an open slot. "I think that one goes here."

Mitch examined the piece in his hand, then slid it into place. "Well, look at that. Thanks."

Jack's fingers went into his pockets. "No problem."

"Want to join me?" Mitch asked without looking up from the table.

He could be kind. He was a kind person.

He pulled out a chair. "Sure, why not?"

Guilt jabbed him in the ribs when he saw Mitch's shoulders relax. He needed to remember that he wasn't the only one dealing with a lot of shit.

The chatter in the kitchen rolled over him, and the sugary scent of blackberry jam filled the air. As he immersed himself in solving something other than his own problems, his nerves unwound like a spool of thread attached to a kite in a stiff breeze.

Kyle stirred the big pot on the stove. "Jack, tell us about your record company."

He shrugged. "There's not much to tell. Gavin Bain and I started an independent record label about a year ago. So far, Gavin's our only artist, but we have our eye on a few more. We're not trying to grow too fast for many reasons, mostly because we don't have the personnel to handle a lot of artists."

Luanne measured sugar and dumped it into the pot Kyle stirred. "Jack and Gavin are trying to provide individual attention to anyone who signs with them. Not like the major record labels that are huge conglomerations, and clients are a number. I really admire what Honey Child Records is trying to do." She pushed her bangs from her face with her forearm.

He was sure his eyes bugged out of his head. The warm glow in his chest at her high praise expanded his ribs and warmed his cheeks.

"What?" Luanne gave him a double take.

Uncontrollable pride coursed through his body. "Thanks."

She shrugged. "It's the truth, and you know I always tell the truth. Like, for instance, you have a grease stain on your t-shirt."

He knew she was trying to deflect the attention away from her compliment. He'd let her. She'd already said it and there was no taking it back. "That I do, counselor."

"Sounds like you're doing good work, Jack." The pride in Mitch's expression was undeniable.

Jack wasn't prepared for the impact of his father's words. "Um... thank you." Mercifully, the doorbell rang, preventing him from having to say more.

Mimi wiped her hands on a kitchen towel. "I'll get it."

He surveyed his and Mitch's handiwork. They'd finished the puzzle's border and never said a single word, but it wasn't a hostile or uncomfortable silence. So that was something.

He could be kind. He was a kind person.

Damn right he was. He'd beat this awkwardness like he'd beaten every other obstacle in his life.

"Jack, Luanne, there's a package for you," Mimi said as she walked back into the room.

"Oh, thank God." Luanne rubbed her hands on her apron and headed for the box wrapped in brown paper. She ripped into it like a five-year-old on Christmas morning, then pulled her phone out and hugged it to her chest. "My baby!"

Jack laughed. He knew how she felt. It'd been like losing an appendage when Pearl and June had relieved him of his phone during the robbery. "I'm happy you two have been reunited."

"My wallet's in here too and...it's full of cash." She threw her head back, closed her lids, and whispered, "Thank you, Scarlett."

Irritation scraped against him. He knew why she was glad to have the money—it meant she didn't have to rely on him or anyone else anymore. Asking for help was a sin to her. Given what he knew about her family, especially her father, he understood, but it still ticked him off that she hadn't yet figured out that she could count on him for help.

"There's something in here for you too, Jack." He went to stand next to her. She handed him the legal-sized white envelope.

"Thanks." He tore the end off and shook out a credit card. The one he kept locked in his office for emergencies. Thank God Caroline hadn't left town before he called, and she was able to get Scarlett the things he needed. He kissed the piece of plastic. "I'm no longer the poor relation. Dinner's on me tonight."

Mimi wiped down the counter. "Isn't that nice?"

He threw his arm around his grandmother's shoulders. "Where would you like to go, Mimi?"

"There is a place." She chewed her lip. "But there are so many of us. It might be too expensive."

Jack laughed. "Money is no object. We'll go wherever you want."

"Well, you see, there's a new truck stop out on Highway 39, and they have a buffet that I've heard is just amazin'. I mean there is everything under the sun on that thing, and people say they have the best banana pudding you've ever tasted."

He could not have heard her correctly. A truck stop? A freaking truck stop? "Mimi, are you sure there's no other place you'd rather go?" He could see Luanne, Kyle, and Mitch over Mimi's shoulder trying, and failing, not to laugh.

"No, this will be perfect." The beaming smile she gave him put any further argument to rest.

"Well." Jack rubbed his hands together vigorously. "Everybody get ready. It looks like we're going to the truck stop."

* * *

Jack maneuvered the rental car back up Mimi's long drive after the family's trip to the truck stop. He had to agree, the banana pudding was the best he'd ever tasted.

"That was fun." Luanne scrolled through her social media sites in the passenger seat.

The meal had gone off without a hitch—no weirdness, no awkward silences. That was mostly due to Luanne and Kyle keeping the conversation rolling. He'd managed to be polite and cordial to Mitch, and at this point that was all he wanted or could manage.

"Thanks to your and Kyle's winning personalities."

She snorted. "That's probably the first time anyone's used that phrase to describe me."

"Don't sell yourself short. You're downright pleasant once you remove that giant chip from your shoulder."

The death glare she laid on him was ferocious. "Do not spread that around. I've got a reputation to protect."

He laughed. "I'll keep your secret, killer." The gasp that came from the other side of the car had him slowing down. "What's wrong?"

"My dad."

"Where?"

She pointed to Mimi's porch, where Marcus Price sat patiently in a rocker, looking perfectly at home. Instead of his typical suit and tie, he wore jeans and a button-down shirt, and tennis shoes. Jack blinked to make sure it was the same man he'd met multiple times in Zachsville.

His hands itched to wrap around the guy's neck for all he'd done to

Luanne, but this wasn't his battle to fight. He knew jumping into the middle of this situation with her father, without permission, would be the end of their fledgling relationship. Besides, Luanne was more than capable of handling her father. Hopefully, she knew that too.

"Do you want to leave? I can turn this car around right now and get you the hell out of here." Even he could hear the menace in his voice, and he didn't give a shit. This bastard had hurt Luanne one too many times.

She chewed her lower lip, and time ticked by until she seemed to make a decision. She released her lip, straightened her shoulders, and put on her game face. The one he'd seen her use on him almost every time they'd interacted before this insane road trip.

"No. This needs to happen."

"Okay. You're the boss." It killed him to let her walk into the lion's den without him.

He maneuvered the car and parked it next to Mitch and Kyle's rental. The couple, Mimi, and Leslie had already made it to the porch. Jack noticed the foursome's body language was closed off as they introduced themselves to Marcus.

Luanne puffed out a loud breath. "I should go talk to him. I'm going to...in just a minute."

He reached out and squeezed her shoulder. "Hey. What's your superpower?"

Confusion flickered across her beautiful face, then she grinned. "Badassery."

"You're the baddest badass around, Luanne Price. Never forget it."

"Damn straight." But when he turned to open his door, she grabbed his hand. "Stay close. I mean not on the porch with me, but maybe right inside the door? I need to do this by myself, but... yeah...stay close."

Two words.

Two little words blew apart his perception of himself. He wasn't fun Jack, or good-time Jack, he was the man this strong, amazing woman could count on. "Always." The kiss he gave her was soft and, whether she knew it or not, full of promises he intended to keep.

* * *

Luanne stuck her fingers into the front pockets of her jeans to hide the shaking. Uncertainty, hope, and a little fear—this was the story of her life with Marcus Price. She never knew where she stood with him. All she knew was that she loved the father that her mother, her grandmother, and she always believed he could be.

She made her way up the steps and stopped on the last one. "Hey."

"Luanne." He had her in his arms in three steps. Panic raced along her nerves. This was the intimidation and overwhelming suffocation she always experienced when hugged by people bigger than her. Now she knew it didn't have anything to do with her size, and everything to do with the fact that she couldn't trust this man's intentions. Ever.

As politely as possible, she extricated herself from his stifling hold. "When did you get here?" She didn't even bother asking how he found her. He wouldn't tell her the truth anyway.

"About an hour ago." He noticed Jack and nearly did to him what he'd done to her.

But before he was wrapped in a bear-hug, Jack stuck his hand out. "Mr. Price."

"Marcus." He pumped their clasped hands with all his might. "Please call me Marcus. How can I ever thank you for rescuing my little girl?"

Jack broke the handshake. "Mr. Price, Luanne's the last woman in the world who needs to be rescued."

Marcus flexed the fingers of his right hand like, maybe, they'd been in a vice. "Yes, well..."

Jack's praise straightened her spine and bolstered her shaky confidence. "Would y'all mind giving my dad and me a minute?"

Kyle stepped forward. "Sure, sweet pea." Kyle kissed her cheek and whispered into her ear, "Draw your boundaries, and remember what you deserve."

The moisture in her eyes crested at her lower lid, but didn't fall. She stared into the face of this kind man and understood that she did deserve so much more than she'd ever gotten from her father. And she had every right to ask for what she wanted. "Thank you."

He winked then herded the rest of the family into the house.

"Sweet pea?" Her father chuckled. "I guess he doesn't know that you're my doodle bug."

Annoyance at the once-beloved nickname pulled her brows together. "What are you doing here, Dad?"

"I've come to get my daughter, who I've been incredibly worried about." He turned toward the front door. "Let's get your things and get on the road. If we hurry we can catch the red-eye back to Houston."

She dropped into one of the rocking chairs. "Let's talk, Dad."

"Talk? We'll have plenty of time to talk on the plane." He checked his watch. "Seriously, Luanne, we need to get on the road. We don't have time for your histrionics."

There was no stopping the sad smile that tugged at her lips. "I'd like to speak with you about a few things."

His nostrils flared as he took a deep breath, and he pressed his palms down at his waist like he was trying to force his emotions into place. "Fine." When he raised his eyes, the genial man who'd met her on the porch was back. "What would you like to talk about?"

She folded and unfolded the hem of her shirt. "First, I'm not marrying Doug."

"Of course you're not." His expression was so sincere she wanted to bathe in it.

She let out the air trapped in her lungs. "Oh, okay. I thought you'd—"

"Not until that boy apologizes. I don't want you to let him off the hook. You make him beg. Do you hear me, baby girl?"

Disappointment replaced the blood in her veins. It pumped and clogged her devastated heart, then rolled up her throat. She swallowed it back down and looked her father in the eye. "No. I will never marry Doug. I won't allow you to use me like that ever again."

His head jerked back like she'd slapped him. "Well, I had no idea you felt that way."

The tears in his voice were almost enough to make her change her mind, but she deserved more than the piddly crumbs he offered. She deserved a banquet of love from the man whose genes she carried. "I do feel that way, because it's true. I want more than anything to have a relationship with you. So much so, that I allowed you to arrange a marriage for me. I would do just about anything to please you, to earn your love. But I won't marry Doug. I won't participate in your business scheme. And I won't settle for your scraps of affection that only come when you want something."

He searched her face, then dropped his head into his hand. Dejection rolled off him like fog in a backwoods swamp. He was upset. Maybe she'd said the right thing. Gotten to him somehow. She would try once more to connect with him, for the little girl who'd dressed in a frilly pink dress to impress her daddy.

She put her hand on his arm. "Dad, I believe we can repair our relationship. I want that."

"Bullshit."

The word was spoken so quietly she wasn't sure that was what he'd said. "What?"

His head came up like a snake ready to strike. Red eyes, a scowling brow, and a sneer had taken the place of the concerned man she'd sat down with. "I said, bullshit. If you wanted a *relationship*, then you would have done what I asked you to do. You've ruined everything for me. You've cost me millions of dollars in this broken deal and for what? Because I didn't hug you enough as a child? Give me a break. You're a grown woman who knows the score. We had a agreement and you broke it." He stood and kicked the rocker. "I'm done with you."

She braced herself for the devastating reality that it was really over, but all she felt was an overwhelming sense of relief. She was sure she'd be sad for some time to come, but not devastated. This man hadn't earned her adoration, her love, her loyalty. He was toxic to her, exactly like he'd been to her mother. "I'm sorry you feel that way."

"I'm sorry you feel that way," he mocked. "Let's see how sorry you are when you're homeless and begging for a job. I'll be taking your law practice, your house, and your car."

She laughed. She couldn't help it. "Are you kidding me right now? I may have acted like an idiot by agreeing to marry Doug, but I assure you that I'm anything but. You gifted me those things, and they're mine." His threat was so empty and yet so cruel that she knew this was the end for her. No more trying to be what he wanted in hopes of an honest relationship with him, just no more. "But you know what, I don't want them. Not one thing. I don't need your money or your things. Take 'em. Take 'em all. I can buy my own." She spread her arms wide. "You bought me a fantastic education, Dad. I can do anything I want." The truth of those words shot confidence to her soul.

His hands went to his hips. "Oh, really. How are you going to do that? You have nothing now." He spit out a half laugh. "You're like your mother. Always wanting someone else to take care of you."

His hateful words, that usually stung, rolled off her and pooled in a scummy puddle at her feet. She wasn't her mother, even though she understood her mother much better now. And she was capable of taking care of herself.

Excitement for a new challenge in her life and freedom from his kind of poison loosened her muscles, and she smiled. "I'm not sure yet, but I'll figure it out. Until then, I have friends who will help and support me."

She'd lived off the scraps of his affection for so long that her heart was malnourished. But she deserved a banquet of love in her life, and she had people ready and willing to give her exactly that. Scarlett and Gavin, Floyd, Honey, and Joyce...but mostly she knew Jack would be in her corner until she could get on her feet.

Speaking of the man, she could see him behind her dad at the screen door with murder on his face. All she had to do was say the word and he'd storm into the situation and deal with her father. But that was her job and her right to send him away. She crossed her arms over her chest. "You should go, Dad."

"Now wait a damn minute." Pink colored his neck and cheeks. "Let's talk about this."

She knew he thought he could bully her into doing what he wanted, and now he was scrambling to find another way to get her to comply. "There's nothing else to talk about. Goodbye."

"I'm not leaving without you." He grabbed for her elbow.

Jack was on him before he ever touched her. He bent Marcus's arm behind his back and Jack growled into his ear, "Try to put your hands on her again. You won't like what happens." He shoved Marcus into the porch rail.

The screech of the screen door and the cocking of a shotgun punctuated Jack's threat. Kyle, Mitch, Mimi, and Leslie all poured onto the porch. Kyle handed the weapon to Mimi. "There you go, Mimi. It's cocked and ready for you."

She wasn't alone. These people cared for her and would stand with her. Amazing. She wasn't one of them, but they had taken her in as if she were blood. This was what family felt like. The sensation fit perfectly in the hole that lived in her heart, filling it seamlessly. Something that made her stronger, better, and braver thumped through her newly healed organ.

The older woman pinned Marcus with the mother of all evil eyes. "I believe you've worn out your welcome, sir. I'd appreciate it if you'd move along now." She leveled the firearm at him. "I hope you do what I say. Cleaning up blood is hard as hell."

Marcus held his hands up and backed down the steps. "There's no need to get crazy. I'm leaving." He pinned Luanne with a glare. "I don't deserve to be treated this way."

As his car sped down the driveway, his last statement hung in the air.

Neither do I, Dad. Neither do I.

Chapter Twenty-Seven

Fury pounded against the inside of Jack's skull. It had taken every ounce of self-control he possessed not to take Marcus Price to the ground and beat the piss out of him. How could a father be so heartless?

"You can unclench your teeth, Jack." Luanne wrapped her arms around his waist. "He's gone."

His jaw ached from the effort of keeping his mouth closed while the man had been spouting his sewage. "I'm sorry, Luanne. I know you wanted me to stay inside. But I—"

"Thank you." The softly spoken word helped quiet the storm raging through him.

"Anytime. But I am sorry that it didn't go the way you wanted."

She shrugged. "I'm okay."

Kyle squeezed her shoulder. "Maybe not completely, but you will be. At least now you know."

"Mother, give me that." Mitch grabbed the shotgun from Mimi. "What were you thinking?" Before she could answer he turned to Kyle. "And what were you thinking?"

Kyle took the weapon from Mitch and broke the barrel apart. "It's not loaded."

"I—" Mitch's anger deflated. "Oh, well."

"Don't worry, Mitch. I'm not in the business of arming senior citizens." Kyle gave him a we'll-talk-about-this-later glare.

"Hey, who are you calling a senior citizen?" Mimi asked.

Pride beat through Jack's chest as he listened to his family. They'd stood up for Luanne. He'd tell them how much that meant to him, but not now. The only person who had his attention was the woman who owned him completely. "If you all will excuse us, Luanne and I have some things to discuss."

"We do?"

He snagged her hand and towed her toward the door. "Oh, yeah."

When they were inside the house and away from his family, she jerked him to a stop. "Do these things involve being naked?"

"Definitely."

The naughtiest grin curled her lips. "Race you." She took off up the stairs. Her laughter trailed behind her like flower petals floating in the wind.

"You don't stand a chance, woman." He caught up to her in three strides. Her squeal filled the air as he scooped her into his arms and ran with her the rest of the way up the staircase. "Get the door."

She turned the knob and narrowed her gaze on him. "Is this how this is going to go? You bossin' me around?"

He kicked the door closed. "Darlin', I can boss you, you can boss me, I don't really give a damn as long as we're naked and tangled up together."

Her fingers slid into his hair and she pulled his head down so their lips were only millimeters apart. "Good answer."

Dizziness swam around his head when she opened her mouth over his. His heart sped to a crazy pace. The intensity of his desire firing off rockets through his bloodstream was making it hard to stand. Fine with him. He wanted her naked and underneath him as soon as possible.

Her lips were warm, sensual, and sinfully soft on his skin. His need for her cranked up one hot kiss after another. He welcomed the ache building inside him every single time she was near. He welcomed it like his next breath.

His fingers lightly trailed under her slender arms, still wrapped around his neck, and down the curve of her waist. Liquid fire burned deep inside him and his thoughts skipped from one delicious part of her to another. This had to slow down or it would be over way too soon. He pulled back enough to bury his head in the crook of her neck.

"You smell so good." Her vanilla and citrus scent filled his head. The smell of her, the feel of her, the taste of her were all around him and in him. With every swipe of her tongue and slide of her lips, he fell deeper and deeper under her spell.

"Jack, put me down."

Her urgent whisper confused him. That was the last damn thing he wanted to do. "What's the matter? Did I hurt you? Wha—"

"I want to touch all of you."

He wanted that too, more than anything. He released her legs and let her slide down the length of him. The pressure of her small body against his dick made them both gasp. One tiny movement shattered coherent thought as she flicked open the button of his jeans. "You're killing me, Luanne."

She glided her fingers over his nipples, through his t-shirt. "No dying before I'm done with you."

He laughed. "You got it." He knotted his fingers in her hair and bent to take her mouth again. Cinnamon and lust swirled on his tongue. Only she would satisfy his hunger, only she would fill his need. He ripped his mouth from hers. "Get on the bed, Luanne."

For a moment, he wasn't sure she'd comply. But then, with a sultry sway of her hips, she sat on the edge of the bed. "Like this?"

"Not quite. I think we discussed nakedness." He stalked toward her.

Her pink-tipped nail went between her teeth. "You first."

Damn, she wanted to play, but he was way past messing around. He took a deep breath then let it out slowly and shook his head. "Uh-uh. You first. Take it all off."

She ripped her shirt over her head without an argument and tossed it to the side. He wasn't exactly sure of the rules of the game they were playing, but he'd just scored. His already swollen cock nearly busted through his jeans when she unhooked her pink bra and let it fall to the ground.

"Perfect." His vocal chords strangled around the word.

He bent and took one pebbled peak into his mouth and was rewarded with a desperate moan when he ran his tongue over the tip.

"Too many clothes." She scooted higher on the bed and propped herself against the pillows, then shimmied down her pants and thong. Unashamed, brazen, and so damn hot that he wasn't sure she wouldn't scald him to death.

"Now you."

There was no slow reveal or teasing show—he wanted his bare skin pressed against hers as fast as he could get there.

She batted her baby blues. "Counselor, what a big...ego you have."

He laughed and gathered her to him. "Come here, baby. I'll show you a big ego."

Her leg hitched around his and she rolled him onto his back. "I think I'll start here."

She circled his flat nipple with her tongue and shivers raced over his body. With every slick pass of her mouth desire wound him tighter, until he was ready to break. "Lou, I want you."

Her wicked smirk almost undid him. "I know. But not yet. I'm still playing. Besides, I owe you."

The slow path she took down his body was better than all his fantasies. When her wet mouth closed over him, he nearly came undone. "Luanne." Her name was a strangled cry.

Her lust drunk eyes peered up his body at him. "Hmm?" She purred around him.

"Don't stop. Please don't stop.

* * *

Jack's strong arms clutched Luanne and hauled her up his body. His beautiful, fine body. There were no two ways about it—Jack Avery was man candy in every sense of the word.

His gaze burned for her. "You got something on your mind, counselor?" she asked him. His lazy grin had the same effect on her it always did. It was like drizzling hot chocolate over her girly parts.

He pushed a lock of hair from her face. "I'm wondering where you've been all my life." His hand slid up and down her back. "Oh, I remember, trying to castrate me at every turn. How do you plead, Ms. Price?"

"Guilty as charged. A girl's got to have goals." She pushed herself into a sitting position until she straddled him. "If it makes you feel any better, I've changed my wicked ways."

His big hands wrapped her bottom. "Mmmm, I hope not."

She arched into his touch, needing more contact. "I have different plans for you now."

"Do you now?" His finger skimmed the cleft of her bottom. "Funny, I have a few plans of my own."

"Are they good? Wholesome?" The broad expanse of muscle and bone of his chest tapered down to the flat plane of his stomach and begged to be touched. Her fingers slipped down along each rib to the dark line of hair that disappeared between the apex of her thighs. He was magnificent.

"No." He drew the word out, making it a promise, then threaded his fingers through her hair and pulled her down to him.

"Oh, good." The game was over. She needed release.

The wet heat of his mouth covered the tip of her breast, the pleasure of it so shocking that she lost her breath. Only this man had ever made her feel this way. How had she lived her adult life not knowing this kind of pleasure, need, connection? That was the difference. She was connected to him on every level, body, mind, and soul.

Every touch of his lips, every word he spoke, every penetrating look went past her skin and her bones, right to her center.

She rose up on her knees, slipped her hand between them, and found him hard and ready. "Ready so soon, counselor?"

An intensity she'd never seen from him before washed over his eyes. "I've been ready since the moment I met you, Luanne."

His words stole her breath, and two words were all she could manage. "Now, Jack."

He sheathed himself with quick, jerky movements. "Whatever you want, baby. I'm yours."

He encircled her hips and lifted her back over him. She slowly lowered herself onto him and stilled.

A hiss of air slid between his clenched teeth. "Oh, my God." It was the exultation of a man dying who'd found water in the desert. Primal and raw, and so sincere that it made her want to cry. "Nothing has ever felt this good. Nothing. Give me a minute or this will be over before it starts."

Gladly. She needed the time to get her riotous emotions under control. He overwhelmed her in every way. Also, he was large and she was small—two things that generally didn't go together. She closed her eyes, let her head fall back, and tried to relax.

"You are a sight, Luanne Price." The praise in his voice only made her want him more.

A chuckled slipped out while she was concentrating. "You think so?"

"I know so. Are you alright?"

"Yes. I'm reluctant to mention this, given your gigantic ego, but you're rather large."

"Am I now?" He clearly couldn't hide the pleasure in his voice.

She snorted. "You know you are."

He trailed his fingers along the tops of her legs. "Go slow. We've got all night."

This was why she trusted him, because he trusted her. Slowly she began to move.

"Sweet Jesus."

Power surged through her that she could make a strong man like Jack feel so much. "You like that?"

A long growl rumbled from his chest. "You have no idea. Come here."

He took her by the shoulders and lowered her to him. He claimed her with his lips, not letting up until she was a mindless puddle. She pushed in closer, stroking his tongue with hers, mating, giving, taking. Her heart tripped into a free fall as he took control of the rhythm.

His hot, harsh breathing broke the silence of the room. "I want to take it slow, Lou. I want to give you time. But I don't think I can." His broken admission only pushed her higher.

"I want it all, Jack."

He rolled them over, and the crumbling dam burst. He drove into her over and over again. Her heart rode the tidal wave, careening and crashing while their bodies moved in time with one another. He gave, and she took. She gave, and he took. On and on it went and with every touch, every point of contact he took possession of her body and soul.

With a final push, he spilled himself into her and she came apart in his arms. Her world shrank to this bedroom, his heart pounding against her breast, and the sound of their erratic breathing. She could live in this moment forever.

Time righted itself and the night closed in around them. Her skin cooled as they lay under the large ceiling fan.

"Are you alright?" His warm voice cocooned around her spent body.

"I'm great." And she was. She couldn't ever remember feeling this whole. This alive.

"I'll be right back." He made his way to the bathroom as she drifted between sleep and wakefulness. Then the bed dipped and he pulled her against his body. "Sleep, Luanne. I've got you."

Much later, deep in the night when secrets are shared in the dark, he reached for her. She went willingly. She had nothing to hide from him. Their love-making was slow and deliberate. He held her face while he moved inside her and adored her with his body.

Incoherent and desperate whispers fell from their lips. She clung to him, giving and receiving things that neither could say during the light of day, words that promised things that would usually scare her to death. But she didn't care. All that mattered was that they both reached that place where everything seemed possible, and consequences were far, far away.

They found it together. They both flew apart individually, but when they came back to themselves they were no longer two people, but their own creation, made of things she didn't have words for but knew she couldn't live without.

As they lay sated and still, she finally understood what all the fuss was about. She also knew that she'd never find *this* with anyone else, nor did she want to. They could be together because they cared for each other, trusted each other, and Jack would never disrespect her by forcing his will on her.

This was what she'd earned from living a life without being cared for.

This was something very, very good.

Chapter Twenty-Eight

Luanne stretched like a lazy cat on a warm windowsill. Every part of her body was relaxed and satisfied. Jack had made sure of that. She turned her head to see his sleeping face, so handsome in the morning light.

They'd done it, finally. Their entire relationship had been one big game of foreplay. And last night was like an explosion. She brushed a piece of hair from his forehead. He'd been so fierce and gentle with her —hungry in a way she'd never experienced, but at the same time giving and generous.

It was definitely something she'd never forget, and she was grateful to him for showing her how sex could be when the partners liked and respected each other.

"So much thinking, so early in the morning. If you keep it up, your head will explode." His sleepy voice sent chills down her body.

She turned to her side to face him. "How do you know I was thinking?"

"You get a little crease right here." He ran his thumb across the top of her forehead. "When you're in deep concentration." He slid his hand down to cup her face. "What were you thinking about?"

"Nothin'."

"Liar."

She shrugged one shoulder. "I was thinking about you."

He propped his head on his hand and gave her his full attention, his signature smirk firmly in place. "Yeah? What were you thinking about me?"

She ran her hand down his chest and the heat of his skin scorched her fingers. This man did something to her, something wild and uncontrollable.

He caught her hand and brought it to his lips.

The moan that escaped her mouth would've embarrassed her yesterday, but not today. He'd made her moan, growl, and beg last night, and she'd loved every minute of it. "I was thinking how great last night was." She glared at him when the smirk got cockier. She didn't even know that was possible. "Like you don't know you're amazing in bed."

He kissed her fingers again. "It's still nice to hear you say it. Last night was like no other for me."

"That's what I was thinking about. How different it is to be with someone you like and respect, and who likes and respects you."

His expression changed for a second, but then it was gone so fast she didn't have time to read it. "Let's be honest. I think we more than like and respect each other, Luanne." He kissed her palm, then her wrist.

She pulled her hand away. "What are you talking about?" The pulse that a second ago was slow and steady jumped and jerked in her veins.

"I'm talking about the fact that I love you and you love me." He caressed her face. "It's okay, I know it's scary. I'm scared too, but we can do this together."

She leaped out of bed like it was full of poisonous spiders. A nervous chuckle rattled from her throat. She grabbed her robe and wrapped it around herself. "Stop being weird, Jack. And stop talking crazy."

He pushed himself to a sitting position and adjusted the pillows behind his head like he didn't have a care in the world. Like he hadn't just told her he loved her, and then told her she loved him. What the hell?

"It's alright, take a minute. I'll wait." He put his hands behind his head.

That did it. He was seriously screwing with her new peaceful world and she wouldn't have it. "No, Jack. I'm not going to take a minute. You're crazy and last night was a huge mistake." She began running around the room, gathering up her things.

"Darlin', I've never been more sane or sure about anything in my life. I love you, you love me, and we're going to get married."

That stopped her dead in her tracks. "What?"

"We're getting married, soon. I know that's a big step for you and it is for me too, but I think that's the best way to keep you from completely freaking out. You won't have much time to think about it."

He was out of his damn mind if he thought she was going to marry him. Maybe reason would work. She hauled in a chestful of air and tried to lower her voice to a calm and reasonable octave. "Jack. I don't know where you've gotten this crazy idea. But you have to know this is a bad idea. I've already had one rushed marriage and it ended disastrously. You don't want that for us. Right? Let's date. Get to know each other, enjoy sex together, and then we can talk about the future." Even to her own ears she sounded like a hostage negotiator. But if she could talk him down, maybe things could go back to the way they were before.

He shook his head. "No, I'm sorry. There won't be any more sex until we're married. It's what's best for you. You deserve to be treasured and valued, not used like you have been your whole life. I won't do that to you."

"You son of a bitch." She advanced on him. "What I deserve is someone who will listen to me and see me as a person with her own opinions and her own desires, someone who doesn't tell me what I should and shouldn't do. Someone who doesn't tell me I'm in love with them and that I'm going to marry them as soon as possible for my own good!"

He took a long breath and blew it out. "I'm sorry you feel that way."

"And that's another damn thing. You hide behind that mask of yours, like everything is a game. It's not. My life is not, and you can't play with it like that. Like my mother, like my grandmother, and like my father."

That must've got to him because his calm demeanor cracked ever so slightly. "I am nothing like your screwed-up family."

"You're no different than them. You want to use me because I make you feel better about your current situation. Well, what happens after your perfect life goes back to normal? What happens when you don't want me to soothe your boo-boos anymore? What happens when you don't need me to make things normal for you? I'll tell you what happens. You dump me and leave me to deal with shit I never wanted to deal with, you arrogant ass."

He got out of bed and pulled on his jeans. "Luanne, listen to yourself. You're the one talking crazy. I'm not going to leave you. I just told you I love you, for God's sake. I want to marry you. It's the only thing I'm absolutely sure about in my life right now."

He moved toward her but she couldn't take it. If he touched her she'd cave. Like with her father. Why couldn't she tell men no? From deep inside a wounded animal rose up and screamed, "No. I won't do this. You can't make me. I've played this game before, Jack. You tell me you love me, you give me what you think I want, but it's only to get what you want. And so today, I. Say. No."

He stopped and stared at her. "You can't see it."

"See what?" she snapped.

"You can't see the difference between how your family's treated you and what I feel for you, for what's between us. It's not the same, baby. It's miles and miles different, and you're about to throw it all away, because you're too scared to trust me. Don't do this."

"And what you don't seem to understand, Jack," she spit the word at him, "is that love makes you weak, and powerless, and selfish to the nth degree." She swiped a tear from her face and straightened her shoulders. "I'm done being weak, and powerless. And I never want to be as selfish as my mother and grandmother. So, yeah, I'm *throwing it away*, because *it's* not real." Clothes fell from her arms as she tried to grab the rest of her meager belongings. She snatched them up and headed for the door.

When she got there she turned to face him. He was leaning his hip against the bedpost with his hands in his pockets. He could've been waiting on his deli order instead of watching the woman he supposedly loved walk out of his life. "I can tell you're real broken up about all of this."

He shrugged. "What am I supposed to do? Nothing I say is going to change your mind."

"That's right. It's not. Don't come after me."

"Don't worry, I won't. You've made yourself very clear."

"Good."

Before she closed the door he fired his final shot. "You're a coward, Luanne Price."

* * *

Jack made his way downstairs. He'd waited in the room for more than an hour until he was sure Luanne was gone. He couldn't see her. He didn't know how he'd ever face her again. He'd opened his heart up and told her he loved her and she'd flat out rejected him. He'd hear the click of that door for the rest of his miserable life.

How could she do this to him, and how could she not believe him? The one woman who knew and understood him best, she should know how hard it had been for him to lay it all on the line. She should've known that he'd been devastated. What had she wanted? Him to cry and grovel? Even she didn't get that from him.

Worst of all, she thought his motives were the same as her worthless father, and that he saw her as a means to an end.

What a cluster fuck.

The house was quiet. The rest of the family must be out. Thank God. He didn't want to talk to anyone, or explain this to anyone. It was too personal, and he was too raw.

He made his way to the kitchen for a beer and found Mitch sitting at the kitchen table watching the birds in the birdbath outside the window. Shit. He was the absolute last person Jack wanted to see. Maybe he could sneak out without his father seeing him. The board under his foot creaked as he turned to leave and Mitch turned his direction.

Double shit.

"Hello, son."

"Hello."

"Trying to sneak off on me?" Mitch took a sip of iced tea.

"No. Why would you say that?"

Mitch pointed to the window. "I saw your reflection when you came through the doorway. And then I saw you turn to leave."

Busted. Jack went to the fridge and pulled out a beer. "Okay, so I was trying to sneak off without you seeing me." He propped his butt against the counter and twisted the top off.

Mitch raised a brow. "A little early for that, don't you think?"

"You know what they say—it's five o'clock somewhere." He took a long pull on the bottle.

Mitch chuckled. "You're a pretty cool character, aren't you, Jack?"

Jack moved his shoulders in a semi shrug. "I don't know. I guess."

"That girl of yours sure left out of here in a hurry. Kyle took her to the airport. Evidently she's going home." His amber gaze never left Jack's.

Relief loosened his muscles. She hadn't tried to drive herself anywhere. "Where are Mimi and Leslie?"

"Mimi's at her church meeting and Leslie's at work. So it's just you and me here. Come. Sit."

Jack sucked down another drink and pushed off the counter. "Can't, I've got calls to make."

"Sit." The command was so emphatic that Jack immediately sat.

"Yes?" He tilted back in his chair, arms stretched out along the back of the chairs on either side of him, like he didn't have a care in the world.

Mitch's long fingers played with one of the puzzle pieces on the table. "I think we need to talk."

"We've already talked everything out. I'm not mad at you, I understand why you did what you did, I'd like for us to stay in contact. What else is there to talk about?" Jack gave him his *we're pals* smile that he'd perfected long ago.

"Why do you do that?" Mitch cocked his head like he was studying an interesting bug.

"Do what?"

"Act like you don't have a care in the world. Like you somehow fly just above all the crap the rest of us have to deal with."

Jack laughed. "You don't know what you're talking about."

"Really? Because in the short time I've known you it's like nothing sticks to you. You throw that cocky grin around like a weapon."

It was the same thing Luanne had said. What did these people want from him? To see him bleed. Well, if that's what this SOB wanted, he'd give it to him. He leaned forward and stuck his finger in Mitch's face. "You don't think I have to deal with shit? You have no idea. I clean up my clients' shit. I take other people's shit for my clients. And I've been wading waist-deep in my life's shit for the past week."

"Poor you." Mitch sipped his tea.

Jack shot out of his chair, knocking it back in the process. "Don't patronize me, you bastard. You're the reason everything is out of fucking control. I've spent my entire life clawing my way out of poverty, and where were you? Livin' it up with Kyle in your syrup compound in Vermont. Is that even a real goddamn thing?"

Once the dam broke he couldn't stop what spewed out. "I had nothing! I wore other people's clothes, I ate free lunches at school, I mowed lawns in the summer until I had blisters and heat exhaustion to pay for my football fees in the fall. And the only thing I had to hold onto was my family." He paced the tiny room. Anger boiled over and obliterated any hope of being kind. Fuck kind. He wanted to hurt Mitch. Hurt him like he'd been hurt. "I knew I had a mom and dad who loved me, who supported me, who would never lie to me. But that wasn't true. None of it was true. She lied to me my whole life. My whole fucking life." He collapsed into the chair like a puppet whose strings had been cut and even though he fought like a lion, a stray tear rolled down his cheek. He had nothing left.

A warm hand touched his head. "It's okay. I'm here now, and I'm not going anywhere."

"She was the one I could always count on." He tried to control the tremble in his voice, but couldn't. "The best person I knew."

"I know."

Jack's fist hit the table. Hard. "And you took that away from me." He dropped his head and more fucking tears escaped past his closed lids.

Mitch stroked his hand over Jack's head again. "I did, and I'm sorry."

Jack nodded and took several shaky breaths. The storm passed and he pulled himself together enough to sit up. He didn't even feel embarrassed. All he felt was relief. Pure, blessed relief. How long had that shit been bubbling inside him trying to get out? Years.

A glass of water appeared in front of him. "Drink it."

He drank. And felt his equilibrium level out, but not completely. Something was different. He was different. He rested in the peace.

Neither spoke, the only sound was the birds at the bird feeder outside.

"I'm sorry." Jack glanced at Mitch, who was wiping his own eyes.

"Nothing to be sorry for."

"But the things I said—"

"Were honest. And you never have to apologize to me for being honest." He folded the handkerchief he'd dried his face with. "Do you feel better?"

Jack snorted. "Yeah."

Mitch nodded. "Good. If I've learned anything in this life it's that you have to be your honest self. People get hurt. You get hurt when you're not."

He guessed Mitch knew better than anyone the truth of that statement.

"You know you're going to need to forgive your mama, right?"

Jack peered out the window. "I know, and I think on some level I've started to forgive her. I won't ever know all of her reasons, but there are things I do know and those are the things I choose to focus on."

Mitch squeezed his shoulder and nodded. "Now you want to tell me why that feisty gal of yours flew out of here like her hair was on fire?"

Jack got up to refill his water glass and resumed his pose against the counter. "I told her I loved her."

Mitch smiled. "Well now, that doesn't seem so bad."

"I also told her she loved me and that we were getting married ASAP."

"You told her." He nodded again. "Aha, I understand. Luanne doesn't seem like the kind of woman who likes to be told what to do. Though I can't really think of any woman who would respond positively to being *told* they were in love with someone, and also being *told* they were going to marry said person. I can't say it was your smartest move." He lifted the glass to his lips. Jack suspected it was to hide a grin.

"She accused me of the same things you did, plus a whole load of other stuff." He came back to the table.

"What are you going to do about it?" Mitch gave him the best dad stare he'd ever seen.

"Nice face."

Mitch beamed. "You really think so? I've been practicing with Kyle."

Jack laughed and it felt good. "Honestly, I don't know what to do about Luanne. I could use some advice. I don't know that I can go to her. I think for this to work she has to come back to me, but I don't know what to do."

Mitch came to his side of the table. "You know what I'm going to say."

"Be honest?"

His father patted his back. "Be honest."

Chapter Twenty-Nine

Pain shot through Luanne's thumb when she bit her nail to the quick. She couldn't remember ever being this furious. And betrayed. She'd been betrayed, by the only other person, besides Scarlett, she'd ever trusted. Jack-ass.

"You okay over there?" Kyle's smoky voice interrupted her tirade.

"Dandy."

"Do you want to talk about it?"

"No."

"All—"

"He pisses me off so much. Do you know what he did?" She turned in her seat to look him.

"Why don't you tell me?"

"He said he loved me."

"That bastard."

She held her finger up to make a point. "And, he told me that I love him."

"Do you?"

"Of course not." But even as the words came out of her mouth she knew it was a lie. "Or at least I didn't think I did, but now that he's said it…"

"Yes?"

No way, she wasn't touching that subject yet. She had too many things to be mad about. "Do you know what else he did?"

"I'm still interested in whether you love—"

"He told me we were getting married. Can you believe that? He *told me*, like I was a child and not a grown woman. What the hell?"

Kyle turned down the radio. "Sounds like his father."

"What do you mean?"

"When I met Mitch I hadn't come out yet. I'd been in the closet a very long time. I didn't want to hurt my family, or that was my excuse anyway. The truth was it was easier to not have to deal with any potential conflict. And Mitch, Mr. High and Mighty, called me on my bullshit real quick. We weren't even dating."

"Sounds familiar."

"We met when we worked for the same tech company. There was a group of us, men and women, that hung out after work. Sometimes we would go to a baseball game or to happy hour. He was out, and one night we'd all gone to his house for a barbeque and I was the last person there. If you think I didn't plan that then you're crazy."

She chuckled and was surprised she still had the capacity to laugh.

"Anyway, I was there and made it entirely clear that I was into him and that I wanted to go out with him."

"And he said yes?"

"No. The rat bastard told me he wouldn't date anyone who hadn't come out. That he'd seen how destructive it could be and he wouldn't be a part of it. I of course was completely offended and conflicted, because he was absolutely right. But I wasn't going to tell him that."

"So what happened?" She didn't know if there was a point to this story or if Kyle was telling it to distract her from her own misery. Either way she appreciated it.

"We would see each other every day, and say hello. I had a wounded pride, but I'd be damned if I let him see it. Then one day, several months later, he brought a guy to one of our get-togethers. I was crushed. I guess I thought he would wait until I was ready to come out." He gave her a sideways glance. "Which would've been never. Anyway, I went home that weekend and told my family."

She pulled her knee into the seat and turned to face him. "Why would you risk your family rejecting you over a man who was dating someone else?"

"Because he was right, for one thing, and for another, I owed my family honesty. It was tough in the beginning, but they've all accepted it and loved and supported us. But the biggest reason was that I wanted Mitch. Period. And I'd do anything to be with him, even if it meant I had to look at my crap and face it to be with him. Nothing was more important. So you see, I know about bossy Rawlings men."

She crossed her arms over her chest. "Did Jack tell you to tell me that story?"

"Jack doesn't know that story, unless Mitch told him, and besides I haven't seen Jack today."

Tears splattered to her cheeks. Misery filled every one of them.

Kyle pulled into a strip mall parking lot. He smoothed a hand down her hair. "Honey, what's the matter?"

"Oh, Kyle, I think I've really screwed up."

"I'm sure you haven't. Is this about your father?"

She nodded.

"I want to kick your father's nuts into his throat." He took her face in his hands and made her look at him. "You are precious, Luanne, precious. You were born into terrible circumstances, but that isn't who you are. You're not part of them. You've risen above their pettiness and forged your own path with your wits and your giant heart. You will not let them define who you are anymore, do you hear me?"

She tried to nod her head, but he was still holding her face. They both laughed, and he handed her a tissue from the console to wipe her face. "Thanks."

"Now what does all this have to do with Jack?"

"I don't know. It's all mixed up in my head." She sniffed and wiped her nose. "In my experience, love is mostly a lie. It makes promises and then it takes your soul. Look at the women in my family, me included, who've sold their dignity for crumbs of affection. I would die if I turned into my mother over Jack."

"Luanne, do you feel weak when you're with Jack?"

She thought about it. "No."

"Do you feel used or uncared for with Jack?"

"No. Though I don't like his bossy *You are going to marry me* crap."

"Good. And are you going to tell him that?"

"Absolutely."

"Would your mother ever have stood up to your father, or your grandmother?"

"No."

"See, you're nothing like them. And Jack is nothing like your father."

"You're right. But if we're going to get married he has to understand that if he tries that shit anymore, I'll cut off his balls."

Kyle's smile lit up the car. "That's my girl."

She stared at her hands in her lap. She really was going to marry Jack, because she loved him. She loved Jack Avery. Crazy.

"Kyle, would you take me back to Mimi's house? I've got a fiancé whose ass I need to kick."

* * *

Jack paced the living room, heartsick and exhausted. He'd royally screwed up and he knew it. But he didn't know how to make things right. Even though he was apparently horrible at relationships, he knew in his gut she had to come back to him. He'd grovel for days, but she had to be the one to return, or it would never work between them. Bottom line, she had to trust him enough to come back and fight this out.

The sun cast tiny rainbows through the stained glass Mimi had hung in the front window. Luanne was probably getting on the plane by now.

He missed her. She'd become so much a part of his life, he couldn't imagine a day without her.

His phone dinged with an incoming text. Maybe it was her. The device nearly flipped out of his hand as he yanked it from his pocket. It wasn't her. It was his dad. With a trembling finger he swiped the screen and opened the text. It was short and to the point and made his knees turn to water.

Ray: I'm sorry I was an ass.
Jack: It's alright.
Ray: No, it's not.
Jack: Can I call you?
Ray: Not yet. Give me a little more time. I love you, Jack.
Jack: I love you, Dad.

The thousand-pound weight he'd been carrying around since he read that letter lifted and blew away. He and his dad could work this whole emotional mess out, but it would take some time. He wanted to tell Luanne. Everything he did or thought came back to Luanne. This was going to be one long, lonely life if he couldn't make it right between them.

He heard Kyle's car come up the drive. He couldn't bear to see him. Kyle probably hated his guts too, after talking to Luanne. She'd come to care for Kyle in the short time they'd been there, and would've shared all the stupid things Jack had done to make her run.

He couldn't face Kyle, so he made his way upstairs to avoid the man.

He heard the front door open just as he closed the bedroom door. Footsteps pounded up the stairs and he squared his shoulders, ready for battle. Evidently Kyle wasn't going to let him off the hook.

When the door flew open he almost went to his knees. His fiery pixie stood there, like an avenging angel ready to do battle.

"Luanne."

"Don't Luanne me, mister. I have a bone to pick with you."

"I'm sure you do." He allowed a spark of hope to crawl through his belly.

She advanced into the room with a can of whoop-ass in her back pocket. He was in for it, and he'd never been happier.

"You and I, we need to get a few things straight."

He shoved his hands into his back pockets to keep from reaching for her. He was thrilled to see her, but he wasn't an idiot. If he tried to touch her right now, he'd probably pull back a nub. "I'm all ears."

"First, you will not tell me that I am in love with you. *I* will tell you that I love you, do you understand?"

"Do you?" He could barely get the words out of his throat.

That threw her. "Yes. But that's not the point. Second—"

"Screw it." He'd risk dismemberment, because he had to get his hands on her. His arms went around her and he crushed her lips with his. She didn't fight him. She was warm and pliable against his body and returned the kiss with everything she had. Then she tried to push him away. But he had her in weight and didn't budge, although he did stop kissing her.

"I'm not finished. Don't try to distract me."

"You're right, I'm sorry." He nibbled up the side of her neck.

"Um...what was I saying?"

He licked the shell of her ear. "Second."

"Oh, yeah, second. You will not tell,—mmmm..." The moan she let out rattled the windows.

"Yes?" He moved to the other side of her neck.

"You will not tell me we are getting married. You will ask me like any civilized person."

He stopped feasting on her neck and dropped to one knee and took her hand in his. "Luanne Price, will you forgive me for being the biggest idiot alive?"

She caught her lip between her teeth, then released it. "Yes."

"Will you also forgive me for not begging you to stay earlier, and for not telling you that you're the only thing of value in my life?"

A tear slipped down her cheek and she let it fall. "Yes."

"And will you put me out of my misery and agree to be my wife?"

She nodded while the tears flowed freely. "Yes."

He scooped her up and spun her around. "I love you, Lou."

She held his face in her hands. "I love you too, Jack Avery. But if you ever do anything like that again, I'll cut your balls off and feed them to the pigs."

"You have such a way with words, darlin'."

"Shut up and kiss me."

Epilogue

"Honey, I think I have enough hair spray." Luanne shielded her eyes from the aerosol attack.

Honey's laugh could be heard back in Texas. "Oh, girl, you can never have too much hair spray, or good lovin'."

Luanne examined herself in the mirror, then glanced around the room at Scarlett fussing with Aiden's bow tie, Kyle coordinating things with the caterer, and Mimi and Leslie arranging the bouquets, and had to agree with Honey. "I guess you're right."

She was marrying Jack Avery in twenty minutes. Who could've ever predicted that? The ceremony was being held in Mimi's church, with only family and a few of Mimi's friends. They hadn't done it as soon as Jack had wanted. She'd had to return to Zachsville to pass her cases off to another attorney in town, close her bank accounts, and sell her house and her car. That last one had hurt—she did love that car—but when she came to Jack it would be with every tie to her father severed.

Not only had it been about finishing with the past, it had been about securing a wonderful future. Details had to be hashed out. Excitement zipped through her at the thought of the new challenge before her. She wasn't talking about living with her new husband, although that was sure to be an adventure. She was now an equal partner with Gavin and Jack in Honey Child Records.

Her birth family was nowhere to be seen, but the family of her heart was in attendance, and treating her like she was the most important thing in the world.

"Lou, look how adorable he is." Scarlett stood Aiden up on a chair to show him off. Aiden promptly stuck his finger in his nose.

"He is adorable. Looks just like his father."

Scarlett laughed. "Aiden, get your finger out of there."

The kid giggled and kissed her on the lips.

Kyle clapped his hands. "Okay, ladies, it's go time. Take your seats and your places and the bride and I will be out shortly."

Scarlett hugged her and whispered in her ear, "You look beautiful, and so happy."

She squeezed her best friend and matron of honor's hand. "I've never been happier."

"You swear on the collective souls of NSYNC?"

Luanne laughed. "I swear."

Scarlett's smile was beautiful. "See you at the altar."

When the room was empty except for her and Kyle she blew out a huge breath. She wasn't nervous at all—she knew beyond a shadow of a doubt that she and Jack were meant to be together. But the adrenaline overload made it hard to breathe.

Kyle smoothed out the fabric of her flowing wedding dress and adjusted the flower halo in her hair. "You look like a fairy princess. The silver in the dress brings out the light blue flecks in your irises so beautifully."

She caught his hand and brought it to her lips. "Thank you."

"You don't have to thank me for a thing." He kissed her forehead. "I loved every minute of it."

How he'd pulled together a wedding in only a few months was beyond her. She kissed his cheek. "Still, I want you to know how much I appreciate it."

"I'm sorry your grandmother chose not to attend." He handed her the bouquet.

"Me too, but I'm really okay with it." She'd invited Gigi, but her grandmother had declined...by text. She'd also received an email stating that she'd been cut out of the will. That had been the most freeing day of her life.

"Thank you for the privilege of walking you down the aisle." He straightened his tie in the mirror and smoothed back his hair.

He'd become more of a father to her in a few short months than Marcus had been in her whole life. "Who else would I pick? You're my fairy godfather."

He chucked her under the chin. "And don't you ever forget it. Ready?"

She slipped her hand through his crooked arm. "Ready."

* * *

It was a perfect day. Not a cloud in the sky, and the temperature was in the low sixties, but Jack was sweating like a pig.

"You okay, son?" Mitch slapped him on the back.

"Yeah."

"You sure? You look a little green."

Jack chuckled and scrubbed his face. "I'm not nervous about marrying, Luanne. I'm positive about that decision. It's just..."

"Your dad?"

Emotion welled up in him and he couldn't speak, so he nodded.

"I understand. He'll come around. This is hard stuff. You can't blame him for needing some time to process it."

"You're right. I know you're right. I'd hoped he'd change his mind and come."

"I get it. There's no substitute for your dad."

Jack squeezed Mitch's shoulder. "Hey, you're my dad too, and I'm happy about that." And he was. Over the last few months, he and Mitch had begun to forge a relationship that he was grateful for.

Mitch looked away and blinked several times. "Me too, son."

Jack's world shifted off its axis and he sucked in a sharp breath.

"What?"

"He's here." Jack could barely speak around the ball of emotion in his throat.

Mitch did cry then. "Well, damn it, now I'm crying. I'm happy for you, Jack, for so many things."

"Thank you. That means a lot coming from you."

"I'm going to find my seat before I make a scene." He shook Jack's hand and went to sit by Mimi.

Jack made his way to his father, who looked small in a suit that used to fit him but was now a size too large. "Hey, Dad."

"Jack."

"I'm so happy you came."

For a minute his father looked uncertain, then he grabbed Jack in a bear hug. "Of course I came. My son's getting married. Besides, your mama would kill me if I missed this."

They broke apart, both wiping tears and laughing.

His dad shoved his hands in the pockets of his slacks. "But I can't stay after and meet these people. Not yet, and maybe not ever. You understand?"

"Absolutely."

"But you bring that new wife of yours to our house, and we'll have a proper Cajun celebration." He patted Jack's cheek. "I love you, son."

"I love you too, Dad."

Ray pointed toward the altar. "Looks like things are about to start. I'll sit back here if that's okay." He indicated the last row of chairs.

"It's perfectly fine. I'll call you in a couple of days."

"You better."

Jack made his way down the aisle of Mimi's little church to the pastor. When he got to his spot Gavin shook his hand. "You ready for this, Jackson?"

"You bet your life I am."

The music started, Beau began to sing, and a hush fell over the crowd.

"Who's that?" Gavin said from the corner of his mouth.

"My cousin," Jack whispered back.

"Did you sign him?" Gavin asked.

"Workin' on it."

"Work harder. We need him."

He agreed, but when he saw Luanne and Kyle come through the

double doors of the sanctuary, all thoughts of his cousin vanished. Gorgeous. A huge smile split his face when their eyes met. But when she saw him, she stumbled a step and pulled Kyle to a stop. His heart froze. What was she doing? He tried to ignore the voice in his head screaming, *She's a runner.*

She whispered something in Kyle's ear, and tried to tug her hand from his arm, while Kyle shook his head and tried to pull her back. When she got free, she picked up the front of her dress.

He'd seen this move before—it was how she'd looked when she ran out of the wedding venue the first time. Panic bloomed in his chest. *Oh, hell no.* But before he could take a step to go after her, she was running down the aisle to him.

When she was only a few steps away, she leaped. He caught her, and swung her around.

"You had me scared for a minute, trouble."

She held his face in her hands. "Don't be afraid. If I'm running, it's only to be with you, sweet talker."

The End

HELLO THERE!

Be sure to sign up for my Reader Group! That's the best way to find out about special giveaways, contest, and new releases, like the next book in the Brides on the Run series, **_Running to a Cowboy_**. Find out if Jack's cousin, Beau gets his happily ever after.
Click the link and join the fun.
http://eepurl.com/c7EJrn

Did you enjoy **_Running From a Sweet Talker_**? If you did, it would mean the world to me if you would leave a review on Amazon for me! Reviews are like gold to a writer and they go a long way in giving a book social credit.

A Note to Readers

It blows me away that you took the time to read my book. I can't say thank you enough.

You, dear reader are why I do what I do. Every story I write I think about you and what will make you laugh and cry. Basically, you're always in my thoughts.

I'm not going to lie, there were days that I didn't know if Jack and Luanne's story would get told. They hid from me for a very long time. It wasn't until I figured out that Luanne could be strong and fragile at the same time that things began to fall into place for the story.

One of the themes of the book is that we all deserve to be loved and treasured. What I've found in my own life is that I deserve and require a banquet of love, a full five course meal of affection, attention, and adoration.

However, there is a person in my life that, because of past trauma, can only give me a Happy Meal of love. This person gives it freely and whole heartedly, so I've had to decide if I could live with their small offering and find the rest of the love I need from other people in my life.

In my case, I chose to take what they can give and be grateful for it.

Ironically, in doing so, that Happy Meal has grown to something far more substantial.

My hope is that this story would reinforce how precious you are, and give you the courage to live a life full of the love and affection you richly deserve.

Yours always,

Jami

Also by Jami Albright

Brides on the Run

Book 1

Running From a Rock Star

Coming soon...

Brides on the Run

Book 3

Running to a Cowboy - Beau and Charlotte's story

Acknowledgments

This book has been so fun to write. I looooooove Jack and Luanne! But like all my books, they don't happen without tons of help and support from other people.

First, I have to tell you how amazing my husband is. HE DOES EVERYTHING while I'm trying to get my books to the editor and to you. When I say everything, I mean everything. He cooks, he cleans toilets, he does laundry, and he listens to me when I think the book is total crap. I dedicated Running With a Sweet Talker to him, because he is everything that a hero should be.

I also want to thank my kids for being so amazing and patient with me during the writing of this book. You three are why I do what I do. I love you guys to the moon and back.

My fabulous critique partners come next. Carla Rossi, Stacey A. Purcell, and Melissa Ohnoutka. They are my sounding board, my support, and my butt kickers. I truly hit the critique partner lottery with these three.

A big ol' thank you to Danielle for coming up with *Tots for Tanks Testicle*. It's one of the funniest and most brilliant things you've ever said. LOL!

Also, a huge thanks and tons of gratitude to Bobbi, who swooped in and made this book cleaner and more error free than I could've done on my own. You're the best!

I have the most amazing writer friends, and one of the best is Maria Luis. She's held my hand and shown me the way in all things marketing, and book promoting. She's also listened to me when I didn't think things were going the way they should or when I wanted to give up. I'm so fortunate to have her in my life.

You guys this book might've stalled out and never happened without my friend Leslie, who let me borrow her beach house, which gave me the space to push through to the end. Thank you, Leslie for such a beautiful place to create.

I want to thank the Brightens, my ARC team for being willing to drop everything and read and review my book for me. I know you guys have lives and responsibilities, so it makes your offering of time so much more precious to me.

A book doesn't just happen. It takes lots of work and people with sharp eyes to create a story that moves and entertains. My editor Serena Clarke is one of those people for me. I struggle mightily with grammar, and Serena swoops in, cleans things up, and makes me look great. It's so important to have an editor that will tell you the truth about your story without trying to change your voice, and Serena does that in such a professional and kind way that it's an absolute joy to work with her.

Thanks to Najla Qamber of Najla Qamber Designs for another AMAZING cover. You rock in every way, Najla!

Let me tell you how fabulous my mother is. Y'all, I could write my books in crayon and on a Big Chief tablet, and she would think they were fantastic and show them to all of her friends. I wouldn't be writing this to you without her. I know that no matter what happens she will ALWAYS be in my corner. She's poured wisdom, support, and unconditional love into me and my four sisters and in turn raised five strong, independent women. I wish you all could meet her. You'd love her as much as I do.

Lastly, I want to thank my readers. You guys were so gracious and generous with your time in reading the books, and I cannot thank you enough. You all took a leap of faith with me, a new author and have shown me love and support. Here's to many more years of reading, laughing, and hanging out together.

About the Author

Jami Albright is a born and raised Texas girl and an award-winning author who writes zany, sexy, laugh-out-loud stories. If you don't snort with laughter, then she hasn't done her job.

Jami is a wife, mother, and an actress/comedian. She spends her days writing and wrangling her adorably mischievous dog, Tug, who may or may not be human.

She loves her family, all things Outlander, and puppies make her stupid happy. She can be found on Sundays during football season watching her beloved Houston Texans and trying not to let them break her heart.

Contact Jami
www.jamialbright.com
jamialbright1@gmail.com

Made in the USA
San Bernardino, CA
19 February 2019